DIRTY VENGEANCE A DARK MAFIA ROMANCE

(MICHELI MAFIA) BOOK 2

ZOE BETH GELLER

KINKY INK PUBLISHING

Dirty Vengeance
A Dark Mafia Romance (Micheli Mafia) Book 2

By Zoe Beth Geller

Kinky Ink Publishing

Cover Design by Shepard Originals
Edited by Elizabeth Anne Lance

You can also follow me on Facebook and Amazon.

Please visit my website at zoegellerauthor.com

❀ Created with Vellum

PLAYLIST

On Spotify

Playlist for Dirty Vengeance

https://open.spotify.com/playlist/6HhuzIfqIoIsUqGFY4P2NY

I am the Fire, Ghost Monroe
Stand by You, Alex Good, Kurt Hugo Schneider, Megan Nicole
By your Side, Lucas Estrada, Alex Alexander
Marry You, Bruno Mars
Girls Like You, Maroon 5
Kiss Me, Malo

GLOSSARY

Glossary

andiamo – here we go
buona notte – good night
ciao – hello
consigliere – advisor
diletto – darling
famiglia – family
Fantastico! – Fantastic!
grazie – thank you
il mio amore – my love
niente – nothing
Oddio! – Oh God!
principessa – princess
polizia – police
rosso – red
saluti – greetings, usually a toast
signorina – miss
scusi – sorry

1

FRANCESCA

I don't need eyes to understand women look at me every day, judging me, resenting me, and possibly wishing they were me. They think I'm a trophy wife for an elderly man, except I don't wear a ring, nor do I have a husband.

It's not customary for Italians to drive extravagant cars in Italy. I toss the keys to my Rolls Royce to the valet. I wink at him and make my way into the fancy boutiques like I own them.

It helps that I have a wardrobe that would have any fashion model peeing with excitement as I walk by tourists in my Givenchy shoes. There is nothing I cannot afford, well, that was until my funds were cut off. Sure I have some secret income, but the extra I get from being in the family, well, it adds up quickly.

I wander around the boutique and refuse to be helped. I'll know the outfit when I see it. Eureka.

I find what I'm looking for and make a purchase before heading to my next stop. I pick up a cappuccino at the train station's café and decide a panini might not be a bad idea as the melted ham and cheese on fresh pressed bread sitting on a plate next to me is too tempting to pass up. I have important errands to accomplish today, the shopping is my cover. The train doors close, making the noise of an airlocked waterproof pod. Which is funny because winter is our rainy season.

The train will take me to another town. I watch the people on the platform disappear as we pull out of the station. The scenery changes from urban to empty fields in the countryside because farmers have harvested their crops. When we're up to speed, it's more of a blur, and I play with my phone to pass the time.

I text my best friend Sophia and figure she's not answering as she works in a café. I remember the last time we were out together was at my dad's funeral two months ago.

Has it been that long already?

His funeral was as unnatural as his death. People stood around to pay their respects dressed in black, but there were no tears. My brother, Mario, whispered to the boss of the Calabrese family because they are like two snakes in the grass. Only my brother is the mongoose, and Angelo Calabrese doesn't know that—yet.

I'm a woman surrounded by sharks, and the made men look at me like I'm bait.

Not the I want to fuck you type of bait. No, their eyes are filled with darkness and solemn faces that turn away every time our eyes meet. They are up to something sinister, so I'm always looking over my shoulder.

Cowards. They may wear tight shirts and show off their muscles, but they don't know what I'm capable of. Only Dad knew and he liked to keep secrets.

I'm not privy to the changes that will inevitably occur

after his demise, but I should be. My brother's moods change faster than the seasons. Summer is still here. The earth is brimming with beautiful foliage representative of new life, but my world is bleak in comparison.

I can't escape fast enough. I need to leave this compound of misery behind me.

Bastards.

What did I do to be treated as an outsider? I look out the window of the modern train as I remember how Sofia stood next to me. We both abhorred my father for his dealings in human trafficking. She's a sweet girl, related to someone in the rank and file of families. She's been my only friend for as long as I can remember. She's petite with straight brown hair and a pert nose I envy.

We met in middle school. She's the only person I ever talked to about my life because she's also inside the organization. We found solace in talking to each other about all the things we couldn't share with anyone else.

That common denominator made us instant friends. There's nothing I wouldn't do for her. We have to stick together especially since we're both women in a male-dominated environment.

She had put her arm through mine as we watched over what was left of my father being lowered into the ground. I'd noticed her extra thick makeup job to cover up the black eye she'd gotten that week and I regretted not having time to talk lately. I need to do something before he kills her.

Try as I might, she loved Guido, and being young, she rushed into marriage last year. It's a decision she regretted shortly after the honeymoon. I never date men in the 'family'—it's a rule I never break.

Besides, my Krav Maga instructor was not only a great

guy but an attentive lover. My only real lover. The time I spent with him was the only time I let my guard down, but not the guard around my heart.

I became an expert at martial arts and any means of defense I thought would come in handy. To me, my mentor provided sanctuary. My family doesn't need to know about him. And in that respect, he is protected, and I only share tidbits about my personal life. No one ever gets the entire story.

He knows I have a dark past and have been knocked around. That rage is powerful enough for me to hurt someone if I want to, even without a gun.

Dad's untimely death triggered many things. There will be a battle for a new don, and my position has already changed. I'm not the daughter of a don if he's dead. I'm no one and that was made clear to me after his death when I wasn't allowed to visit the girls in their squalor 'safe' house. The girls are a commodity. Traded, bartered, and worse. Forced into prostitution they are hooked on drugs, and they will never be the same even if they can escape. But no one ever escapes.

I was pissed when I heard a rumor that the girls are off-limits to me now. That, and the building tension between Sofia and Guido escalated my own anger issues and the current way I'm feeling is that I have nothing left to lose. Mom left with a man she loved for years and had to repress so I'm alone. Mom won't suffer from my actions, seeing as how she left after the funeral.

I'd love nothing more than to beat Guido to a pulp, but these matters are to be kept in-house and I'm not exempt from following family rules. My brothers are not to be trusted, and I must be careful how far I push the limits of their non-existent patience.

I showed Sofia some defense moves but she's not me. We both knew she was fucked but neither of us said it. As a last resort, I suggested she try to make him happy. But we all know that men who beat women don't do it because they are unhappy, it's control. The type of control that is subtle in the beginning, a sentence here and there that one makes allowances for. Then, as time goes on, the realization hits that everything out of his mouth is demeaning.

I wish he would fuck up with the family so they could take care of the problem for us. Sofia isn't part of our inner circle so there was no protection from my dad, or as it stands now, the Calabrese family.

I thought I'd take the matter into my own hands seeing as how I excel at tech things and have connections of my own. I used to follow my brothers without them knowing it, so I learned how they operate and how things really worked behind the scenes . . . as much as anyone could from the outside.

But in this matter with Guido, I can't use their resources. It would give away what I know and raise questions I don't want to answer. I've become streetwise and savvy at many skill sets, all of which I keep to myself because it makes life easier for a potential foe to underestimate me. I always have a backup plan, too. By that I mean, I know how to disappear before someone disappears me.

So here I am, a month later, using a disguise because there are security cameras everywhere. I'm on a train to take me to another part of Italy for fake identification. I'm having two passports made, one for me, and one for Sophia. With today's holograms, pictures, and chips, it's a real art form ... and expensive.

Two weeks later, I pick up the documents, but when I return home Sofia isn't answering her phone. I assume her husband was around and she couldn't talk, but when that night stretched into the next day, I got a sinking feeling in my gut.

I know better than to ask her husband, who is openly seeing another woman. I can only assume he did something to Sofia, the new version of divorce. His new girl parades around in her unnatural curves built by butt and boob implants. She is definitely top-heavy by design. Her gloss-covered lips are overstated and akin to that of a porn star. I'm sure fillers were involved. No one has lips that plump without it.

Guido parades her around like a prized filly when he meets my brothers for guys' date nights, the nights not meant for the wives.

I'm mourning the loss of my friend. I have no idea what might have happened to her, and I fear the worst. Did he have her killed? Has she been sold into prostitution? She might be in one of our houses for the girls being trafficked. They'd be stupid to keep her this close to home so there's no telling where they will send her to avoid someone in our community from recognizing her.

The men don't tell the women anything, but we stick together and have a way of finding things out through our network. I say 'we' because I'm a woman and I'm disgusted by these man-pigs who treat us like property.

I've managed to dodge the bullet because of my birthright and status. Plus, I have come from money and money comes in handy. All my life I had the protection of my father, but do I have it with my brothers? Or the Calabrese family?

I've been to where the wives are sent after their husbands discard them. It's a condo building that's run more like a ghetto with armed guards. Sure, they have a roof over their head and the kids are fed but they are not free to leave.

The sons are usually taken away from their mothers and given to grandparents until they can be trained as soldiers. Mafia husbands don't trust angry wives and when the relationship hits a dead end, it's the women who pay the price.

I do what I can to help but it's limited and fleeting.

Sofia's disappearance bothers me. I have no idea if she's dead or alive, but I'm making it my mission to find out.

Knowing how cold-blooded her husband is, I have to be careful. I'm a Conti but hey, in the mafia, there is no limit on how many family members can be killed by their own blood.

I'm on thin ice already for helping the girls in these shitty brothels, but the organization tolerates me as my presence keeps the girls calm.

Sofia's husband, Guido, lives up to the stereotypical American bastardization of the name as a bad guy. It's evident something is wrong. Sofia's parents are afraid to even speak to me when I knock on the door of their apartment. All they can do is whisper through it to let me know they haven't heard from her. Then they asked me to leave.

It pisses the men off when I try to mediate on behalf of the girls and get them much-needed medical attention. I abhor what's happening in these above-ground dungeons, but I can't set the girls free because my own family would kill me.

Dressed in sneakers and an old shirt and jeans, I drop by the compound to take food and some womanly items to the women. On my way in, I see my brother and as I brush past him, he puts his arm up.

"What are you doing, Fausto?" I ask as he stops me at the door.

"You're not allowed in. We got a new crew of guys and new girls. The word is you aren't welcome around here. Your access codes have been revoked too, just thought you'd want to know. You aren't on security anymore either, so I guess you are out of a job," he taunts.

"Give me a break, you know some of these girls will be beaten to death," I try to reason with him, but he's not budging. Amazing how his voice is like Dad's and now his behavior follows suit.

With my martial arts training, I could break his arm before he could stop me, but I don't take the bait. It would ruin the element of surprise and the less he knows about me, the safer I am.

"Where did the girls go?" I look toward the woods as if to ask if they're buried in a ditch. The drugs take a toll on their bodies and the girls never last long. It seems the only way out of here is in a garbage bag.

"Dunno, you can ask Angelo if you want," he suggests in a mocking manner as if I really want to talk to the new don. "Or you might want to check out the Micheli family."

"Fuck Angelo," I spat at him which is dangerous since he's in the ranks, but he's also my brother and I rely on the blood being thicker between us than him, and Angelo. They can both be sons of bitches. "What about the Micheli family?"

"All I know is that money was exchanged, and we got word to move the girls out in a box truck. That's it. Sofia is gone."

"I doubt that we would do any business with the Micheli family." I sneer, knowing we've had a long-standing feud with them.

How did he know Sofia is missing? Is he implying she went to the Michelis?

"Watch it, sis," he hisses in my ear.

Weird that after Dad dies, and most probably at Dante's hand, we're in bed with them. I haven't given Angelo

Calabrese, the new don, enough credit for patching up those old wounds. It crosses my mind that Angelo might have been in on my father's murder if what he's saying is true. Angelo certainly stands to profit the most now that I think about it.

As I turn to leave, Fausto mentions something about our rivals in Florence getting in on the trafficking. After they looked down on us for the same thing, I find this hard to believe. And if that's a fact, he's telling me something I wasn't supposed to know. I can't figure out his end game. Things in this world are rarely as they appear. Even with my experience growing up in this dark world, it's still hard to separate fact from fiction.

These men are cunning, otherwise, they wouldn't be good at their jobs. My brothers lie out of both sides of their mouths. They make a living at it, and they've been doing it for generations.

I can't say I was surprised when my brothers, Mario and Fausto, joined the Calabrese family, because they outnumber us and Angelo was the *consigliere* for my dad, so it makes sense. Of a sort. By my brothers giving the Calabreses their support, they sold out for top positions.

How long they will be content with that? Didn't they plan to get Dad's spot? Now they act as if everything is fine and it's not sitting well with me. Something is amiss. I view it as them selling out for an easy ride.

Traitors!

After Dad died, that prick, Angelo, had the nerve to push me aside like I'm dirty dishwater that needs to be tossed out the window. When I ask for basic items to make life tolerable for the hostages, he gets nasty and now he's denying all my humanitarian requests. I'm sure it will cut into his profits.

Little does he know, if he or anyone else comes after me, I will kill them. I've been watching my back since I was a kid, and now I'm on high alert. I have no one to protect me. I could be a liability, even though it's uncommon to kill off a don's daughter. Besides, I am the person who makes public appearances for our donations to charity. I frequent the gym, and trained some female boxers and by no means do I splash myself around on social media.

My brothers love their luxurious sports cars and act like big shots around the others, often running up huge bar tabs and picking them up for everyone. I'm sure both of them are capable of having me killed so he can get more of Dad's estate. Oddly, my family has more to gain should I meet an untimely end, and I'm beginning to think I'm not safe in my own home anymore.

Instinct kicks in and I'm beginning to see myself more like Sofia—trapped with no free will. My every move is being watched around here. I hate these men and what they stand for. The thought of Sophia being prostituted sickens me. She must be found, and the clock is ticking.

ANTONIO AND FAUSTO think I'm no longer relevant, but I'd love to show them. Growing up with every privilege imaginable I had no idea what it would be like to live without family money.

Due to the issues with the estate attorney, I curse my brothers for trying to screw me. They make me look like I'm a thief and it's terrible to hate the only blood family I have left. But I do.

I am so blinded by anger I don't know how sane or insane this mission is, and once my mind is made up, it rarely changes.

The Calabreses didn't even have the balls to tell me of

their new rules, nor did Angelo apologize for cutting me off. No concessions were made and my blood boils judging from my racing heartbeat. My brothers must be thankful that they weren't taken out in the vacuum that follows an empty seat at the head of the table. I find it odd how the regime changed over without the blood bath that always takes place after a don's death.

I box up my apartment and use a fake ID for the storage unit before leaving town. I have to protect my personal possessions. I don't care about the lush furniture and material items I've collected over the years.

Sentimental items can't be replaced so I protect those in the event that my apartment is torched. Besides, I have to leave a number of items, so no one is the wiser that I'm not off visiting Grandma, which is something I normally do, but particularly true after Dad's death.

Is Sofia out there? Could she be in Florence? Maybe. I owe it to her to check it out. And there is only one way to find out. I've done a week of research on the family and my impression leads me to believe Sal is easier to get to than Dante.

Besides, a hit on Dante would spark fury at home and it wouldn't end in my favor. I doubt Angelo wants to spend money on war as his first order of business as the new don. His agenda doesn't need to be written, he's trying to earn respect and put more money in his men's pockets.

I pack all my hacking gear, workout clothes, and tons of designer items for every occasion as I'll have to infiltrate the Micheli family and find out who they are and where they are weak.

It's risky, but it needs to be done. I will do this under the cloak of darkness starting tonight as my brother isn't home. I text him I'm going to visit Grandma in Sicily. He knows I'm not the type to take an actual vacation. Grandma is different and won't look suspicious.

I make a quick call to Grams. She just needs to cover for me, and my getaway is complete. I have one last detail to cover before assuming my alias. I break my phone, stomping on it the hard heel of my boot before I open my Zippo, squeeze lighter fluid on it, and light a match. I switch to my burner phone. Now I'm off the grid. I took care of the GPS in my car the day it arrived in my driveway, but I check for portable trackers just to be safe. One can never be too careful.

I slide into the plush leather seats in my luxury car and make the trip to my brother's house. He's working nights so no one will be there. He's predictable, a creature of habit. It's also a dangerous way to live in our world.

The hard rock music on the radio bothers me so I turn the station to Italian music and take a sip of the iced coffee I grabbed on the way over. It's the perfect drink when it's too hot for coffee. I can't wait for winter to come.

Oddly, I was a precocious child and after asking a million questions I came up with my own solutions. And they clicked when I started with karate around the same time Dad insisted on kicking me around like a soccer ball. He assumed it would toughen us all up and my brothers got their licks as well. At the time, there was no way I was going into the family business.

I was taught I could be abducted as the child of a don, but my motivation for learning self-defense was due to its usefulness to me on a daily basis at home. It was my first silver lining that I took advantage of to ward off not only Dad but eventually my brothers, with a few well-aimed kicks.

The music can't keep my mind from the past and in retrospect, I can blame Dad for not having friends in my life. Dear old fucking piece of shit Dad. The one that will fuck a woman with his eyes, then his dick. I don't know how Mom put up with it. But he was Dad and I loved him as all children give unconditional love to their parents. He was the only man I ever loved until I met Alessandro, my mentor, and Krav Maga instructor.

Life changed for me the minute Dad watched me beat the shit out of a female opponent in the boxing ring at the gym. After that, he never hit me again. But the years of abuse had already taken a toll and left me with issues I'm still not ready to deal with. The door on that shall remain closed indefinitely.

I did hang out around the warehouses where Daddy had his office when I was little. It was our only father-daughter bonding time and as I matured, I studied the hot guys who came in and out of his office but never imagined myself married to one of them. They were rough guys who did bad things on the street.

Flirt with them? Guilty. However, I consider myself damaged goods due to my anger issues over men. That's only one issue. But why marry into the mafia and worry about what will happen if I disagree when my husband has a mistress on the side? No, thank you.

I take the familiar turns to get to my brother's house. I make my way into his office circumventing his security cameras. I enter his computer because he's so pussy whipped his password is his girlfriend's name.

What an Idiot.

He handles the electronic transfers and I quickly locate the information I seek as I stand flipping through his desktop files. I find an accounting program and after opening it I can see he received an electronic transfer from an account that he has noted in a spreadsheet that is from the Micheli family. I will check it out for myself. It could be money for coke or use of the docks. Mafia dealings are all convoluted.

I'm careful to wipe my fingerprints off everything and turn the alarms back on after I leave. I love knowing exactly where people are when I use skills my family, who are now my enemies, don't know about.

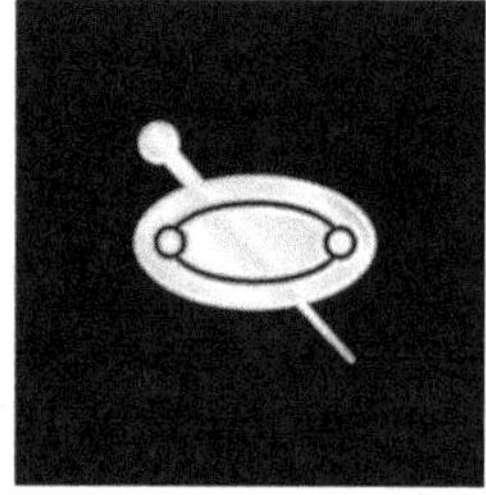

2

SAL

I observe the club, the music is loud and I'm ready to go home. Pushing back the cuff of my designer dress shirt I glance at my Breitling Aviator watch. It's not the most expensive from my collection, but it fit my mood this evening when I dressed for work. Seeing as how it's one-thirty in the morning, we'll be closing soon.

It's not as busy as I'd like, but I can't complain, there's never a bad day, and it just means I can dump more money into the till to launder it. I stroll around, check in with the staff and greet a few guests with familiar face and heavy spending habits. I give them attention as it's all part of the VIP scene.

I notice a woman with light chestnut brown hair and ashy blonde highlights. The lighting is low, but as I circulate closer our eyes casually meet. Her calm green eyes give me an unabashed going-over. She turns away and begins to fidget with the paper napkin under her Cosmo. I have a feeling we're both checking out my club. Only she looks more like she's casing it, while I'm looking for intruders who come in many forms.

Namely-gangs and other mafia personnel looking to score.

If she's trying to be inconspicuous, she should have brought a date for cover and lost the rope-size gold chain with the large diamond pendant. Wearing jewelry like that begs for the wrong kind of attention and a clunk on the head.

Normally, girls come here to get picked up, but I see men approaching her, making what I assume is a light conversation, and leaving a minute later. She remains solo in an area designed for guests to mingle when the dance floor is packed.

I can't figure out what's up with this chick and find it nearly impossible to tear my eyes away from her, she's unique. Thirsty for a closer look, I walk around the room again, pretending to check out the patrons and the servers, but I'm kidding myself.

I check out her round, firm ass as she leans lightly over the high-top table for two with one knee slightly bent, showing off her toned legs and thin ankles in her four-inch-high heels. I notice a black rose tattoo on her ankle as I walk by.

The loud music with its booming bass makes the top-of-the-line speakers vibrate, almost matching the pressure in my eardrums. It is too noisy to make conversation, which is why the guards and bouncers wear earpieces. I do too, occasionally.

I love music, it's a universal language—a language of love, lust, or passion. I only allow myself to experience lust. There isn't room for long term commitment or love in my life or line of work. Sure, I had Carla, but I can't get serious enough to keep a good thing. It's been a few months, mostly, I'm just horny. And she deserves someone better.

We picked the name The Red Grotto for the club because my family is used to bleeding—bleeding blood, pride, and at times, money. We've taken all that and more from others to get where we are today. When we're threatened, blood will be spilled.

This year, Florence delivered an exceptionally hot summer, and even though it's September, it's way too hot, and some days are in the nineties. Between the heatwave and Dante and Juliet crawling all over each other, there were times they had to leave the room before we all got a steam bath.

I'm happy for them but can't let Dante live down the fact that he swore he'd be a bachelor forever. I guess true love can do that to a guy.

I stand behind the bar and check my phone. I'm not stalking my ex . . . I just like to see where she is and who she is hanging out with on social media. We were a couple close to a year, and I do miss the friendship, but I am what I am.

A player. I like to flirt. I'm the life of the party and I'm only serious about work. Not only do I run this bar, but I'm involved in the construction side of our business as well.

I don't have time to wine and dine women but when they find out I'm the owner of the club, their panties hit the floor. I use my father's condo here in Florence as a crash pad and for one-night stands. Carla is the only girlfriend I ever brought to my house in the hills overlooking Florence's vineyards in the countryside.

She was right to leave my sorry ass. I kissed another woman. It was a dare, but I have to admit, I liked it. Everyone knows Italian men are excellent lovers who find it difficult to be faithful. I'm not sure I'm capable of being faithful to one woman for the rest of my life—I'm afraid I'll lose interest and be miserable.

This club definitely delivers when it comes to the unspoken language of flirtation with its dirty dancing, wanton looks, and knowing smiles. It's all fun regardless of the outcome. Foreplay is the fun part where bodies bump and grind into each other until it leads to a heated hook-up. See, no words are needed, and most of the time, that's just how I like it.

With a name like The Red Grotto, the walls are painted a dark red to look like the inside of a *rosso* cave. The decorating is sheer genius and it's a comfortable vibe that our customers love.

We spared no expense building this club and have hand blown Murano glass lights hang over the numerous bars that give a touch of modern elegance to the marble bar tops. One lounge area even has a waterfall cascading down a wall, providing the ambiance of the coast. Italy has many fountains, and we decided to decorate by bringing the outside —inside.

This is our version of the Blue Grotto, only it's red. The real one is situated off the coast of Capri and is such a gorgeous place to visit that if I close my eyes, I can pretend I'm heading into light waves with sand sticking to my feet. It is a routine destination for the Etruscans of Italy as well as tourists from around the world.

Lost in my thoughts, I find myself under the staircase leading to the upstairs VIP room. I turn back for one last look at the mysterious girl. She's still in the same spot, her body gently moving to the beat of the music. I watch as she sways her hips just enough to allow her clingy mini-dress to showcase her voluptuous ass. I find myself aroused and turn away. She interacts with her waitress and watches couples on the dance floor.

Observing and reading people is partly my job and necessary for my survival. But even I know that a woman can make a man come undone and subsequently be the death of him. The luxury of being distracted is one that I can't afford.

How is it that she's here by herself? She's far too attractive not to have a date with her. It's not her dress or her looks, but something tells me she's not from here. We're very cosmopolitan these days. Around here, girls don't go to clubs alone unless they are desperate to get picked up or they are prostitutes, and I can tell she's neither. I try to place her. She seems vaguely familiar, but I can't make the connection.

I pause when I notice two strange men who don't look VIP-ish walking upstairs to the VIP area. I follow them. Remaining casual and inconspicuous, I breeze past them, pretending I don't see them selling drugs to the guests in the lounge. It's unacceptable, but I'm not surprised.

The hottest DJ in the city is pumping up the crowd and yells into the microphone for them to make some noise, and everyone yells, just as word comes over my earpiece, we are at maximum capacity. The music changes to hip hop as the DJ knows to mix Italian with American and other European hits. Italy has laws that dictate how much of the music on the radio stations has to be Italian to preserve our culture and the Italian language. Who says modernization and change is always good?

The dance floor is packed with girls grinding on guys they wanna take home for the night, or vice versa. Sirens go off, confetti drops from the ceiling, and the crowd goes wild as fake fog envelopes the dance floor, bringing with it a cool shift in the air.

I circle back downstairs, annoyed about the men upstairs using carte blanche to pedal drugs in our house. They are from another syndicate and should know better.

We own many clubs in the city and employ full-time managers, but this is a business that generates a lot of cash. I need to keep an eye on the till, and the alcohol pours to make sure we're not giving away money or products. The graft is everywhere, and I should know. My family makes an incredible living off it.

My blood runs hot, but I can't overreact to the mafia underlings with drugs. I send a waiter upstairs with free drinks to see if he can pick up an accent. He returns with the dreaded, but not unexpected news, Albanian.

Fuck!

I storm to my office and look at the security cameras to see if there are others. They know who owns this place, and they know they are not welcome here. It's a brazen move on their part, but they are encroaching on territory everywhere. And not just our family—it's every family in the business.

The cameras show no other suspicious activity in the parking lot or the rest of the club. They could be acting on their own, which is one more reason not to make waves that could escalate into something over nothing. I make a note to keep an eye on it. The Albanians usually don't come down this way, but I can't rule them out entirely as a potential problem.

After I take a deep breath and exhale, I leave my office and approach the waitress station.

"Maria, club soda, please." I need something in my hand so I don't punch someone.

"Sure." The bartender fills a glass with ice and uses the fountain gun to fill it with club soda before garnishing it with a wedge of lime.

"Thanks." I sip the drink and try to distract myself as my eyes scan the club.

Everyone seems to be having a good time, but my night is ruined. The Albanians are cutting into our business, and it needs to stop. Before I know it, they will be taking the place over, which is probably their intent. Or they will bring up crime in the area, so no one comes, and then buy the establishment for under-market value.

I hope they aren't spiking drinks with drugs or selling shit that could kill someone and blow back on me. We trust our own clans to a point, but to trust a rival organization? Never.

It could be just guys making their bones, a hazing, or a more elaborate setup.

Testing, always testing. I hate uncertainty. I hate rival mafia and gangs who think they can come here and deal on my turf. Clearly, they don't know what Dante's punishments are for their crimes. Let alone the things I am willing to do to send a message.

I empty my glass and set it on the bar with a loud *clunk*, not realizing the force I used.

"You alright?" Maria asks as she takes the glass.

"Yeah." That's always the answer, even if I'm not.

No one will know my mind, it's the Micheli way.

The break from the surveillance and the cool drink has calmed me down. I enjoy alcohol but rarely drink it at work, preferring to keep my senses sharp. I can see the exits, and, with my earpiece, I know where my guys are.

There are hundreds of customers here, and none of us want the undue attention of the police, so I keep myself in check even though I want to bounce those Albanian losers out.

We've remained in control of the criminal element in central Italy by thinking things through and not acting on impulses or emotions. Actions, good or bad, have consequences.

Dante's genius is knowing when to take risks. We knew it was risky going after Conti earlier this summer. Fucking with Juliet's father proved to be more dangerous than we could have ever anticipated. However, the authorities still haven't figured out what went down the night Conti got whacked on the rooftop of our luxurious five-star hotel. And we planned it that way.

We're very effective when we all put our heads together with our skill sets.

My phone vibrates in my pocket. I pull it out. Dante.

"Hey, what's up?"

"I just got word that Angelo Calabrese took over Conti's position as don for the Roselli family and other clans."

"We know anything about him?"

"Not much, can't be any worse than Gio Conti, in my opinion. I understand that there wasn't much bloodshed and that everyone is glad Conti is gone. His sons are on board with the changes."

"So, we can rest easy now?"

"For now, it seems."

I imagine Juliet is with him because he sounds happy, and then she giggles in the background.

"All good there?" I don't want our relationship to become all work with no brotherly connection. "Tell Juliet 'hi'."

"Will do. How are you?"

"I spotted a couple of Albanians selling coke upstairs earlier. I'll keep my eye on it. Other than that, seems pretty normal."

"Good, so I'll see you at the gala tomorrow night?"

"Wouldn't miss it."

"I don't know how a mask is going to hide your ugly mug. Do you have a date?"

"Going stag, in between annual flings."

"Looking forward to it, actually, I get to introduce Juliet to everyone."

"Well, her ring will arrive in the room before either of you."

"Thanks," he chuckles, "nothing is too good for my woman."

"*Ciao*," I say and hang up.

Good, maybe now that Commissioner Manara has backed off, life will get back to our abnormal but normal life.

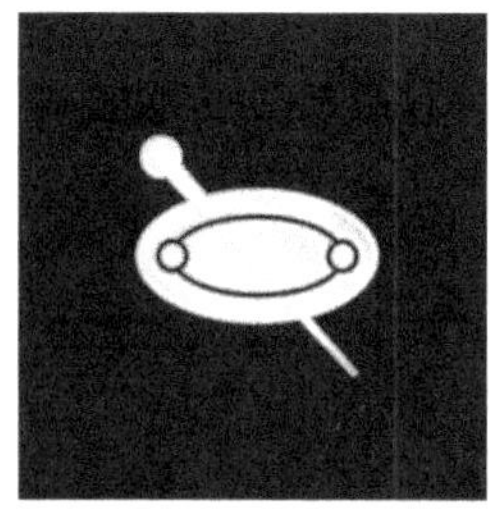

3

FRANCESCA

A warm shiver runs down my spine when his eyes run over my body. A man of his stature should know I am not some young chick looking to get laid. My gaze buckles under his. I look away, hoping he missed me staring at him. I'm not used to taking a back seat in any situation, and the past few days have me reeling.

Dad died unexpectedly. The new management has cut off my monthly allowance and fired me from overseeing the women my dad human trafficked and some side jobs that only he knew about. It played to his advantage that he was the only one who knew how skilled I was at ground warfare and hand combat. Never show your enemy all your strengths, he used to say.

I abhor that he did that, but if I was too vocal about it, I'd be silenced, so I decided to build myself up to not be fucked with by anyone, and I became a go-between for the girls he used. Turning them loose would result in my head being ripped off . . . and not in a gentle manner. Dad came down on us harder than anyone else as we had to be tougher than everyone, and he thought a bit of slapping around would help him achieve this.

I don't know what the Calabrese family has in store for the organization, but I do know they are not fond of me or my fight to end this barbaric tradition that has become a huge money-maker for them. We have brothels everywhere, and it's also a haven for selling drugs to clients. Another lucrative business we're into, especially with the profit margins of cocaine.

The slimy operations repulse me, and I have to be careful of enemies within my family, which are too many to count. They exist everywhere— shadows with no faces. My brothers would be the most likely candidates the Calabreses would send if they wanted me gone. The oldest trick in the book is to be taken down by those closest to you.

I'm quiet and don't advertise what I do with all my time at the gym, and they are not privy to as much of my life as they should be. I like to learn. If I make a mistake, I go back and learn why and fix it. One can never go directly against an organization this large. One has to be streetwise and plan a strategy. Or have powerful allies.

Being without a job is new to me, and I don't relish being broke any time soon. Not that I don't have a lucrative side business after I coached a woman boxer who went on to claim a title. I won a deal on outerwear with my brand on it. But no one knows the woman behind the company that would give it away. Anonymity is what public relations firms and numerous shell corporations give.

I have money saved, but I have expensive habits, and everyone knows it judging from my car that costs more than most middle-class homes.

I was the fucking *principessa* of the most feared don in Italy. How dare the Calabreses to treat me like I'm just any other woman in the street? One would think it was the Dark Ages for the lack of respect I get, and I'm only allowed on the fringes of the men's world. And God forbid they try to marry me off. Some girls are auctioned off or sold into slavery once their husband doesn't favor their bed anymore.

I demand respect but it appears to have slipped their mind. Since my father was gunned down, I've gotten snide remarks and slurs about being a woman and knowing my place. Any time I don't agree with my brothers or the man in command, I am greeted with comments most American women would slap them for. The most offensive comment is that I'm good at taking a dude's cock in my mouth.

It disgusts me that we have to put up with this treatment. But one day they will get theirs, and maybe I'll be the one to show them what retribution is all about. Maybe then they will look at me with respect.

I hoped it would be cathartic for me when my father died. He didn't think twice about inflicting his cruelty upon his kids. There are too many occasions to count when I hid under my bed or in the wine cellar until he fell asleep at night. But he still gives me nightmares.

I might wear the latest and most fashionable clothing and carry the most expensive designer bags. It doesn't escape my mind that I probably paid the most out of everyone for the privileges I received. I wasn't always so lucky at escaping his wrath.

I don't understand what makes a man do those things to his own flesh and blood. I hate men who bring their work home and use their wives and kids as punching bags. I hate men in general.

What the hell am I supposed to do? I'm twenty-five and have no future except one living behind the lines of society's laws. Sure, my two brothers can join the new rank and file as part of the restructuring, but it's clear that as a woman, I'm considered to be their property.

They will marry me off if I don't get out of here soon. I'll be an indentured servant to a husband who will expect me to pop out some kids, so I'll be stuck forever. I don't even like kids. I don't know if I want to risk being married to someone in the organization. Trusting men doesn't come easy.

All the anger I stifled for years broke like a dam this month when Sophia disappeared. No one will say it, but it's true, she's gone. I know too much not to pick up on the signs that this might be a problem for the new don. Even if the Calabrese doesn't pursue my father's killers, I want the people responsible to pay. Maybe if I prove my worth, I'll regain some position in the ranks, or they will let me lead my own life.

But, if Sal Micheli has the enslaved girls, maybe I can find Sophia, Perhaps that's why they were moved so suddenly.

My heart is filled with anger and vengeance. It appears my father died under dubious circumstances at our rival's hotel, and even though there is no conclusive evidence, it's enough for me. What I want, I get. And at times, you only get if you take, and Fausto made it sound like I'd find Sofia with the Michelis. This fuels my hatred of them even more.

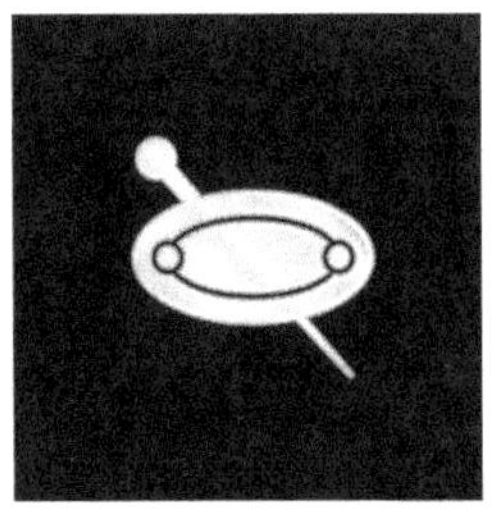

4

SAL

At the end of the night, I circle around again, looking for little Ms. High Society, but I can't find her anywhere. Trust me when I say that if I can't find her, no one can because a woman that gorgeous is hard to miss.

I swing by my office to make sure everything is in order for the deliveries tomorrow, and I empty the cash registers to put the money in the safe to be washed. After we declare it as sales, it's clean money.

When I put the key in the doorknob, I find my office is unlocked. Who could have been in my office? Only I have a key, as my assistant manager has his own office and safe, so no one comes in here.

I check my desk, and everything is just as I left it, and there isn't anything out of the ordinary. The list of booze to arrive tomorrow is here, and a message that Carla called is lying loose on my desk.

As if I need a note to remind myself that she probably wants to make up, gain closure, or just fuck.

I'm at a loss to know what that woman wants. I tend to

create my own drama with women as they usually bore me after a few dates.

I open my laptop with the security feed, and with one button tap it plays the footage to my office hallway. According to surveillance, no one has been here, but the hair on the back of my neck goes up.

Something isn't right. I can't piece it together. I need to be extra careful. Just because Gio Conti is dead doesn't mean his family has forgotten where he died.

I will omit the part about my office when I talk to Dante unless anything else happens, as he would go off on that. But there's nothing that I keep there that would incriminate us in anything. I have special places for anything that could jeopardize the family.

I'm perplexed at my weird evening and hope it's not a bad omen. Italians are very superstitious, and when I get a feeling in this line of business, it usually leads to something. It's only a matter of time before it all comes to light. Now is the time to take precautions and remain vigilant.

This is another reason I take my downtime seriously and look forward to going home and having a scotch as I lounge in my house in the country with my security staff. My phone beeps. I glance at it. Carla with an innocuous message.

The single life isn't as fun for girls as it is for me. Maybe Carla needs a good fuck, and I'm the one to deliver. Who wants to train a new guy when the last guy can't be beaten?

I knew she'd get tired of the boring dates, the cocktail hours that never progress to a dinner date because the conversation is enough to make one want to pluck their eyeballs out from boredom. It's times like this I catch myself thinking I need to get up and walk out. But it's not polite, so you sit for another hour. Another hour of life that I won't get back.

Work is always on my mind, and it's safer for Carla to not

be with me since Conti died at our feet. But we were cleared of involvement, and Commissioner Manara has backed off considerably.

We've laid low all summer, which has slowed cash flow a bit, but it's why I don't want the obvious drug sales in my club. It's the easiest way to go to jail forever short of racketeering and money laundering. I don't need some two-timing thug to open that door.

Especially when it's not our guy.

I stare at the video feed of the bar and recheck my hallway upstairs. It's so still as if the air conditioning isn't even blowing dust, so my radar is up. But no one can enter my office without a trace. Or can they?

And if they did, I'd want to meet them. I'm a people person and I like to learn new things, so if they can pull off this little caper, I can't imagine how badass they might be in other areas. Someone broke in undetected, and that's never happened before. Changing the locks won't help. If that's the case, I'll have to figure out a better system. But who was here?

Because I want to hire them.

I shrug it off as an odd occurrence but keep my eyes open as I tell Maria goodnight before checking in with the manager closing for me tonight. The valet turns to me and when our glances meet, he tosses me the keys to my sports car. He made sure no one fucked with it, so I tip him well.

Only then do I see a grey Rolls pull out of the valet station.

"Who drives that car?" I question the valet, who is eighteen but looks more like fourteen with no facial hair or body fat.

"I don't know, but she was hot and gave me a big tip."

"Was she blondish hair by any chance?"

"Yeah, she was. How did you know?"

"Thanks," I say, then drive off. I don't answer to anyone I don't want to unless it's Dante or Riccardo because neither of them ask me dumb questions, and they are both responsible for the entire organization.

Riccardo is the man who gets things done, and I wouldn't want to be on the wrong side of him. In fact, I respect him immensely.

One thing's for certain— that Rolls made a fast exit and is not cheap. Florence has no shortage of sports cars, but they are usually seen at fancy parties or in the mountains, where it's fun to maneuver the hairpin turns at breakneck speeds, just like the motorcyclists on the weekends.

I'm curious about where the woman was when I didn't spot her in the club. Her looks are distracting enough. Who is she? Does she have a sugar daddy?

Now she has me thinking about her naked in the backseat of that Rolls and what I'd like to do with my lips. I have an overactive imagination, and now it's all riled up. I'm pissed that I didn't hit on her before becoming distracted by the Albanians.

Gripping the wheel of my car I try to relax on the ride home because my boner needs a seatbelt, and it's not a comfortable feeling, especially when there's no one in my life to help release the pent-up Stallion in my pants. The steering wheel is still too close to my engorged cock.

There's something about high-end sports cars and custom leather seats that can be adjusted. You wouldn't believe how many women want to get laid in it. They should have designed it with a tilt adjustment one can make while driving.

I take my time as I cruise around the bends that take me up the mountain. I'm enjoying the drive where the landscape overlooks Florence. It's two in the morning, and the full moon's glow reflects off the blacktop illuminating my way home like pixie dust.

Maybe I'm a lucky man.

As I pull up to my house gravel crunches under the weight of my tires. The only light is from my headlights, illuminating the pale yellow walls and green shutters.

I like retro style, and the outdated wood shutters add a touch of old Italy to the architecture. Newer houses look more modern, but I like the old-world vibe best. The house has been in the family as long as I can remember.

It brings back fond memories of when Grandpa and Grandma lived here. I like to think that I'm on the cutting edge of everything new. When it came to wiring this place with the best security, there is nothing retro about it.

My guards let me know all is quiet before I go inside. The home I walk into gives little indication that I have spent the past year and buckets of money to renovate this place. Even at that, there is a laundry list of things that still need to be done.

It's way too hot to open the house, and I can't wait for winter to get here. We don't have three seasons anymore. I drop my keys on a ceramic plate that matches the décor of white, grey, and pale green.

My decorating vibe runs toward minimalist when it comes to furnishing the house. I chose lightweight drapes and white sheers to accent the clean white walls. I'm the money guy, so I like organization and being anal about details.

"Hey, Enzo," I greet my head guard on the back patio. He normally works for my brother, but I needed extra guards with everything happening in the south.

"Hello, sir, have a good night." He heads out to patrol the perimeter.

"Thanks, you too," I reply, dimming the lights in the

house. There is a small room at the bottom of the original wooden step by the front door worn thin from years of use. An antique armoire with a bench and hooks for coats is where I sat as a kid to take off my boots when we visited during the rainy season.

I pour myself a drink and head upstairs taking sips along the way and savor the flavor of a twenty-one-year-old scotch from Ireland. When I reach the landing I unbutton my dress shirt.

My phone dings and I hope it's not Marchello, who's always in some bind with his friends or playing cards. He's the only one of who can drop all this stress and worry like it's nothing. He simply lets it roll off his shoulders—like a duck in water.

He seems insulated from the violence around us and has a great sense of humor. I'm happy one of us doesn't appear to be as emotionally damaged.

"Pronto," I answer. "I better not have to bail you out of jail."

"No, not at all. I just ran into Carla, and I'm giving you the heads up, that she'll be at the gala tomorrow. You're still coming, right?" Marchello asks.

"Of course," I sip my drink, "it's business as usual." My voice is void of emotion. Carla is cute and comes from a good family, yet I still refuse to take the bait and settle down.

Now, with Dante engaged and a wedding being planned, it will keep Mama off our backs for some time. This leaves me free to milk the single life for five or more years. And if there is a grandbaby before then, I'm golden.

I can't pinpoint exactly why I grow bored with girls so quickly. It's as if they are the newest flavored alcohol that I have to try. Once. Maybe more than once, if I like the flavor. But it never lasts longer than a year. I think the three of us all play a game where one of us dates a girl to keep Mama busy, and we give her hope that one day we'll all be hitched and expand the family.

She'll be busy planning Dante's wedding, so Marchello and I have a short reprieve. I'm Italian, we philander and have mistresses. I can thank my ancestors for that. Or curse them. It seems to get me in trouble, and all I did was partake in one innocent kiss with another woman.

"Everyone will be there tomorrow night?"

"Yes, just like always. We need to raise a ton of money for the new children's wing, so we will be rubbing lots of elbows over the surf and turf," he chuckles, "and cigars and whisky at your club as an afterparty if we're able to get away afterward."

"Great, I'll see you tomorrow night, little brother. *Buona notte.*"

"*Ciao.*"

If this was springtime, the windows would be open, and the curtains would be blowing in the wind from the mountain, bringing cooler air. But not tonight.

It's technically past our official summer, but the humidity clings to me, and the temperatures now remain as high as the nineties until late September. It's hot enough to set my fucking balls on fire, so I peel off the rest of my clothing and finish my whiskey.

I take a lukewarm shower, but the emerald-green eyes of the hot, dirty blonde haunt my thoughts. Carla will have to wait if I call her back at all. I haven't decided yet.

The serenity I find inside my house is what I crave. This is my refuge, my escape, my get-away-from-it all. Life has so much drama. I breathe easier every time I come home.

I kept a few working fireplaces, so I guess there is a bit of romantic buried under this dark heart. One fireplace is located in a small room just inside the front door. The other is in the cozy living room with French doors that open onto the terrace that overlooks my modest vineyard.

The property has plenty of unused acreage and some outlying buildings, like the detached garage and greenhouse that sit two hundred yards away from the house.

I haven't had much time to deal with the vineyard, so I pay someone to maintain it. I have much to learn, but one of these days, I hope to create an incredible Chianti. For now, I leave it to the professionals.

My brother, Dante, can be a bit of a taskmaster, and between the club and the construction company, I'm never at a loss for something to do. Thankfully, I have people I trust and delegate work to, but it still leaves many other details that only I can carry out.

Days off are Sundays, and even then, we get our most important conversations in at Mama's house. The backyard is our most prized office space, as we can drink, have a cigar, and talk without the confines of walls or moles that might have infiltrated us. However, I doubt that.

I throw my phone on the charger before I remove my bath towel—reveling in the freedom I have to do so because my life is micromanaged for my safety—then slip into bed butt naked.

I SLEEP IN, and I'm still sleepy by the time I roll over and crawl out of bed. Today will be a long day. We've booked six outrageously expensive tables to enable us to work our deals under everyone's unsuspecting eyes. Eyes that are focused on friends, politicians, fashion, luxurious food, and ambiance, not dark criminal figures conjuring deals in public.

We accomplish an unprecedented amount of business in a few hours while eating food made by famous chefs and drinking expensive champagne. Mama doesn't need to know it's our annual meeting with local and foreign contacts.

The event is filled with decadent food, alcohol, and gorgeous women. Millionaires and billionaires? Oh yeah, and did I mention an abundance of pretty women who are divorced and very wealthy?

We've reserved tables for our construction company one for Micheli Enterprises, and our counterparts in crime have their tables near ours. Families of various names that most people wouldn't think twice about as our business affiliations on or off the books. Most have forgotten the days of my grandfather and the mafia wars. Today, we blend in with high society and build legit businesses.

That's why I put the university's dean next to our table along with others who aren't connected to us. Knowing what I do and how we work while everyone else visits is funny. The irony isn't lost on me. The fact that no one suspects a thing makes it the perfect meeting place.

I throw back the soft sheet covering my hard abs and walk to the window that overlooks the rows of trellis filled with ripening grapes. It brings a smile to my face.

Soon it will be time to harvest them. That's when the open bed trucks will slow down traffic as they congest the double lane roads to take the grapes to be processed over old roads.

I throw on some workout shorts. I jog on the treadmill downstairs before whaling on the punching bag. It gets my heart rate up, and when I've completed my forty minutes of aerobic activity, I pour myself some orange juice and make myself some hardboiled eggs and thinly sliced bacon that takes just a few minutes to cook.

I drizzle some olive oil on the peeled eggs and sit down with two espressos. It sucks eating alone, but it's the least of my worries. My mind wanders to what Carla will be wearing tonight. Then, I chastise myself for thinking of her when my heart isn't in it.

What heart? We're just meeting basic needs. Sex. Lust. A one-time hookup. Maybe that's why she was texting me yesterday. I'm such an ass; I need to stick to girls who aren't looking to settle down.

I like what I like. If a woman doesn't captivate me at the first glance, I don't bother because you can't fake chemistry. Fucking is no fun without being aroused to the point of oblivion. It sounds terrible, but we all have standards.

I know enough to stay away from the girls that are ten, like the girl at the club. The dark-blonde with highlights from last night has high maintenance written all over her, and I think her car might cost more than mine. She must be married to a wealthy man, but I doubt he would let her out late at night alone. I don't know why I'm still thinking of her. I doubt I'll ever see her again.

Besides, I can't have a woman hotter than myself because I'm enough high maintenance for two, and I'd hate competing all the time. There's plenty of that between work and my two brothers.

I surf the channels to relax before sinking into my soft sofa in the living room, killing time until I get dressed. This is one of my favorite rooms with large paned windows that cost a fortune to install.

The incredible view of the vineyard and the hill slope behind the house is picture-worthy. The cost of the new windows was worth every penny.

Mom calls. She's worried her dress isn't perfect. This is the event of the year and something she always attended with my father, so I know that she's missing him, and it's not the dress that makes her nervous. She goes through this around his birthday and the anniversary of his death.

"It will be okay, Mama." I try to console her before she breaks down in tears.

"I know," she says, but a sob catches in her throat as she tries to be brave for me.

Granted, he was my dad, and I certainly miss him, but it's been a few years. Dante took over for him, which was to be expected.

"Mama, Mama, come on. It will be fine. Look, I'll save the first dance for you," I offer, hoping it cheers her up.

"Oh, that would be wonderful." A doorbell buzzes in the background. It's one formality that time hasn't changed in Italy. There are buzzers at every door to get into all condos and apartments. "Hold on, that must be Isabelle." She covers the mic of her phone but calls out to her guests just the same.

Her heels move swiftly over the tiled floor as she walks to the door. I'm not surprised that the voice I've identified belongs to Isabelle. She comes to help her dress and do her hair.

"I'm fine, Sal. Isabelle is here." With the lighter tone in her voice, I know she's fine. I am consoled by the fact that she has someone besides me to talk to.

"Great, Mama, I'll see you tonight."

"*Ciao*."

I watch football, but when the Brazilian team takes the lead, I lose interest, and the next thing I know, the TV shows a different game. I must have fallen asleep, but I shrug it off. It's the beginning of the season, so there is time for Italy to make up for the loss.

I SHAVE with care before donning my outfit for tonight. Men like me who go to these formal events all the time don't rent tuxedos. We own one, sometimes two. We all look the same from a distance, but there are subtle differences: double-breasted or single-breasted, cummerbund or vest, bow ties or regular ties.

I don't complain. In fact, I kinda enjoy dressing up in a tux with the tail and a wing-collared shirt. I change it up just a bit with a blue square of silk in my front pocket to match my cufflinks.

I open the top drawer of my dresser and pull out a box the size of a desktop cigar humidor, only it holds my watches and cuff links. I select the cufflinks with a double row of sapphires that wrap around a square group of individual diamonds. They look more like rings than cuff links, but I like them. Not many men wear them today, but I'm a traditionalist, and these are sentimental. My grandfather and father wore them, and now I wear them.

Before I leave, I make sure the motion sensor alarm is on inside the house, and two guards are on duty. This is a gated estate, but I still retain armed guards. Dante agreed to have Enzo here with another regular. Matteo will be at the event, posing as a valuable employee for our construction company.

Now that things have settled down with the Conti family, Dante is more than happy to share our most loyal protectors. The bodyguards blend in with our world without a second thought. They don't need to advertise what they do for a living.

I rev the engine and hear the tires squeal as I round the first bend down the mountain to Florence. I look forward to seeing my family and knowing we are all safely meeting at the prestigious San Ferdinando Hotel near the Uffizi. It will be like old times, only without Dad.

. . .

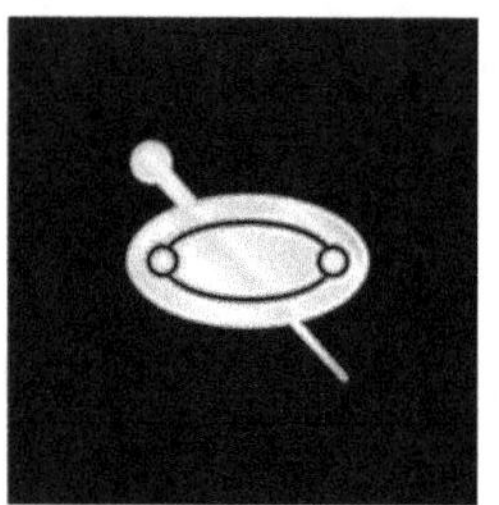

5

FRANCESCA

I journey north enjoying the scenery, and I regret not traveling more. I've taken so much for granted, so this might be a new beginning for me if I play my cards right. I continue to travel under the moonless night that serves as my cloud of obscurity.

I drive north to Florence to check out the situation, checking into a hotel that is not worthy of my stature, but it saves me money, and no one will recognize me, not that anyone should. No one expects me here as I usually stay at the five-star hotel downtown. I wear a ball cap, tattered jeans, and a pair of white sneakers, even if they cost two hundred euros.

I lived the princess lifestyle and spent my days ordering help around, shopping, and doing things with my few friends or boyfriends. As far as boyfriends, my daddy had everyone keeping their eyes on for one misstep. They never lasted long before someone ran them off with cold stares that even gave me a chill.

I'm doomed to a life without lovers, except for my trainer

and instructor. We could easily hook up at the gym for hot, sweaty sex after an intense workout.

I fight a marriage of convenience to bring in more clans, money, or power. God only knows how old that man might be. I could be one of the marriages that end with the woman being sent off to what we call the 'she left' divorce.

Granted, the Calabreses are thankful to my father for building the empire they now control. I am usually good at reading people, but I can't read them.

For all I know, my head might be on a chopping block next because I haven't pledged fealty to the new don. I'm sure that statement won't be lost on Angelo.

Personally, I don't care who takes over and since I'm not an acting member of the family I don't understand why I should have to kiss his ass.

But if I can find Sofia and the girls, I can get back at my brothers, Angelo, and the Micheli's, effectively knocking off three birds with one stone. I suspect Dante was behind my father's demise. I'm thinking killing Dante's brother Sal is easier than hitting Dante and will give him a life filled with regret and remorse.

Besides, killing a don will get me killed faster than if I kill a relative of a don. Killing relatives or bosses can be fixed. It will be safer in the long run, and maybe I can get information out of him before he goes.

I've mapped out the family and know their faces and schedules, and now it's time for the one-on-one recon.

The club is hopping tonight, and the vibe is tantalizing, or maybe it's the tall Italian in the tailored suit taking everything in and then some as he notices the pretty women. The club is popular and even known in southern Italy, making it easy to find Sal Micheli as I order another Cosmo.

See, it's not so hard. He could come right up to me and

not know who I am. Daddy kept me hidden well for fear I'd be kidnapped. In retrospect, it was just another way for him to control me.

The waitress is nervous under Sal's scrutiny and spills some of my drink on the table. "*Scusi*," she mumbles.

"Watch what you're doing the next time," I bark at the waitress who looks a few years younger than me. Now, she looks like she might cry.

Shit.

I don't want to draw attention to myself but as usual, my quick tongue has made that nearly impossible. It's the Italian in me. I can be abrupt at times. One reason I am sure Gio Conti was my dad.

I've heard talk of other children by his mistresses, but it's all very hush-hush. Rumors circulate and I'm anxious to meet the latest arrival on the family scene. Juliet.

I'm a hunter tracking its prey as I eye my mark. Like an eagle, I watch him walk around the bar. Sal has no clue what I have planned. He has the usual number of bodyguards doubling as security for the club, and the place is packed.

Dante is too difficult to get to, Sal is definitely the easier target. He is likable, judging from his interactions with his staff. Killing him will fill Dante with a lifetime of regret for killing my father and bringing this upon his family. He will be hurt like I've been hurt.

I've already scoped out the home where Sal lives, and from there, I followed him to work. I try to blend in while I take inventory of his guards and identify any routines I can take advantage of during the hit. I must admit the club is impressive. I can't help but enjoy the music as I sway to the beat.

It's obvious the bar is popular and must be making bank. The ambiance is intoxicating, and I find myself lost in thoughts of happier times as people dance and get liquored up around me, and for a second, I wish I could join them and be just another normal twenty-five-year-old out with her friends for a night of fun.

Sal's eyes are checking me out again, and he's sizing me up to see if I meet his criteria. However, killing him in his bed is too . . . normal. No, for him, I want to make a large splash.

Luckily, my car and clothes fit in with the crowd. I decided the bar is too visible for a shooting. I know the annual half-mask gala is coming up to raise money for the children's hospital, and everyone who is anyone will be attending. I have it on a good source that the Micheli family goes every year.

It's always good to mix business with pleasure at huge and very public events, especially if you have to speak with people who might raise an eyebrow, like the owners of cash operations and houses of prostitution. I mean, it's no secret that elected officials use these places from time to time for free.

It's the oil that keeps the machine going.

Until the gala this weekend, I will use what I have picked up over the years to make this hit successful. Then my clan will want me back in due haste because it will mean we've avenged our father's death. Something they were too weak to do themselves.

Granted, I'm not a made woman yet, but I want to have my allowance restored on a general principle. I have an adequate standard of living without my family's money because I know it's a brutal world, and I trust no one to provide for me.

I believe in being in control of my destiny and maybe

that's why I can't commit to a relationship. Giving up control in this world shows weakness, and I'm not weak.

Do I deserve to be paid by the organization? Yes. I deserve compensation for my father's years of service and ultimate sacrifice. Once I have that, and once I make that right, I'll be untouchable.

I pick up my phone to check the time. I stayed later than expected. No one knows where I am, plausible deniability.

I pay for my last Cosmo with cash as I turn another potential suitor away and make the decision that the annual ball must be the place. It's a masked ball, and I can cover my face around cameras.

It will be at night with limited lighting for dancing. The fact that the place will be packed with other syndicates will help to keep eyes off me. Who would suspect me, the only daughter of don Conti, of being ballsy enough to take on the Micheli family?

Besides, it's been months and there is no talk of retaliation from our side. They probably think they are in the clear now and will help me even more if security becomes lax.

The anger over my dad is one thing, but the anger of the girls missing and the fact that Sal or Dante is behind it disgusts me. He's busy with the Albanians, whom I happen to recognize by their clothing and posture, which will keep him distracted so I slip up the other staircase where I assume his office is. He launders money here for sure, so it makes sense that he keeps his books locked away somewhere. I just want to find evidence that he paid Angelo.

Personally, I didn't think Angelo would do business with our worst enemy in the history of the planet. I doubt it was a popular move unless the money made him overlook many details.

I pull out my lockpick set from my tiny handbag and pop

open his drawer no problem. I carefully rifle through his papers and ledgers that are in code and take pictures of them.

I slip out under the cover of night, mingling with the Florence crowd on the street. Dad had so many enemies. He didn't want my death to be on his conscious and kept me away from prying eyes. But I'll show the family I can do what they can't or won't.

I don't have to tell them that I set the girls free once I find them, but I have to find Sofia. She's the main focus. She must be found even if I might have to do some unsavory things to find her. What is Sal's life worth if I can set twenty innocent girls free?

I'm the best at what I do. And sneaking away to learn ground fighting on the rough streets was easy and even though I got hurt, I realized it would come in handy at an early age.

If my husband ever raises a hand to me, he'll pick his teeth off the floor. Worst case scenario, I'd have to make his death look like an accident if that is the path my life will go down.

I'm undecided about where my future will be—going home the victor or striking out on my own with Sofia.

For now, I'm just happy to be out of my family's town. But if I'm gone too long, the Calabreses' will come to their own conclusions and depending on what that is, dictates whether I live or die.

The gala is an extremely public event, and security nowadays relies on electronic wands to catch everything. I could strap a gun made of plastic to my leg the night of the masked ball. Or better yet, I will leave a gun at the event location beforehand. Everyone has watched *The Godfather* movie and knows to hide a gun beforehand. What else is the back of a toilet good for?

I will show everyone that I'm not to be fucked with and that you never say no to Gio Conti's daughter. I will never willingly enter an arranged marriage or be with a man in the mafia.

Fuck that.

I'VE BEEN in Florence for a week now, and as I'm going after Sal, if I get caught, it carries a less formal punishment than killing a don. I'm pissed as hell that Dante has gotten away with murdering my father. An inconclusive police report, my ass. I want to know how much he had to pay the commissioner in Milan for that. Why Daddy went there just to settle a score older than me is a question I'll never have an answer for because I don't trust my brothers' lame stories.

After scoping out everything and planning exit strategies for the gala beforehand, it's finally here. My evening is long. My plan is to park near the Uffizi, then walk a short distance to the event. I'm dressed to kill but it's not just sexy, it's also practical.

An almost skin-tight black dress is not as flowing as other young ladies, and I wear a cover designed to tear away in case I need to use my combat moves. I chose black for this occasion to blend in with the night.

I put my makeup on with care and make sure my mask is tied securely so it won't go anywhere. The hotel doesn't have that many cameras, but why take unnecessary risks?

My hair is styled in an updo. I had it bleached at the salon to match my new ID. I wore a wig for the pictures on it as I couldn't be blonde at home.

Today, I had my hair coiffed at the salon and they did a great job, the only difference is I replaced the metal clip with a large decorative pin laced with poison in case I get into trouble.

I finish dressing, sliding on my three-inch heels. I have developed my legs and can walk miles in any shoe. I have an escape route planned and will escape to my car on foot. I have a ceramic knife sheath on my leg, just in case. It never hurts to have a backup plan.

I slide behind the steering wheel of my beloved Rolls, inhaling the rich leather interior. It's the most expensive thing Dad bought me. Then again, my home was extravagant compared to most.

Now that my mother has moved on and the estate has been taken over by Angelo. He's modified it with secret rooms and such, there's no better way to continue building the empire than to stave off an attack.

I drive to the event running potential scenarios through my head. Sal has to be alone to do the deed, obviously. Where and when will that happen? What if I never have the opportunity? I fret over the details I can't plot and have anxiety as I'm not in control of the surroundings I'm entering. Not a good combat move.

The night air is humid. I have a pocket in my outerwear for my keys, tissues, and a burner phone. I use the white square to blot the sweat off my face as I join the line to enter the gala, having purchased my ticket under an alias.

Upon entering the luxury hotel, I am immediately aware of the energy and excitement as everyone laughs, talks, and mills about in anticipation of the big gala. Soft music floats over me as the string orchestra plays, sitting in an ancient alcove.

Little do they know how eventful tonight will be. Cameras go off before I reach the entrance. I make sure to dodge the limelight and others who are using their phone to video the evening with my mask securely in place.

Bentleys, Rolls Royces . . . you name it, everyone flaunts it tonight—their cars, jewels, and other finery. I can't say I blame them for being a mafia princess. I love the lifestyle, too. I realized too late that not having a backup plan when you were being supported was the biggest mistake of my life.

Many women are wearing the same black and gold mask as mine. I made sure to buy it in a store that sold hundreds so it couldn't be traced to a special purchase. I've watched my share of murder and mystery TV over the years with the series *Elementary* being my favorite. God, I love Jonny Lee Miller. Kitty is my role model. The abused, scorned girl gone rogue, a vigilante for justice. Love it.

I find my way to the ballroom where dining tables are lined up as if in a private parade. There are hundreds of people, wealthy people who can afford the outrageous price of admission. This expense is nothing to them, compared to maintaining their fancy homes.

I should know. We had an incredible compound with a pool, tennis courts, horses, and stables. Dad didn't earn everything we had. I'm sure he did his share of just taking what he wanted.

The crystal chandeliers are beautiful, and for a second, I feel like a princess in a fairytale. Only this is the Micheli territory and if they had a daughter, she would be the belle of this ball.

No expense has been spared tonight. Each table brims with fresh floral arrangements of exotic orchids, baby's breath, green leaves, and white dust to resemble snow as the seasons are all represented in centerpieces. The buffet table has a carving station, a table of side dishes, and a dessert table. Large ice sculptures depicting the four seasons statues on the bridge next to the Uffizi grace each of the four large food tables. It is after all, the Four Seasons of Florence Annual Gala.

Photographers dressed in suits abound, flashing overhead lamps as if Prince William of England was in the room.

A line of couples stand in queue as they wait for their turn to use the requisite photo booth for tiny snapshots that resemble the first Polaroid instant developing pictures that were before my time.

Everyone smiles when they exit the booth, whether they are in couples or groups. They laugh at the funny faces the camera captured for their scrapbook because the memories will fade in a few days.

I've studied the hotel's floor plan as well as Dante and Sal's houses. Now, I need to find out where Sal is sitting because those are always the last known bits of the necessary information that can't be acquired beforehand. As luck would have it, I spot him on my way to the check-in table.

The tall darker, haired man next to him is the incredibly handsome Dante who escorts his mother and what I can only assume is my half-sister.

Her hair is dark like mine and neither of us is exceptionally tall, but I beat her by a few inches. I'm glad I changed my hair color as it would be obvious that we are related if anyone were to catch us standing together.

Strange that I have a sister I never knew about and that we're so alike with our facial features and petite frames.

I turn my focus back to my subject, and it looks like the gang and a few bodyguards posing as guests are all here.

Fantastico!

I slide behind a group of people and make it my mission to study them and find out where they bought tables. I should have done more than just one week of recon on him, but he's fairly predictable, going to work daily and living in such an isolated place.

I could have killed him at his isolated farmhouse but the guards and the rough layout of the vineyards made an approach out in the open detrimental to my end game.

It would be nice if I could have gutted him and left him decomposing until his brother found him. But no, that is not going to be his fate.

He will be sorry to be a Micheli tonight, but not before I extract information from him. He launders the money, he's the brother of the don, he'll know what's going on and lead me to Sofia.

Classical music floats across the room from the string quartet, but I can't let that distract me. Alessandro taught me that any discipline worth learning has to be done to perfection. Now, it's second nature to block out unnecessary distractions as the swirl of the festivities fades to black. I focus on my hunt.

The other men around Sal act like familiars. They seem to know each other enough to make friendly conversation. If I had to guess I'd say they are on the fringes of the inner circle and are making points with the brother to the don. It's safe to assume the trust only goes so far because one of the nearby tables has another mafia faction seated at it.

They look familiar, but I wouldn't know them by name. These are the types of men that move at night and behind the scenes and only one man high up in the organization would know.

Dante's brothers know their place and don't upstage the don for attention. In fact, the brothers don't even have a companion with them.

I make my way to the open bar. Red wine seems fitting

for the evening I have planned. I set out to identify the rest of the players in tonight's game.

Ah, at last, I think I've identified Dante's right-hand man. He's handsome, forty-ish, and when he's not flanking Dante, he steps away here and there to talk to men at other tables, then carries news back to Dante. Their heads are close, so I'm sure they are conducting business right under the nose of high society. Yes, I'm sure he's Dante's man, Ricardo, is his most trusted person next to his brothers.

And the other man at the nearby table is…I recognize him from the news. He's from Florida, Viggiani. Yeah, Antonio. Wow, this is turning into a real 'who's who' in the world of organized crime. No wonder a wall of men in suits surround him like a human shield. He's in his late seventies, and the years have not been kind to him as the head of the crime syndicates' American connection.

Probably too much sunshine, I muse to myself, lost in thought. However I'm not surprised and let out a tiny *huff*. It seems fitting he's in Florida at this age, having started in New York and moving south like they notoriously do.

My plan to carry out my debauchery in plain view of this esteemed guest list is brilliant, and I want to laugh out loud at the sheer irony. But I hold my snicker in. Besides, it's bad form to celebrate before I pull off my mission. It's bad luck, too.

Shakespeare would be so proud that human nature is playing out flawlessly. Money, greed, power, and death all represented and came together at the year's greatest and most publicized event.

Dante is laughing with his brother as they walk to their table. When they take their seats, I glance at my sister hanging on Dante's arm. Is that a humungous diamond on her finger? Engagement ring? How progressive of him, but a good call, seeing as how he was a sworn bachelor for so long. He makes the most eligible bachelor list in Florence every year.

Sal flits around like a butterfly, one minute flirting with the server, bringing him a glass of French champagne, the next minute snagging an appetizer off another server's tray as she passes by. He turns to his younger brother, who joins the family at the table. My research says his name is Marchello, the youngest in the family.

The family lies low, and their name is unblemished, tied mostly by their family history of a huge war that raged with our grandparents and their sons. It's amazing what a great public relations company can do for the family name. I'm not surprised as they are the Mafia royalty of Central Italy to those of us who know the name and history. They are the equivalent of my family in the south, before my father carried everything too far. His arrogance did him in, and Dante is to blame for me being an outcast.

The press paints the Michelis as legitimate, focusing on their charity work and ribbon-cutting ceremonies. You'd think Dante was running for office by the way he works the room tonight.

Men pay fealty while women bat their pretentious fake lashes at him and some even grab his butt as he gently moves their hands away. With his charismatic face and engaging smile, the title 'Mayor of Florence' would look good on him.

The woman next to him hangs on his every word, and he acknowledges her by softly placing his lips on hers for a kiss that isn't long enough to be considered bad manners at the prestigious event. Juliet, a sister I had longed for since I was little, but I never knew she existed until a few months ago.

The rumor is she was the beginning of the end of my

father, but no one will explain to me what that means. Did he meet her? Did he know she was his all these years?

Juliet is gorgeous with her black hair and smoldering eyes. I can see why Dante fell in love with her. Tonight's event must be her first plunge into society. Her face is aglow, and her smile can't be contained as she's welcomed by people who line up to meet her. She has all the tell-tale signs that show she is a socialite virgin as she demurely accepts the attention.

I swear, sometimes it's as if Europe has returned to the dark ages. If a woman is too sexy, she's asking for it, but this woman is wearing a long off-the-shoulder dress that mixes conservative with sexy, and the winner is sexy. The light catches on her ringed finger as she swings it through the air as she speaks.

I'm stunned that Dante is allowing himself to be vulnerable with a wife and future family that can be used against him. Does he think our silence is a truce between our families?

Hum. . . accidents happen all the time. So does mayhem.

This truce isn't talked about, but there is a lull in the air that implies it as months have passed since Dad's funeral. And to think that I will fuck it up for the sake of finding Sofia will not go over well at home. Making a point to my brothers and Angelo Calabrese is a side benefit for keeping me out of the loop.

I'm pissed over the fact no one will say Sofia's name. It's bad enough that we had the illegal girls, but I could help them somewhat and intercede on their behalf, telling myself I was a better person for keeping them alive.

I have nothing to lose as I look for the girls and my BFF. I've lost my father, my mother to her long-lost lover from high school, and my brothers are with my despised enemies.

My brothers, who are clones of Dad, and a bit psychotic, didn't have their rivals killed off fast enough is my guess.

What a pussy for not taking his rightful place where Dad sat.

I can't love family that I have no respect for and there is no one in the world I love more than Gran and Sofia. I love Alessandro but he didn't want to be a part of my heritage, and I can't hold that against him.

Sofia is my only connection to my life right now. I need to find her and set the others free.

I have nothing left to lose as I gaze at the handsome Sal. Hmm. I purse my lips together. He's tall with a slim frame, toned, agile. His tux fits him like a second skin.

He is devilishly sexy as he moves like a sleek cat, making his way to his mother, Mrs. Micheli, where he showers her with attention. He's quite the charmer, and she lets out a light laugh just before a bell rings. It's time for everyone to take their places.

I can't risk being seen, so I hide near the long, heavy curtains used to divide rooms for smaller functions. I raise my right hand and lightly touch my mask, making sure it's in place. I would have painted it on had it not made me look different from everyone else. I cannot risk someone remembering me after Sal's murder.

The beating of my heart pounds in my ears as anxiety swells in my chest. Fuck, this needs to move faster. The first rule is a quick in and a faster out when doing a job. It's one of the many things I've learned over the years while listening to the men talking in the war room near my father's office.

Despite my father's ruthless and disturbing reputation, I'm not my dad, and I have no doubts about taking a life. To be on the brink of a kill, yes. But I'd only kill out of necessity, a forgone conclusion that I must in order to live another day. With one exception. Sal.

But first, I have to get Sofia's location from him.

The endorphins of being in a real battle take over and will be a hell of a rush if I come out the victor.

I'm not in denial that Dad was . . . unbalanced, void of empathy and emotion. I try to relax and smile politely as a few women in heavily beaded gowns walk by, making their way to the ladies' room or outside to smoke.

On the stage, introductions are made, followed by one boring speech after another. Only people who know the speakers care. I tap my right foot, anxious for the next part of this pomp and circumstance rodeo to end. Rome has the same fancy events.

Italy is a place where outdoor concerts are held inside what was once home to Roman soldiers. They lived inside fortresses. Our piazzas hold holiday concerts all over the country as we are very much into opera and pop music. A country dedicated to art, culture, music, and—mafia wars.

That's the double standard with organized crime families. It's all so formal. There is respect and loyalty, but often it is given based on one incredible feat or a moment, and it may not be authentically earned.

For instance, Daddy got it through fear and intimidation. Violence originally occurred years before the unfettered fear factor. In his final years, intimidation brought about the results he was after without violence. . . most of the time.

A real leader gains respect due to a special skill set such as strengths beyond that of the others in the pack. To be successful, one must be surrounded by loyal and skilled people. Otherwise, the don won't last long. Dante is young however, I believe he's proven himself in the dark world in which we operate.

I refuse to be afraid as my eyes detect Sal heading toward the men's room down a hallway. I figure now is as good a time as any. Sorry to all the people who made large contributions just to have their night ruined by a little murder.

Sal is alone and unsuspecting as he casually swings the bathroom door open and slips inside, none-the-wiser.

I pause outside the door to give him time to pull his dick out for much-needed relief after an hour of drinking cocktails. I push the door open with my shoulder, slowly and without a sound.

It's reflex that he will glance in the bathroom mirror in front of him and it's now or never as I leap like a panther, landing on his back and clamping my strong thighs around him. My heart is pumping fast enough to cause a heart attack, I'm sure of it.

He swings around in an attempt to fling me off, but my grip is too strong, and I stick to him like my life depends on it. And it does.

Instinctively, he knows this is a hit and pulls at my hands clinched around his throat as he realizes his move is redundant. Even if this hit is not ordered from our Don, a hit is a hit. I'm not a man, but he knows this is real.

I've always been a bit of a rebel. Some habits are hard to break.

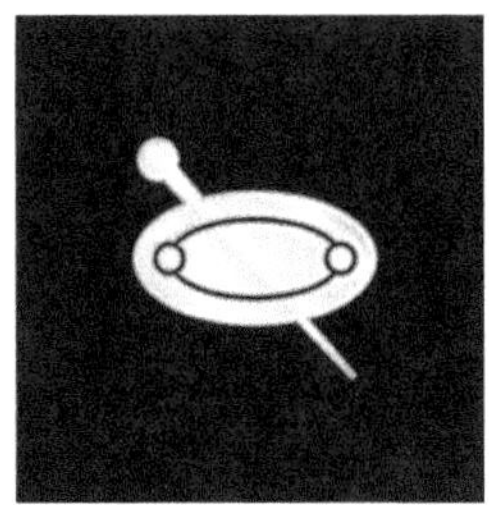

6

SAL

Out of the corner of my eye, my brain gets a fast glimpse of a gorgeous woman moving with the swiftness of a cheetah and she's on my back before I can blink.

By the time I jiggle off my dick, she's on me before I can blink, her arms have the strength of a giant for someone so small. Her hands are more like an octopus wrapped around my neck for such petite hands, but they are strong enough to strangle me.

I turn quickly, this way and that. I can't shake her, but her choke hold restricts my oxygen.

Oddio!

This might be the end of me if I can't get out of her vise-like grip. I've known men that have died with the first leap if the person is learned in martial arts.

Strong thighs are clamped around my waist. Survival is all I care about. No use yelling. I grab her arm in an attempt to leverage it to throw her off enough as I attempt to get a hold on her. She's no play toy to be tossed, and I realize all too late that she's trained. And trained well, as in a trained killer, but I can't process anything other than sheer survival maneuvers.

"Tell me where Sofia is." She gets her arm under my neck as if to snap it like a twig.

"Don't know." I gag with the little air I have left.

I use this as an opportunity to run backwards slamming her back up against the tiled wall in the urinal area.

The next think I know, the pressure on my neck is gone and I hear familiar voices as I crumble to the floor and gasp for air.

My breathing is irregular overcoming my brush with death and I calm down to regain my composure now that help has arrived in the form of . . . Dante, who is standing over the woman he knocked off me and is now wrestled to the floor. Her face is down, and her arms are behind her as Dante kneels over her.

And here I always thought a bullet was the most lethal way to die in our world, not a cat-like martial arts aficionado that strikes in one of the most public events of the year. And who the hell would suspect a woman?

Fuck, she's brilliant, is what I'm thinking. Well played, indeed.

Dante lifts her to her feet and restrains her arms as she protests and kicks. Riccardo enters, blocking the door behind him so we aren't disturbed. Using zip ties, he pulls them snugly around her locked hands, placing them behind her back, which I know from experience is more uncomfortable.

"You . . ." I gaze at her, looking so perfect, her hair is mussed a bit, but other than that, one would never know what transpired a minute ago. "You were in the club last night." I stand and approach her to get a better look at her face.

Her luscious lips are full, but not with filler. Some tendrils have fallen out of her high society up-do and give the impression that she had a hot make-out session with the color in her cheeks and her elevated breathing.

She spits on my shoes.

I slap her face hard enough to make her head turn as far as it can go. Under normal circumstances, I would never hit a woman. But she's out of control, out of her league, and worse yet . . .

We don't know who she is.

And she tried to kill me!

"Who sent you?" I demand.

She looks at the ground.

"The silent treatment, hmm?"

"Are you okay, Sal?" Dante asks, turning her over to Riccardo.

Voices are approaching the door. Dante reaches into his vest pocket and jabs the woman in the neck as Riccardo bears her weight to hold her upright as she slumps against him.

"What did you do that for?" I'm shocked. But he's the don and this is the event of the year—the event where we conduct business under the noses of officials, lawyers and our friends. The masks cover more than our faces.

"She was going to scream." Dante's voice raises more than one would want in this situation. "People are coming. We need to move her now. And she'll look drunk," his voice lowers as his calm demeanor returns. He cocks his head as we prepare to roll out, and it's business as usual.

Only it's a woman we're carrying out.

Riccardo pulls out a pocket knife and cuts the zip ties on her wrists. I take one of her arms and put it over my broad shoulder, where I hold it in place.

"We need to get her out of here without making a scene. Dante, you'll be missed. Let Sal and I take her to the interrogation room," Riccardo says.

"Yeah, I got this." I give Dante a quick look. "Thank you, how did you know?"

"She's been studying you all evening, and when she headed this way, I followed her. I'm surprised you didn't notice."

"She was at the club last night."

"Hmm, that's not good. She's been stalking you. But there are so few women assassins. No bother, we'll get to the bottom of it, just not now. But do put her in four points because she's as lethal as a tiger."

He straightens his suit and checks himself in the mirror, running his hands over his hair to make sure it's in place as there is another knock on the bathroom door.

"Coming," Dante replies, unmoved by the past five minutes. "Coming out with a slightly intoxicated woman," he says before Riccardo opens the door, and Dante falls behind us so he can slip out without being seen.

I glance in the bathroom mirror and notice red marks on my neck.

"My night's ruined anyway with this." I gesture to my neck before I walk forward with the woman's toned but limp arm around my neck. I'm surprised by a warm tingle that travels up my spine.

It must be from the lack of oxygen, I tell myself.

And what a body she has as it bumps into mine. She's dressed in a tight black leotard top that flows into a type of dress that gives her a great range of motion.

Her thin overcoat hides how lethal she is, and the covering makes her outfit sexier even though it covers her arms and shoulders. I'll need to check to see if she's hiding anything on her. And in due time we will get her whole story. One way or another, she has messed with the wrong family.

I nod to Riccardo and exit the bathroom as men begin to

pile in curious as to what caused the commotion, and I catch a glimpse of Dante walking past them with his back turned to avoid being seen.

"Too much to drink already?" a stranger asks.

"You know these women who just get carried away," I comment with a wry smile, hoping they don't look too close at my neck with welts.

Dante casually turns back to make sure we get out of the mess, not giving anyone a clue that he knows me.

He'll return to the family table and in true Micheli style, switch from his current look of concern and back to his poker face. He will carry the night off with his chivalrous attitude and no one will be the wiser.

"Where to?" My voice is barely a whisper.

"The wine cellar. It's set up for this."

"The old torture room?" I can't help but chuckle because it's been around longer than me. Actually, it's on a vineyard that the family operates.

"Sure, it has a bed and is made for this. It's been a long time since we had a wild one like this."

"Indeed." And my mind is piqued with questions. I wrap my left arm around her tiny but firm waist.

"Let's go out the exit right here," Riccardo suggests as we attempt to keep up our appearances with smiles. But Riccardo never smiles, so he nods. The band is announced, and as the music cues up I thank God for the distraction. The timing couldn't be more fortuitous.

We manage to hold the limp body between us, and it reminds me of the movie *Weekend at Bernie's*, only she's not dead but she can't move either.

Another minute in that bathroom alone and one of us would have been dead.

The narrow corridor ends, and we exit, walking faster

through the parking lot behind the hotel. Our cars are all valet parked to avoid the paparazzi. Plus, Dante's fiancée is wearing stilettos and those are a twisted-ankle-waiting-to-happen on cobblestone streets.

We are greeted by the paparazzi at the entrance to the hotel but they have to stay behind the ropes put up for the event.

"Shit, no keys," I growl, clearly annoyed.

"I'm back here." Riccardo nods in the direction of the black Rover.

"Great." I'm not surprised. He might be Dante's right hand man, the *consigliere*, and he's always prepared for every occasion, that's what makes him so valuable, that and the fact that we all trust him with our lives.

"What about my car?"

"I'll send someone to get it but later, and I'll make sure all the security cameras are on the fritz as well." I can't say I remember him smiling, but he takes pride in his work and being able to handle any situation. In the darkness that engulfs us I feel better knowing he's got my back and he'll tidy up any loose strings.

"Are you okay?" he asks me as he pulls out his key fob and his vehicle chirps once in protest, but the doors are unlocked, and I place the mysterious woman in the back seat as Riccardo starts the car.

"Yes, a few scratches. How long will she be out?"

"Hours, actually, you need to go back to the gala, so you're seen. I'll have Enzo follow behind us to drive you back."

I put the seat belt on mystery girl and sit beside her to keep an eye on her and check her breathing to make sure she's okay.

I wrestle with myself as to why I care if she lives or dies

from the drugs.

Why do I care? Anyone else would be in the trunk.

"Is that necessary? I want to know who she is." I'm eager to find answers and there's no denying that I want to know what else she has under her black attire and I'm not limiting myself to weapons and a belly button.

"It would be best." He concentrates on the curvy road and the downtown traffic, but his voice is unwavering, and I find it soothing to my erratic heartbeat as I am now processing the fact that I could be dead.

"Who the fuck would come after us? And a woman of all things. I mean, wouldn't it be easier if I seduced her, and she murdered me in my sleep?"

"*Basta!*" His voice is deep and sharp.

Okay, apparently Riccardo has a limit as he declares enough, but my mind is racing just like my heart earlier.

"You can't say you're not curious," I continue.

"She came here to kill you so that's revenge. If it's unsanctioned, we have an even bigger problem."

"You mean another mafia might have sent her?" I don't know why I find it so incredulous. Some women run cartels in Mexico and are even more ruthless than their male predecessors.

"Exactly."

I turn my head to take in the petite women beside me and as we pass under streetlights, I'm able to make out more characteristics. Like her high cheekbones, her perfectly tanned skin, and the fact that her clothes aren't cheap.

In fact, she fit in with everyone else tonight, just like a hitman would. But I don't feel like it's an act with her.

Riccardo is probably correct and even though my neck is red, I don't want to kill her. I should, but right now I'm too intrigued and I don't want to return to the gala. I want to be with her when she wakes up.

We wind through the hills out to the country where we have an old house that no one would ever suspect we use for the torture and containment of enemies.

The house has an old stone wall around it and is surrounded by fields. It's a place the enforcers use, and now that Dante's been don for a number of years, I haven't thought about it as much as we try to keep our fingerprints off the messy situations.

I watch her chest rise and fall, making sure she's still breathing. Why was she casing the bar? She's been stalking me, and I can't believe I didn't pick up on it sooner. I'm mesmerized by her perfect lips and her breasts that fit perfectly in her dress.

I don't know why I should care so much when she wanted to end me earlier. But now, she's a good source of information and with some luck, we'll find out who sent her.

One thing I learned from my years coming up the ranks is that everyone has a weakness and a threshold for pain. She might look tough, but I think taking away her Jimmy Choo's might hurt her as much as a broken arm. She's someone I can't wait to learn about.

"Wait, I know her car, she tore out of the club in a Rolls Royce, like the most expensive one there is." Suddenly, I'm putting together some pieces of the puzzle and I feel better because I wasn't totally off my game, just too relaxed at the gala.

But in hindsight, it should have been the one place any of us would be an easy target as we rely on the security there but there is always a way to get to someone if the desire is there —and the money.

Money is no object for me and I'm coming to the realization that it might not be an obstacle for her either.

"She's young," I comment as the moonlight reflects off my window and I glance up at it to enjoy a minute of tranquility in a night filled with unrest.

"Keep it in your pants, Sal. The last thing we need is an enemy in the house. It won't bode well for the family to get involved with someone who is clearly against you and the family . . . I'm sure of it. Plus, she can kick your ass." Riccardo lets out a rare chuckle at my expense.

Everyone knows Riccardo doesn't show joy. I can count the occurrences on one hand when he's cracked a grin, and it's only with Dante. The man is a rock and loves his code of being emotionless—the Lone Wolf. We've endeared him with the perfect nickname.

He would be less of a tight ass if he got laid now and then. Maybe he feels like us and doesn't want to be liable for another woman's wife. I heard that he lost his wife in Israel. He never talks about it. He's never spoken about what his life was like before he joined our family.

I can't read him either. I can only predict his actions based on how he operates methodically and with expert precision. But he's still a wolf. He always goes it alone if he can.

I have always taken life for granted, being the second son and tonight, my life could have come to a screeching halt. I'm not ready to go yet, and not before I fuck that adorable mouth of hers.

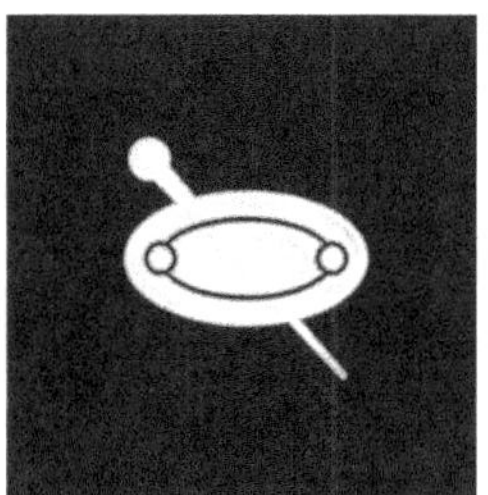

7

FRANCESCA

I wake from a restless sleep, nightmares of being slapped around as I toss and turn in a bed with no sheets. As I come to, my first thought is I should have just gone for his heart with the knife.

My eyes open. I'm staring at four walls of rough rocks. I try to focus through the foggy hangover from the drug they used to knock me out.

I'm dying to move my arms and legs. They know how skilled I am so it's unlikely I'll be untied and allowed to use any extremities while in captivity. There is a first time for everything, or so the saying goes.

Pain shoots up from my right leg and I stifle a wince by biting my lip. How long have I been out? Long enough for my legs to cramp, and, in my experience, that takes hours. What the hell did Dante hit me with?

I remember a prick, a short buzz, and then nothing. I need water. My mouth is parched, like someone who has smoked too much pot.

My jaw isn't broken but it is bruised for sure. Unfortunately, I know the difference. I didn't expect him to hit me so hard. Damn, not a bad wallop.

I broke my own rule of engagement by underestimating my opponent. Fueled by emotion and not strategic thinking, this attack may be my undoing. If I can just get free, I can fix the situation and save myself in the process.

Peeking through my eyelashes, I glance around the room. It's dark but I can make out a small sink and a toilette that still has a pull chain. This must be a wine cellar the family has used over the years to torture and even kill their enemies.

I'm lying on some sort of mattress that is so thin I feel the slats under it and my back hurts. But what hurts more are my arms from being strapped to the bedpost in such an unnatural position. The pain is blinding. I focus on my breathing to remain calm but my efforts to keep the pain levels tolerable aren't going to work.

Damn! They fucking drugged me. Now I really want to kill Sal.

I need to make use of my time and observe my captors. There are two in the room. As my head becomes clearer, one is larger and older with a neatly trimmed salt and pepper goatee.

By larger, I mean stacked, with muscles, he probably eats a dozen eggs for breakfast and works out non-stop. He's ruggedly handsome, but I instinctively know he's all business and will never cut me any slack.

Fuck, an enforcer. With the posture of a commanding officer in an elite force he stands with his legs apart to keep himself from being knocked over. His training has made the way he carries himself second nature, giving him an aura of confidence and strength. Make no mistake about it, he's a worthy opponent.

Damn, damn, double damn!

I can't look down my legs but assume they retrieved the knife I had strapped to my thigh since I don't feel it against my skin. Of course, they would search me. One doesn't go up against the likes of them without retribution.

"She's awake," Sal announces as he approaches the bed in four long strides.

I fully open my eyes, and the game of possum is over.

"My arms are killing me. Release me," I demand.

"You don't call the shots," the man with the goatee speaks, moving closer and crossing his meaty arms across his broad chest. "Who do you work for?" he inquires.

"No one."

"You have a name?" Sal asks, and I find it hard to resist telling him.

I've been known to be manipulative, and I've been appeased most of my life, but this man . . . definitely a worthy opponent.

"Fine, we have a way of dealing with uncooperative prisoners." Without untying me, he takes my hand and puts my palm on a glass surface to get a print.

The machine searches until it gets a result and lets out a beep.

"Francesca Conti," he volunteers, and suddenly, he's not perplexed.

"Ha, you are here to avenge Conti's death?" the goatee man says.

"Something like that," I concede.

"Well, Dante is the head of the family, and there is no proof our family was involved in that," Sal suggests while licking his lips in thought as he sits on a chair that is too close for comfort. "Why go after me?" he asks, as calmly as a man propositioning a woman over a cup of espresso.

"I want Dante to be miserable, knowing he is the reason I

killed you. Family is important to him, and it is the most destructive form of revenge, short of killing him." I make it clear that I still intend to finish what I started.

Sal chuckles, and I notice he's gotten more comfortable, having removed his tie, jacket, and even unbuttoned the top buttons of his shirt. There is something manly and primitive about his hairy chest popping out of his open shirt.

"You're not capable. You botched it," he taunts.

"You got lucky," I argue.

"Luck, you say? We'll see who's lucky. You made an unsanctioned hit against another family. There are consequences for your actions." He leans in close, and the earthy scent of bergamot wafts under my nose, causing me to become excited.

I feel the wetness between my thighs and a tingling sensation. My nipples betray me and turn rock hard under the skintight bodice, immediately giving away my state of arousal.

His gaze cuts through me before moving down my body, caressing me with a hint of sexual desire. His blueish eyes are almost grey and remind me of the sky before a winter storm. They draw me in, but I can't get past the icy wall between us.

Danger is omnipresent with two of them and only me.

I am so screwed. No one knows where I am.

The Conti men use women for sex and babies; I assume the Michelis do the same.

I want to wither under Sal's intense stare, but instead, I return his stare with mine and don't flinch. That would be defeat. I know he and the goatee guy over there can kill me with no retribution. My blood is boiling even in the dark and dank cellar. It's cooler down here, and the warmth spreading through my body doesn't appear to be from my anger.

I'm supposed to be handling him, but he's got all the

control. There's nothing I hate more than a man having control over me. I tug at the restraints around my wrists but it's a mistake as the zip ties cut into my tender flesh and blood drips down my arms.

"Don't hurt yourself. We have plenty of time for that later," he mocks me before turning away.

"Your family thinks they are so untouchable," I spit out the words as anger takes over my emotions. But I know my family won't fight this battle. There's nothing in it for them. I'm invisible and of no use to them. Or so they think.

Sal would be correct in identifying me as a loner. I am. Maybe he is, too.

He paces and turns on his heels, throwing out an arm. "So, you just think you can murder me at the most public event of the year and get away with it?"

"I almost did."

"Almost, but now you are my hostage, and in the aftermath of your father's death, you are persona non grata, without friends and family," he says as his eyebrows furrow in thought.

They will find out soon enough. A call might be made. An insider will be contacted. Backdoors exist everywhere to accomplish missions many assume are impossible.

"We need to give her water," the man with the goatee states while retrieving a bottle of water. He makes sure he cracks the seal in front of me so I know it hasn't been tampered with, and to build trust.

Sal takes the bottle from him and holds it to my lips. Lifting my head as much as possible, I guzzle the refreshing liquid so fast that some spills on my chest, but it's a relief. There is no airflow down here, and if there was ever a place to have an encounter with being claustrophobic—this would be it.

I can't help but notice scratches on Sal's hands and know I am responsible for them.

I lick the water off my lips, but I can't reach the droplets on my chin.

As if he reads my mind, Sal leans over me and uses his slender fingers, taking his time to wipe away the moisture for me. His hands are warm, and soft, more like a businessman than a thug.

He pulls his fingers away quickly, as if he's been shocked, and I try not to take offense.

I should have killed him. My problem is that as much as I enjoy fighting, there is a big difference between training to kill and actually killing someone.

I know now that I can't kill. I would have hunted red deer over the years with my father if I could. Wild boars are edible nasty creatures and overpopulate Europe so hunting them was easy for me, and I didn't have guilt afterwards. It also gave me an opportunity to fit in with the men and earn praise from my dad.

It figures my only bonding experience with my dad was a hunting trip to kill something. I realize now that killing a person takes more of my father's darkness than I can muster.

Sal puts the water bottle on a small table beside the bed and resumes pacing.

"What time is it?" I ask.

"You have somewhere to be?"

The sad part is I have nowhere to be, and this is the loneliest I've ever been. Instead of obtaining a personal life, I spent my time getting in shape and training for a man's world filled with more limitations than possibilities.

"Maybe it doesn't matter. Maybe none of this matters." I give up. I don't want to show my cards, but he sees right through me and knows right where to land his verbal punches.

"What were you doing at the club? Aside from casing the joint, you were studying me. What did you find?"

"You're predictable, you don't deviate much from your schedule, and you like routines and order. Your house is well guarded and in a good location so it would be hard to get the drop on you there."

He stops pacing, sits in a chair he drags to the bed before rolling up the sleeves of his shirt. A shirt that was clean and pressed at the gala but now it's wrinkled beyond recognition as he slept in it.

He put an elbow on his knee and his first finger rests on the apex of his square chin lost in thought.

"You're very perceptive," he says and turns to the goatee man, who nods in agreement.

"We can't take you out of all your restraints, you are too lethal," he concedes, pointing to my hands. "But we have your knife and you've been checked for other weapons, so I'll give you the use of one arm and leg at a time. We can't have you getting nerve damage. You're far too pretty to have permanent damage to your extremities at such a young age."

I should thank him, but I don't on sheer principle.

"I have a proposition for you. My friend here, Riccardo, is my brother's head of security and he will need to return to other duties. I can't trust you, but you might be useful to me."

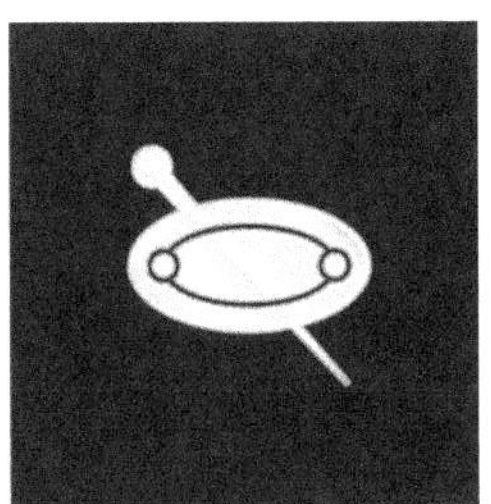

8

SAL

My mind is spinning when we leave the wine cellar. Riccardo drives. We're both quiet. How can Francesca feel loyalty to her father, a man who was disliked by everyone?

I can't imagine what kind of a father he was, but hearing how he treated his daughter, Juliet, and how he talked about his mistresses, I doubt he had a nurturing bone in his body.

"What do you have in mind, Sal? You need to be careful. She's still the enemy no matter how sexy she is," he warns me.

I turn to Riccardo with a grin. "You noticed that too, huh?"

"She's trouble. Spoiled, too, if she owns the car you said. After the upheaval following her father's death, she probably feels displaced and unable to fit in anywhere. I sense major anger issues, my friend. Tread lightly. For her to try and kill you with her bare hands is pretty fucking ballsy." I take in his stoic face that cracks just a bit. "And at the gala, of all places," he scoffs.

"Right? But if you think about it, it's the mafia way, better executed obviously."

"Obviously, but she's like a ghost. My God, I felt her there and then she was on me in one leap. What is she, part cat?"

"Ha, you would be so lucky to have a woman that flexible in the sack." Riccardo's comeback surprises me.

I haven't been with anyone since Carla and I'm horny as fuck. I had to turn around when we left the wine cellar because my cock was hard and visible. I didn't want her to notice.

She's very observant and has a knack for reading people which comes in handy in this line of work. But not so handy when I want to hide something.

"What are you thinking, Sal?"

"I'm thinking she would be a great head of security for me. I mean, if she got the jump on me, someone else can too."

"True, but how can you trust her? Her dad was psychotic, and she's probably not stable herself. You need to be careful."

"I know, trust me."

We arrive at my house. My car is in the driveway just past my gate, and I know Riccardo took care of that for me. He's a man of his word.

"Thanks for tonight." I shake Riccardo's hand and make my way into my house, dropping my keys in a glass dish in the entrance way, and turning on the TV to stream Italian music.

I slide off my jacket hanging it in my closet along with my pants to be dry cleaned. I feel dusty and dirty from the damp wine cellar. Standing under a hot shower, I let the water wash over me and when I close my eyes, Francesca's tight little body makes my dick hard. I can't deny that I'm horny for her; all thoughts of Carla are obliterated.

How can I be so attracted to someone who is on my family's list of enemies?

On one hand, Dante was able to bridge that gap, but his situation is different. Juliet didn't grow up knowing her dad or living amongst mafia families.

Francesca was raised like us, but her father was a real psycho, and it led to his demise. I must tread carefully because I don't know anything about her.

She has studied me and has the jump on me there, as well.

She pointed out all my shortcomings but thankfully, she agrees my house is safe. Great, I don't have to sleep with one eye open. I'm tired, and I haven't eaten much today. I was able to get a few bites of delicious food when I made a quick appearance at the gala while Francesca slept under a guard's watch.

Just one more hit to fluff my pillow, and I will be asleep. Instead, I'm haunted by her emerald-green eyes.

I wake up to my phone ringing, it's Riccardo.

"*Ciao*, Sal. I made some calls, and it turns out that Francesca has a bad rap of being spoiled and interfering in the family business. She's currently without a county. She hates her family, so it seems like we hold all the cards."

I know better than to ask Riccardo for the details of his connections. He plays everything close to the vest.

He is all work, always on the job, there's no room in his life for anyone other than Dante and our family. Because of this, he is The Wolf. He came to us that way and he's remained the same over the years. Our home is his den.

"Thank you, Riccardo. I'll put some men on her."

"Keep me posted."

I hang up and roll on my back. What do I do with a

woman who is filled with rage and too much strength for her small body?

My phone rings. It's Dante. "*Ciao.*"

"Little brother, I hear you found a wild cat," he snickers into the phone.

"Relax, nothing is happening. I mean, she's in the cellar."

"That should suit her just fine for the time being, but you need to think long-term here. What are we going to do? We can't have this." His tone turns serious. "You are known to be fun, but you don't have my obligations. Don't be fickle."

"I won't, brother. I do my job, and I will do it well. Thanks for saving me in the bathroom, by the way."

"Not a problem. Besides, it would have been very bad for business," his deep voice reminds me it could have been my funeral they would be planning tonight.

"Gee, thanks, what about me?"

"Obviously you come first. What are you thinking?"

"She's good at security issues, that's for sure. How she got the drop on me, I don't know. But I won't let it happen again," I mention unapologetically.

I mean, it could have happened to anyone. It's weird that she thought she'd punish Dante by taking me out instead of going after him. But even I know his schedule is constantly changing to avoid being predictable. I like routines, so it's harder for me.

Plus, I work in a business with established hours when I need to be there. Even if I stagger in late, I'll eventually show up.

"Well, proceed with caution. She's an outlier, an unknown. I can't lose you."

"I know. I'll see you Sunday at Mama's."

"*Ciao.*"

Great, now Dante and Riccardo have both put their two cents in.

It's late, or early in the morning. Does it matter if she's locked up? I dispatched my righthand man, Matteo, to the cellar with food and liquids as I need him to check on the situation.

I also instructed him to alternate the restraints carefully. I don't have to go, but it's in my best interest to check on her, or so I tell myself.

I throw on a fresh shirt and a nice suit to look respectable. What would Francesca, a spoiled princess with anger issues, crave the most to take off the edge of her anger?

A latte?

Most likely the coffee will be cold by the time she drinks it, but it's the thought and effort that counts. She has to give me points for the attempt.

And she owes me an apology. No one can do what she did and live, unless we deem it to be so. Her life is in my hands first, and Dante's second. If Dante had his way, he'd send a message, but because she's a woman and one who is strangely connected by name, it muddies the water.

I get that.

I throw the covers over my bed instead of making it look like a show room. I wish I was more of a neat freak, but I don't have it in me. The housekeeper who comes by weekly can make things clean and pretty.

On the way to the kitchen, I open the French doors overlooking the Tuscan hills dotted with olive trees and cypress pines. It's a view I never grow tired of.

It's turning out to be another hot day for fall. Fortunately, the cellar stays below seventy. I can't deny that I would love to experience Francesca sweating, and I don't mean the kind of sweat from standing outside in humidity.

I listen to National Public Radio when I want the real news without Italy's political slant on it. I check my phone out of habit to find out what's up in the world while I eat a balanced breakfast of eggs, thinly sliced bacon, and wheat toast because Mama insists it's good for me.

I'm not worried about inheriting Dad's heart issues. He loved his steaks, pizza, and pasta more than he loved his fruits and vegetables. I'm more conscientious about what I put in my body and too vain to let myself gain weight.

I leave the house, waving to my guards as I pass by. They have no clue where I'm going as I'm totally deviating from my routine. I find a coffee house and grab a latte with cocoa on top for Francesca.

The drive to the farmhouse is relaxing and gives me time to think. Now that I'm in my late twenties, I need to focus on how I live the rest of my life and where I'm going in the organization.

But all I can think about is that little spitfire in the wine cellar and I can't wait to get the report on the night. Surely she's behaving—as one in her position should.

Who am I kidding? She's not behaving—she's trying to manipulate Matteo into turning her loose. I'd bet money on it.

The farmhouse comes into view, and my stomach flips in anticipation of seeing her. Only a few guys at the top of the organization know about this place because the house is registered in our grandmother's maiden name, a name no one outside the family remembers anymore.

It's a shame that none of us use this place. We pay for the basic upkeep, but one day, it might be worth sinking money into. I park on the gravel driveway and grab the coffee as I head into the house.

I open the door with care now that I know she loves to attack from behind but instead, the sunlight hits the wood floor illuminating the entranceway. The heavy wood door lets out a groan as it shuts behind me and I make my way to the kitchen, and to the door that leads to the cellar.

"I don't want to eat," she hollers.

She has lungs, I'll give her that.

I open the door and the light fades with each step I take as I descend into the cellar.

"You leave me with this Neanderthal," is her greeting.

"He's a great guy, calm down." I sound nonchalant because I have a wait-and-see attitude unless the situation calls for urgency.

It's probably why I'm considered the fun one in the family. I'm definitely the sticky glue that keeps everyone together and the chill pill that keeps everyone calm.

"Good afternoon, Sunshine." I start the salutations over in a positive light.

"Fuck you. It's not sunny in here so I wouldn't know." Her foul mood fills the room. I imagine Matteo is ready for a break.

The walls are rock, and the floor is Terrazzo tile, and oddly enough, there is still wine in the wood racks that line the walls, along with an empty olive oil barrow we pushed into a corner.

"Maybe we can make it a better day."

"Doubtful. The only thing that would make it nice, is if you untied me."

I chuckle and roll my eyes.

"You, a lean fighting machine, want to be cut loose. Don't think so."

"Asshole."

"I can't help it if you had a shitty plan. You have to think and act without being blinded by your emotions. Besides, your dad was a real asshole and should have been dealt with years ago."

"I loved my dad," she snaps back, but I doubt her.

"You loved your dad because he's the only dad you had and your only male role model. I won't get into the psychology of it but even you can't deny he was a twisted piece of shit."

Frankly, I worry about her stability, but I can understand being without your family and a home and having to fend for yourself without the proper skills.

She has great potential to do many jobs, she just doesn't know how to apply herself to go about it the correct way is my assumption.

"Can I get some different clothing to wear? I'm starting to stick, and the air in here stinks like moss." She's still in the same clothes from last night but I need to keep her uncomfortable.

"Hmm, well, your actions put you in this predicament, but I might have a solution."

"What do you mean?"

Was that an inkling of hope in her voice? Maybe she doesn't want to die.

"I can use more staff and think you'd be a great addition to my personal detail. You'll have to be watched, I'll never be alone with you, you won't have weapons—but you don't need them," I add.

"Is that coffee?"

It seems I might understand this little minx better than anyone else. But the question begging to be answered is, can I trust her?

"Yes, I'll give it to you. Then, the three of us are going for a short walk. You look a bit green. I think you need some fresh air."

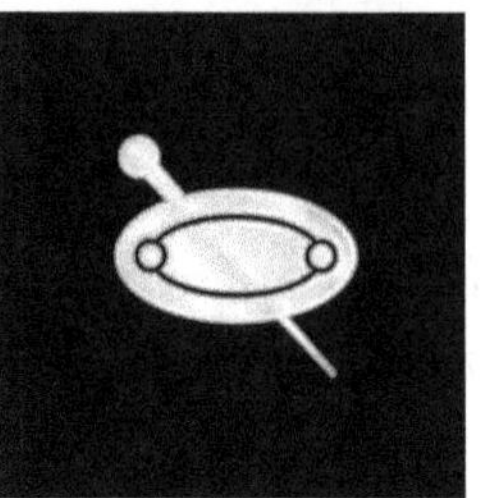

9

FRANCESCA

I have to pee. I've been holding it for what feels like days, but my mind knows it's only been hours. However, the need has reached critical mass. Matteo unties my ankles but leaves both arms tied behind my back. This is gonna be tricky.

Matteo looks increasingly uncomfortable as he helps me to the toilet, pulls my panties down, and lifts my dress above my waist. This is humiliating but preferable to peeing on the bed and smelling of urine when Sal returns. I doubt they have many female hostages from the perplexed look on my guard's face.

My strong glutes and quads hold me up as I squat over a toilet that looks like it hasn't been flushed since Mussolini was in power. Good thing I'm in great shape. When I'm finished, Matteo averts his eyes and pulls up my undies before helping me back to the bed, where he re-ties my ankles and anchors my wrists.

He's been switching out the restraints to give me some semblance of comfort. Now it's time for him to free one hand. I use it to readjust my clothes. I'm not accustomed to someone else dressing me, especially some mouth breather Sal uses for babysitting and possibly dig my grave.

"Can you just let me go? I can make it worth your while. I have an expensive car I can give you if you let me escape," I implore Matteo, who has resumed his post and picked up his AK-47.

He says nothing, smart move.

How did I get myself in this mess and how am I getting myself out alive?

I could fake a panic attack. It's doable. A heart attack, too difficult to pull off when I can't grab my chest. But even if I got out of this shit hole, Matteo could easily outrun me.

How is it that I end up with the one guard who isn't a snowflake Millennial with a poor work ethic and an unwavering need for caffeine and fattening snacks? Or a video game addiction?

It's been hours but I assume Sal's coming back. I know he will have more questions for me, not that I intend to answer any of them. He must be busy checking with his boss and maybe they are discussing if I live or die.

Dante is the don and makes those decisions, but I hope he'll be forgiving since I wasn't trying to kill *him*. Mafia rules are not written down anywhere, but they don't need to be. Everyone knows the rules and follows the rules. If I'm allowed to live, I will have to pay a price, of that I am certain.

I'm tired of laying on this filthy mattress thinking of all the things that Sal might do to me. I should be worried about being sent to my family in a duffle bag or being found floating face down in a river. Instead, I find myself fantasizing about the texture of Sal's chest hair and how hard he wants me to pull it.

I blame my erotic daydreaming on boredom and frustration. With my hands and feet bound I can't fight my way out of this situation.

If my dad were still alive, I'm sure the Michelis would torture me for information about his operation. Would Dad have saved me? Or just his sons? Or not give a shit?

Women, especially those dependent on men for financial survival, are viewed as immaterial and exploited all the time. The spoils of war. Why should they view me any differently?

I've heard my father didn't give a shit about Juliet, my brothers said he didn't care if she lived or died. I hope that's not true. But if it is, I can't say I'm surprised.

He was a narcissist and hated any sign of weakness. Any time I failed at something, it was followed by a verbal assault and an ass-kicking. The same for my brothers, but with them, they could take their anger to the streets and be commended for it later.

Me, I had to hold it in, where it festered until I learned to take out my aggression at the gym.

I'm nothing to the Calabrese family and my brothers will do as they are told, the loyal soldiers my father groomed them to be since they could walk and talk.

As for Sal and Dante— they will do their research. All they have to do is throw around some money and rough up the right person, and they'll get the information they need.

The echo of a man's shoes on the tile floor above, suddenly gets my attention. Paralyzed with anticipation, I hope it's Sal, the man who holds my destiny in his hands, beautiful hands at that.

I have a flashback to the altercation in the bathroom and can't understand why I didn't just snap his neck as soon as I had the chance. I'm perfectly capable but I hesitated a fraction of a second too long and his brother Dante, of all people, saved him.

No doubt those two bastards are gloating over my foiled attempt.

A whiff of lavender arrives before Sal. It's the same earthy scent with a hint of musk that he wore last night. As he makes his way down the steps, the first thing I notice is his dark aviator sunglasses.

I've lost all track of time, but I'll take it as an indication that the sun is up. When he reaches the side of the bed and takes them off, I feel naked under the penetrating gaze of his steel-grey eyes.

My body betrays me as my stomach flutters and my nipples harden, pushing against the thin fabric of the tight-fitted bodice of my dress. Why am I drawn to him like a moth to a lightbulb?

It's exciting to feel parts of my body wake up from their sexual hibernation, but at the same time, I cannot make the mistake of sleeping with this man. I have more to lose, and he has everything to gain.

As these new feelings wash over me, my breath catches in my throat and my pussy tightens. She has a mind of her own and her timing sucks. I need to concentrate on getting out of this mess, not on getting off.

Any movement, even the slightest, sends bolts of pain through my wrists and ankles. I remain still and helpless while his presence drives my hormones into overdrive.

Is he into kink? Does he like seeing me tied to this bed? The rumor is he's ruthless in business. Maybe he's just as ruthless in the bedroom. Thinking about it makes me long to feel his hot breath on my body and his Machiavellian mouth luring me into something sinful.

Instead, I get, "Coffee?" as he hands over a Styrofoam cup.

I take it from him with my one free hand. He pulls up a

chair, takes off his jacket, hands it to Matteo, and sits down. He loosens his tie and leans forward, putting his elbows on his knees and the stare he gives me has the intensity of a tiger studying its prey before the kill and it unnerves me.

It's hard to resist not picturing what he looks like under his fitted custom suit. I imagine his skin is smooth, tan, and hot to the touch. He rakes a hand through his black as-night hair and I experience a weakness in my chest. I don't understand why my body betrays me when discipline has always ruled it.

My body won't give me a rest, my façade of confidence and indifference left the minute I opened my eyes in the cellar. Surrounded by betrayal—by my body, my family, and even my mother. Why should Sal be any different?

I need to keep that in mind when Sal opens his mouth he cannot be trusted. He's the enemy, we've always been enemies, and it's our birthright to hate each other until the end of our days or when hell freezes over, whichever comes first.

And in between those two events, our families will wage little wars with each other until one day it will boil over into an all-out war.

But what harm is there in accepting a cup of lukewarm coffee?

"I'm only taking it because I need the caffeine," I state in all honesty because my head is pounding from the lack of it.

"Of course," he says as he smirks and lifts his eyebrows, telegraphing his doubts.

Sitting up with one arm still tied, I wince in pain as my body is stiff.

"You can undo her other hand for a minute," he states, and Matteo swings his gun behind his back and moves in to untie my other wrist.

Wrapping both hands around the cup, I guzzle the coffee, hoping this helps the pain that presents as daggers in my forehead. "So, what's in store for me? Will it be waterboarding or a bed of nails?" I can't help but make light of the grave situation.

"What you deserve is a double tap to the head, but I think you might be of service to me."

"You can forget about me being your mistress or some whore!" Somehow, I manage to refrain from crushing the cup in my hands.

"As much as I like where your mind is going, I've come up with something equally important. I imagine your abilities are stronger in self-defense and security than they are between the sheets." His cocky grin pisses me off.

"You're so like all the others. Italian men, all men, only care about getting their dick hard and sticking it in as many women as possible." I practically spit the words at him as I vent my anger when I should have saved my breath.

Misery loves company and a miserable person loves to spread it like a contagion. I've said too much and given too much away with my words.

I shouldn't have revealed my weakness, but anger drives my thoughts and actions when it comes to the Micheli family. Or is it just me supplanting the anger I have against my own family?

"I think you need to get outside and walk off some of that hostility," he comments before his phone rings.

One swift nod to Matteo and I'm tied up again. My brief respite is over as he abruptly stands up and leaves the room.

Damn it.

I can't think straight in the presence of this man and when he's gone, I fantasize about him—the man with the haunting, hungry, grey eyes.

Eyes strong enough to pop into my head while I lay here, wanting to hate him but finding I wanted to touch him. Even with my strong discipline and years of training, I have a difficult time pulling away.

When he returns, I throw an angry look in his direction, knitting my eyebrows together and sending him a death threat with my eyes. He's still the enemy. My dad was an ass, but he was blood.

I hate men, I hate Dante, I hate Sal, I hate the world they have created.

I owe the Michelis nothing. I know they killed my father, and they don't get a pass on that, not from me. I might not know everything in the criminal world, but I do know that it is an eye for an eye and justice hasn't been served.

"You're in a pickle, Francesca. Your family is broken, they don't want you back. In fact, they just offered us money to keep you," he gloats. "You are safe for now, we used sources for the information. But you tend to cause trouble." His eyes are summing me up as he puts his hands in his pockets.

He's feeling comfortable around me. Not good.

"Please untie my hands, they hurt, and my back hurts," I ask trying not to sound weak. It's just a matter of time before I start begging because the pain has been constant for over twelve hours.

"We need to come to an understanding. I don't trust you, and I'll never trust you, but you have skills I can use."

"Like what?"

"You can read people. You're quick and skilled with your hands and I assume proficient with knives and guns."

"Are you sending me into a war or are you in the business of giving compliments? Really?" My sardonic voice hurts even my own ears.

"Neither. Merely stating my observations. You need a home and money. You've made it abundantly clear I need better security." He pauses, and pulls his hands out of his pockets now that he's not walking, instead, he sits back down next to me.

"Let's make a deal. You head up my security and be my bodyguard and in return, you not only get to live, but you'll also live in my house. I'll even pay you so you can get on your feet. Who knows, I might even find a way to use your skill sets in my business."

"So, I'm at your beck and call?" I sneer.

"Yes, unless you like living here in the basement, staring at these four damp walls as life goes on." He looks around, punctuating the reality we both know to be true.

"How do you know I won't kill you in your sleep?"

"I have other guards." He smiles and stands up. "And I have a few tricks up my sleeve." He's trying to be coy, and it's working.

Now he has me thinking about what he's capable of doing in business and in bed. No doubt he's a skilled lover judging by his looks and the charm that rains on me even though I'm his prisoner.

He drips sex appeal like a candle drips wax. Right now, that warm wax is coating me like a glove of lube. But I'm so wet it's the last thing I need.

My eyes are drawn to his crotch, and it's impossible to miss the bulge from his massive hard-on. I know it's only a matter of time before he's overtaken with lust, and I begin to think that might be the in I need to gain valuable information on the girls' whereabouts. Maybe he can be useful to me, as strange as that sounds.

"Fine, but after six months, I'm free to go," I offer. After all, we're negotiating.

"Fair enough," he agrees. "Help me get her to the car, and follow us to the house," he gives the order to Matteo. "After that, I assume you need some rest."

"*Grazie*." Matteo bows his head out of respect and helps with the restraints around my ankles.

Sal unties my wrists, and as I sit up, I bite my lip instead of moaning from the pain as I rub my arms and wriggle my legs to get the circulation going.

"I have painkillers in my car if you need some. I guess I slammed you pretty good last night."

"Hmm, anti-inflammatories would be great," I murmur without admitting my back is killing me and he may have actually hurt my jaw.

As I stand, I feel light-headed, and my knees feel like ricotta cheese. I struggle to regain my balance as pain shoots up my spine and my lower back muscles spasm causing me to double over.

I take a deep breath and try to stay lucid.

Sal wraps an arm around me to help me and Matteo grabs me on the other side as we make our way up the steps. Matteo's body is rigid, and Sal tightens as if he's on guard.

We're so close right now that I feel the warmth of his body through his suit and find myself thinking thoughts that would make a Catholic girl blush. My mind shifts to thinking about what he looks like with nothing on and standing this close to me.

After being in the dark for so long, the afternoon sun is blinding at first but after they adjust I can make out a barn in the distance. The fresh air feels good on my face, and I take a deep breath hoping it will make me feel better.

Sal puts me in his car and zip-ties my ankles tighter. He's clearly a man who doesn't take chances.

It feels good to sit upright and the plush leather seat feels like heaven compared to the old mattress that was as thin as a slice of stale bread.

He tugs on my seatbelt and puts the shoulder straps around me, making it a failsafe. But as he does so, his hand brushes my sensitive nipples, and they harden with desire.

He recoils as if he touched a hot stove jerking his hand away. But it's too late, my pussy, like my nipples, aches for his touch and I find myself frustrated in ways that are new to me. So, this must be what they call sexual frustration.

Fuck.

Fuck, and fuck me.

Of all my conquests in battle, I have to find the one that turns me on now? The most dangerous endeavor of my life?

I need to stay focused. Now that we have an arrangement, I feel like I have a future. Maybe out of my failed attempt to kill Sal, I have found something that I can do and do well. If I pull this off, I can command a higher price for my services in the future. Maybe I can get enough money together to buy the girls' release.

One thing I know for sure is, that six months from now, I'll be free of my obligations to Sal, and no man will ever touch me unless I want it.

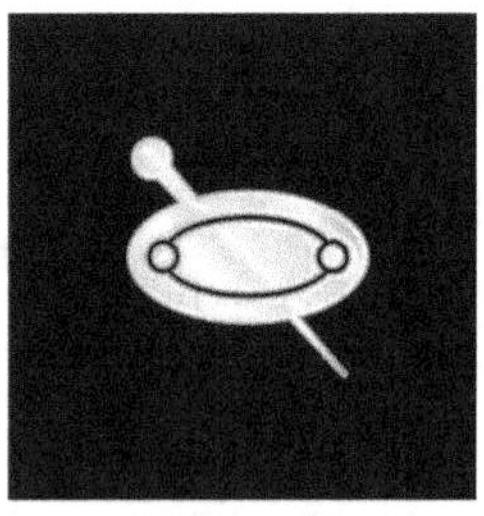

10

SAL

I drive through the rolling hills of central Italy in my Maserati heading home while Francesca stares out the window in a trance.

She's a million miles away and yet I still want to know what she's thinking. She mentioned something about 'where is Sophia when she attacked me, but I thought better of grilling her over it.

And to be honest, I have no idea what she was talking about, which made me think she might be delusional at first. Although her grasp on me was one of survival.

She's not an easy person to read, but she must be hungry. I'm starving. She's just too hardheaded to ask for anything. God forbid the woman should need a man for anything is the vibe I'm getting.

We're heading to my estate because there's no point taking her anywhere else, she already knows where I live. I'm not worried about having her under the same roof because I don't think she has what it takes to kill. She could have ended me last night, and she hesitated. The hesitation that could have cost her own life.

"Oh, I forgot," I say, opening the glove box and pulling out a bottle of pills. Holding the steering wheel with one hand, I extract two pills and push them past her lips.

She pulls away. "Relax, it's just ibuprofen, you need to get it in your system."

She swallows the pills without any water. That tells me she's in serious pain but too stubborn to admit it. She's not only stubborn. She's tough.

And feisty.

Definitely not like any woman I've ever met, and I'm sure I wouldn't want to meet another one like her. Then I remember that Juliet is her half-sister, but they definitely have different temperaments.

She says nothing and I can't imagine it's easy to feel unwanted by the people who are supposed to love her unconditionally.

It sounds like the Conti conditions are part of the rift in the family. Who can attest to what her life was like and what her brothers' dispositions are? It's safer to not make assumptions without knowing Francesca's side of the story.

She's the outlier like Dante said. She's someone who can't be measured against the norm, and we'd best remember this, as she's in our clan now.

I don't know if it's that or the fact that she's sexy as fuck sitting there in her crushed dress and not quivering with fear like anyone else would.

Considering her psychotic father, there's no telling what she went through growing up. Maybe I can find out if I spend time with her, but first, she has to open up. It sounds like she was raised by wolves, maybe something worse than wolves. And we knew her father so there's that piece of reality. Anger is a different animal, and those issues are clearly visible.

We arrive at my house where Matteo greets us and helps

Francesca out of the car. Better him than me. Not that I don't find her attractive, just the opposite.

Her hair may look like I just fucked her brains out, but it's kinda cute, and she looks good even if her lipstick is gone, and her eyeshadow is smudged. Just sitting close to her in the car makes my dick hard. I long to explore every inch of her body. She won't be easy to tame.

It's hard to concentrate on what I need to do when she's near me because all I want to know is how she'll taste when I kiss her. How soft will her skin will be when I run my hand down her back, and . . . I have to stop these thoughts right now as delectable as they are. She's dangerous, in and out of the bedroom.

I have to give her credit for the outfit she wore to the gala. It fits in all the right places and must have cost her a week's allowance. The stretchy fabric also allowed her the flexibility she needed to get the jump on me. She's a wild cat with impeccable fashion sense.

Carla, by comparison, dresses up to walk to the mailbox. And she'd never go into town without spending an hour on her hair and makeup. I recall her spending more time with her hairdresser than me.

Maybe that's why it never worked out, not that I was looking to settle down. It's all for the best. She was fun for a while, but not what I need long-term. If I ever decide to have a long-term relationship, that is.

For someone so proficient in martial arts, and the art of war, Francesca flinches when I help her into the house.

I take her arm as she is stiff from being slammed and tied up. The uptick in her breathing leads me to think she's anxious and has been abused in some way. Matteo follows armed and watchful.

I'm not one to force myself on any woman. That's one

rule I've never broken. I'll give her time and she will want me, I'm sure of it. I detect her shallow breathing when I'm near. If it's not from fear, then she's keyed into the chemistry between us. I doubt she has health problems.

I can have any woman at the snap of my fingers. I'm a patient person in matters of the heart, or rather lust. Lust is quick and easy, but love, that's complicated. I don't do complicated.

My father was a poor role model when it came to being a good husband. He kept up the Italian tradition of having a mistress most of his married life. It's a double standard that has gone on for generations.

After Baboo, our dad, died, we found out about his other women. It was easy for him as he had his mistresses living in the condo in the city, the one that now belongs to Dante. We gave the last mistress the boot and never said anything to our mother.

It bothered me at the time, but I got over it. Dad was gone and knowing it after the fact isn't such a big deal. I have a gift when it comes to moving past the dark things I must do at times.

I deal with life by taking few things seriously. I find a sense of humor goes a long way in cutting tension in situations that are morbid, like death and dismemberment.

You won't find me kicking a severed head around like a football, but I can laugh about it. It's my reality as we see pretty gruesome shit.

Once inside the house, I hand Francesca off to Matteo and instruct him, "The kitchen, I'll cook something."

It's noon so I'm thinking about making paninis for an early lunch.

I'm confident Francesca can't hurt me as Matteo straps her to the chair.

"Nice place," she speaks at last, looking around and testing Matteo's knots.

"Thanks, I've worked on renovating it for years. I prefer to be on the outskirts of the city."

"I can see, between this and the farmhouse, I'd say you are reclusive in nature, like the spider," she adds, digging in with the cut-down.

Me, a poisonous spider?

Ouch. I hope she's not like the typical Italian mother figure who complains about everything and borrows trouble.

I shrug it off. As long as she's behind enemy lines and not sure about what to expect, she's going to be defensive. On the other hand, maybe she always has to get the last word.

Matteo leaves to check the perimeter and Francesca's shoulders sink into a comfortable state of resolve. Either she's had a change of heart or she's looking forward to lunch.

"I'd like for you to train me, y'know, in the stuff you do . . . that kung fu shit. I also have a little problem at the club. You might be able to help."

"Ha, good luck, getting up to speed on my, as you put it, kung fu shit. A fitness retreat is not what I was expecting, but I can teach you how to throw some better punches," she snickers, making me keenly aware that she's teasing me. "As for the club, just let me know what you need."

"Says the woman with no friends and no family. I heard your mother ran off with a wealthy man and left the country," I lash out, not wanting to be soft in front of her. "And we need to do something with your car. I don't want your brothers breathing down my neck."

"Oh no, don't get rid of it. The trackers in it don't even work. I parked it downtown, but I'm sure you have room for it here in an old garage . . . or a barn. Do you have a barn? It's the one big thing Daddy bought for me, so it has sentimental value," she pleads, giving me the sob story of why this car is important to her.

The question is, why? She doesn't appear to need the money and her dad was a prick so I'm not buying the sentimental bullshit.

But what do I care? At last, I concede. "We can find a place for it, I'm sure. Why does your family hate you so much?"

She's quiet.

"Hmm, cat got your tongue, eh? Did I hit a nerve? Seems you like to be a smart mouth, but you don't have much to bargain with, you might want to reconsider that."

"*Niente*."

Nothing, of course, we're back behind the wall of silence and one-word answers. I still have to monitor her and remember that she can't be trusted.

Blood runs deep even when family members hate each other and for all I know, this could be an elaborate smoke screen set up by her brothers.

"That's all you have to say?" I pull up a chair to feed her bite-size pieces of the panini I made. If she's not going to use her mouth to answer my question about the falling out with her family, she might as well use it to eat.

While she chews, I take a bite of my sandwich. My mouth waters and I remember it's been hours since I ate. Food is always better when I have an appetite, but when someone else cooks, it's sublime.

Now that I have something in my stomach, I can think straight. Maybe she's a trojan horse, a gorgeous woman who gets inside a man's house and waits for him to drop his guard? Should I be concerned she'll spin her web with me in it?

I already feel like she's inside my head. I haven't been

this horny since I was a teenage boy and found my uncle's secret stash of porn. Doesn't every single man have spank bank material?

Bottom line is, she's from the enemy's camp and I can't trust her, and she'd be a fool to trust me. I don't need her around stressing me out and possibly spying on our organization. But what am I to do with her? If I can't keep her, I have to kill her.

And I can't bring myself to give that order.

She's a good addition to my security staff. She also knows how the Conti and Calabrese family work and who the players are. She might prove to be an invaluable source of information if she's pissed enough with them maybe she's already changed her loyalty but her way of showing it was misguided at best.

Even though some of the key players changed after Conti's death, the organization is too big to make large-scale changes overnight.

A new don still has a learning curve and there is a time following the takeover when he can't trust those around him until he becomes entrenched.

"I'd like your help with a situation at the club. You accused me of being predictable. Tell me what I need to do to get rid of the Albanians. They are selling drugs right under my nose and it needs to be dealt with. I think they broke into my office too."

She coughs on the piece of sandwich in her mouth.

"What?" I pound her back and look around for something for her to drink. She waves me off shaking her head no, but I leave my hand on her toned back, enjoying the feel of it under the palm of my hand.

"Um. That was me."

"You?" Fuck me, this girl is unbelievable.

"What were you looking for?"

The silent treatment again.

"Look, we're not going to get anywhere if you don't talk. I need something from you, and you obviously need something from me. What is it?" I pull her chair toward me and lean forward, peering into her eyes with my elbow on the counter. I want answers.

Her eyes widen and her body stiffens. "The girls," she says, as if she's had an epiphany.

"What girls?" My eyebrows knit together like a small caterpillar.

"The ones who are being trafficked. They should be here by now, in a box truck. Supposedly you paid for them. Where are they?"

With this new accusation, my face and my mood darken. Pissed, I lean back and cross my arms.

"I have no clue what you are talking about. We don't traffic women."

She doesn't believe me, but I can tell the wheels spinning in her head.

I stand up abruptly. "I'll leave you with Matteo. I have some calls to make. I'll have your car found and brought here." The way she carries on about this car, I want to have a closer look.

"Thank you." For the first time since we met, she's agreeable and the chip on her shoulder seems to melt just a tad.

It's just a glimmer of her softer side and I find it encouraging. I have no illusions that it will remain, but I know the crack in her defense can be chipped away given time and a hard as fuck pickaxe.

Her softer demeanor makes me nervous. Fuck, did I just step into one of her traps? Her body is here to tempt me, like a Russian spy in the Cold War. A red sparrow in my house.

I walk outside, calling Dante. I should have done it earlier, but that gorgeous woman in there is distracting my mind and my cock. So much so, that I find myself thinking about her constantly.

What can I say? Knowing she can kill me with her bare hands might excite me. Or is it her icy, light green eyes that can cut like a knife one minute and suck me in like the relaxing tide of the ocean the next?

What the fuck am I doing? I'm the one who likes my solitude and no attachments. I get more than enough human interaction at work and Sunday dinners where Mama pries into our personal lives and picks out our wives for us like we're still children.

We know she has the best of intentions, but these Italian Mama's are a breed onto themselves, and with Dad gone it only gives her more time to obsess over us.

Dante answers, interrupting my thoughts, and for once, I'm relieved.

"Hey, yeah, she's here. No, there's nowhere for her to go, and trust me, no one is going to look for her here. Not right away, it seems. I mean, we have some time. She's convinced that we have a shipment of girls that have been trafficked, and she's looking for them. I think this vendetta against us to atone for her father is a rouse to get into our camp."

"It looked like she was intent on killing you when I came into the room," Dante reminds me.

"Mmm, well, I don't think she's crazy in the head, just crazy with skills. I want to keep her long enough to help me resolve this problem with the Albanians selling in our club."

"A message needs to be sent," Dante agrees. "Let's let it sit for now, gain intel. We have time."

"Yes, but I'm thinking, what if we can follow them and figure out what else they are into? I mean if we cut them off now, they'll just send replacements. I think we should find the mother fucking nest with the rats still in it."

"You make a valid point. Why don't you pursue that angle and let me know if you need support? But we need to resolve this issue with Francesca. Sounds like the Calabrese family is a royal fuck up."

"Sounds good. I think Francesca can make herself useful, especially if she thinks we might have the girls she's looking for. Who knows? I'm sure the Albanians are into every illegal activity known to mankind."

I can tell Dante's amused. He likes the games, which is why he's great as a don. It doesn't stress him out like most. I can tell from the way he remains detached that he's observing everything and making connections in his intellectual mind. He figures out what motivates people, and I just unwittingly played to his strength and bought Francesca an extension of life.

I hung up without telling him my plan to keep Francesca with us for six months. That's plenty of time to get to know her and plenty of time to work my charms.

I'm sure she felt our connection. It's just a matter of time before she's begging me to take her any way I want.

I can't suppress my smile as I turn to walk back into the house. My only issue now is, how do I know she won't try to kill me in my sleep?

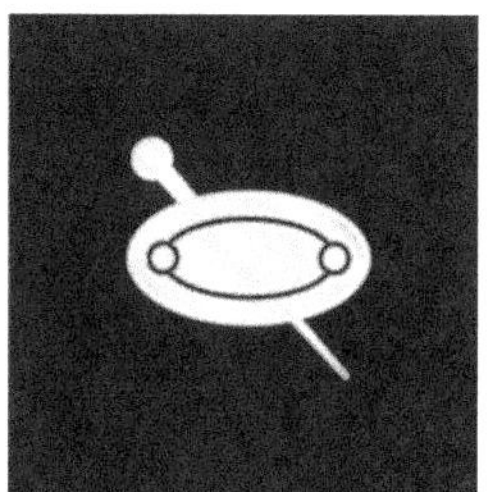

11

FRANCESCA

I never imagined my superior martial arts skills would land me in Sal Micheli's living room tied to a goddamn wooden chair. What a fucking inconvenience this is turning out to be. Quick in and quick out. Why can't I follow my own rules?

The breathtaking view of the valley and vineyards outside his French doors is the only thing keeping me sane right now. I must say, it's a refreshing change from the Conti compound of concrete walls and eyes everywhere. I can actually relax and take a breath without unwanted noise.

Sal left the room a minute ago with his cell phone to his ear. I hope it's not going to be bad news when he returns. Every time the phone rings, I worry it's someone calling to order my termination.

Now, it's only me and Matteo in the room. He's huge and intimidating with that don't-fuck-with-me look in his eyes. I admit, I cannot survive a toe-to-toe fight with him but if I had the element of surprise, it would be a whole different story.

I think he knows that because he never lets his guard

down. He's always watching me, even when Sal is in the room.

"Any chance I can change my clothes?" I ask sweetly.

This tight dress felt good when I put it on yesterday, but it's two days old now, and I'm getting ripe. The breeze blowing through the open doors feels nice, but I need more humane treatment, like a hot shower and clean clothes.

"Working on it," is all he says, unmoved by my pleading. He just stands there, poised to pounce like a killer tabby cat if I so much as move a muscle.

"Well, how about taking off my shoes?"

He lets out a haughty laugh. "Are you kidding me? I know better than to go within five feet of you."

Damn.

Sal returns, "Your car will be here soon."

That's good news. I'm relieved it won't be towed somewhere.

"Don't worry about the Calabrese's or my brothers. They think I'm in Sicily," I offer, letting Sal know my clan won't be following my car here with guns blazing.

He doesn't need to know just how unimportant I am to my brothers. I'm sure I could be gone for quite some time without them bothering to look.

My brothers are the closest thing to human cloning I've ever seen. They both turned out just like Dad in looks, too.

Sal puts his phone down and starts going through the items they took off me after the attack. Holding my knife up to the light, he asks, "Specially designed?"

"Of course."

He looks at me as if I have more to add, and he waits me out, hoping I will let something slip.

"What?" I ask as he continues to stare at me.

"I have some clothes upstairs that will probably fit you

for now," he offers, surprising me. I wasn't expecting those words to come out of his mouth.

"Great, because formal stuff is fun to wear, but the thrill is gone after the first twenty-four hours, y'know," I joke, but I'm not laughing.

A chuckle escapes his full lips as a low masculine laugh greets my ears. I find it sexy, and he tosses the knife back on the countertop.

"A burner phone?" His question sounds more like a foregone conclusion. I am a professional, after all.

I shrug my shoulders.

"You surprise me, Francesca." His eyes are a dark blue today and filled with desire.

Is it a desire for my mad skills? Or for me? Or both?

The wetness between my legs is hard to ignore. "Clothes?"

"Oh, yes, you can't leave the room, your wrists will remain tied, and Matteo will watch you and help accordingly."

"Great," I murmur.

"You can't blame me. Let's not forget you came into our territory and attempted an un-sanctioned hit on me. You're lucky you're not at the bottom of a lake right now."

I can't argue. My dad would not have thought twice about killing a woman, which is probably why human trafficking came to him so easily.

He gives Matteo a nod, and I'm taken upstairs with the gun in my back. To make a play would be stupid. I need to earn their trust and maybe Sal will help me.

They don't know that I'm finished trying to stick a knife in Sal or Dante or anyone else involved with the killing of my father.

I'm moving on to my next mission, finding and freeing

those girls. My brothers set Sal up to look like he took the girls, and they have no idea about it. My family has no way of knowing I'm here . . . in the enemy's house. I'm getting a different story.

The Calabrese won't care if the girls are released now. They got their use out of them, and they've been sold. What better place to hide than with the enemy? But there is a nagging suspicion in the back of my head that tells me this is just way too easy.

Sal's face was shocked at the thought of human trafficking, and I've never heard the Michelis associated with it before, but that's not the gospel—just rumors and innuendos.

Who really knows the truth about anything when men who make their living off of lies, double crosses, and violence?

Matteo leads me into a room that reminds me of summer. Sheers in the large window with green and yellow curtains pulled to the side that fit snugly into a glass and stainless steel tieback hooks that match the curtain rod. The color continues to the quilt on the bed and matching bed linens.

This room is very feminine for a guest room, and I assume his mother, or a girlfriend helped him decorate it. Or maybe he had a girlfriend live here at some point in time. The jealousy I feel is pushed down, because I have nothing to be jealous about. Sal and I together would be a disaster of epic proportions.

My eyes come to rest on the bed where jeans, a t-shirt and boat shoes are all laid out as if they knew I was coming.

A bathroom adjoins the room and glancing in, I'm greeted with a row of jars and bottles that look like moisturizers and bottles of expensive perfumes on the marble countertops. Now, I feel like I'm intruding. Does it belong to a current girlfriend or one from the past?

Matteo cuts the rope around me feet and I waste no time in pulling my dress off. I don't even care at this point if I'm naked in front of him. I slide my panties off, letting them fall to the ground all too suggestively hoping to distract him. I step out of my tight dress when I fail to unnerve him. I hope he gets excited and has to jerk off in a paper napkin later.

I don't even cover myself as I reach for the jeans and slip into them. They're a tad big, but a welcome change as far as comfort goes.

Matteo is looking extremely uncomfortable with me in a strapless bra as I hold my arms, and he slips the shirt over my head, then, one arm at a time. While he re-ties my wrists, I check my look in the mirror.

The t-shirt logo is a big red mouth with a tongue sticking out. Ha, how appropriate. I recall it was one of those eighties bands, Aerosmith or The Stones. It's hard to be sure when both lead singers have big lips.

I'm allowed a bathroom break with the door open and enjoy a refreshing splash of cold water on my face as I wash my hands. Matteo instructs me to hold out my hands, re-tie my wrists, and check my knots before we head back to the living room. I'd love a shower, but I'm not pushing my luck.

Matteo reties me to the chair. I hear Sal outside the house. There are numerous voices outside, and I have no clue what is going on.

An hour passes. Sal returns carrying bags of cash, my cash, and the fake IDs I had made for me and Sofia.

God damn, him. He's smarter than I thought. I knew I overplayed the sentimental value of the car.

Damn.

He reads me like the simple instructions on a container of microwaveable macaroni and cheese. Somehow America's gooey cheesy dish is the latest, hottest trend in Italy, the land of pasta.

We can thank the American burger joint that made melted yellow cheese so popular it had to get its own spot on shelves in the stores that only held European cheeses for centuries.

"How did you know to tear my car apart?" I ask him, but I already know the answer. I should have been a detective instead of trying to be a smuggler.

When it came time to hide that stuff, I knew better than to put it in the trunk. Instead, I had the doors inside lined with the money and the IDs, thinking no one would look there. Well, no one but Sal, apparently.

"You're not very trusting, are you?" He eyes me, but it's not out of contempt. A devilish grin covers his face from ear to ear. "I don't like to underestimate my opponent." He walks closer to me. "Care to explain?" He waves the ID in my face and sits down in front of me. I'm on the losing end of this, and I know it.

"Look, I came with what I could, not knowing if I would ever go back home. That's everything I have. I had to take it with me, naturally." My voice grows softer as my anxiety increases.

My heart feels like it's having palpitations, and I could use a stiff drink right about now to circumvent hyperventilating.

"Naturally," he agrees with brooding eyes that study me.

I casually look at his high cheekbones and breathe him in thinking I shouldn't be this hot in cooler clothing. "Look, I'll help you in the club with the Albanian thing and you help me with finding the girls. Sofia may be one of them. This is real, and I need to find her. No one deserves the life those girls get, least of all Sofia. Her husband is a ruthless pig and is already parading around with some skank he picked up in a striper bar."

Sal puts the IDs down and grows quiet. His pensive face must mean he's considering my proposition.

"Where do you think they are?" he breaks the silence.

"No clue, Fausto, my brother led me here. But the girls haven't been gone that long and must not be too far. If I had to guess, they are up here somewhere since they come in at the Port of Civitavecchia. And in case you missed geography class, there isn't much south of that Port, so I assume they went north." I shrug my shoulders. "It's logical."

He covers his eyes with his hands for a minute before standing. "I get your point. I don't know why your brother put you on my tail. I don't want the syndicate world to think we are traffickers. So, I guess I have some skin in this game too. How dare he blacken my family name?"

His face is one of indignation. He has a valid point. I wouldn't want to be blamed for something I didn't do either.

He paces around the living room in a foul mood at the thought of my family making him look sleazy, and my brother hit their mark if their intent was to get under his skin. Apparently, the Michelis are just as proud of their family name. He returns to me from where he is sitting on the bar stool next to mine where I remain tied.

"After some thought on this, I don't want to piss someone off by stepping on their trafficking toes. Those human traffickers are ruthless and can't be trusted. But at the same time, I can't have them blame my family for it so I will help you find your friend. I assume one of those IDs has her real picture on it."

"It's in the wooden box in my suitcase."

"I'll have the guys pull it and see what I can find out," he says as he stands up to leave. "Can we agree to a truce? A six-month truce where we work together and form an alliance?"

"Yes, you have my word. Ask around. It's golden."

"I will, and it better be all that and more," he threatens as he turns and leaves quickly.

I second guess myself that he was just here, in front of me, smelling like summertime and juniper trees, and that I'm not delusional.

I'm stuck here, and like a teenager with a first crush, I'm upset he left. Suddenly, the room feels empty without him.

The sun dips below the hillside before Sal returns. "You'll be locked in your room at night, no weapons until you need them, and no burner phone . . . for now."

It's to be expected. "Fine."

My concession is not from weakness, these parameters are necessary if we are to work together. He wants to get the Albanians pushed back, and I want to find my friend.

"It's agreed then. If you pull anything, I won't hesitate to kill you. I despised your father and if you are anything like him, you are not long in this world." The blackness I find in his eyes shows me he is dead serious.

And I wouldn't want it any other way. I'd do the same if I were him.

"Well, I hated him too, and I'm not like him. You'll see." I plant the thought that I might be a better person than he thinks mostly because I am.

I don't mention the fact that my brothers are despicable, I'll save that for later. Being useful means I have the information he needs. And the longer he needs me, the longer I have to find Sofia and stay alive.

Sal nods to Matteo and I'm cut out of my restraints.

I rub my wrists and stretch my legs but feel naked without my knives and guns. Sal probably locked them away.

Meanwhile, I'm guessing how long it will be before my family realizes I'm not in Sicily. And how long before they question what I'm really up to? Sitting here for so long, I think Fausto set me up.

Maybe he wanted me to kill Sal or Dante and save him the trouble. Or worse yet, start a war the Michelis have been staving off for years.

Sal motions for me to follow him into the kitchen and asks, "When you were at the gala, did you see your half-sister?"

"Yes, I did. I heard a rumor after Dad died. He had other women all the time, so I'm not surprised. She's pretty and looks happy with Dante." My voice lacks emotion. I didn't plan to meet her or get to know these people, but now I'm thrown into dealing with the reality of family, blood, honor, and possible deceit.

"Yeah, yeah, they're engaged too. She's sweet—you'll like her, I'm sure."

I'm not comfortable thinking about more family, and I'm exhausted from it and struggling to keep my eyes open.

Sal moves around the kitchen pulling food out of the refrigerator.

"Are you making dinner? Because I need lots of protein and I'm starving. That might be why I'm suddenly so tired."

His looks to me and I swear there was an inkling of concern in his eyes. He shifts his gaze to Matteo with instructions to go to the butcher and pick up some steaks, and shish kebab with beef, lamb, and chicken.

I don't know what has me drooling more– Sal in the kitchen with his dark blue dress shirt rolled up to his elbows or the fact that I'll finally be able to eat real food for the first time since lunch.

My stiff muscles buckle in protest from lack of exercise and proper nutrition so a steak is a good start.

Now that I'm in the Micheli camp, I have to work with the enemy of my family, no matter how confusing this is. I'm torn between my family that doesn't want me and one that does. I need to be focused on my new mission. It's time to find Sofia and what my family is up to. But first, I need some answers.

12

SAL

"Wakey-wakey. Time to go running," Francesca chirps like a personal trainer jacked up on caffeine and candy bars. Maybe some Red Bull and steroids for all I know.

I hide my head under my pillow as if it will make her disappear, but it only prolongs the inevitable.

"You have got to be kidding me!" I yell back when she pounds again on my bedroom door at seven o'clock. Birds are chirping outside my window, and it's a welcome sound only not this goddamn early in the morning.

"I worked last night. You weren't up until midnight like me."

"You're wrong about that. I was up late doing research. I need to go shopping later to buy some stuff, y'know, to blend in and all that." She pauses, and when I hear nothing, I hope she's gone.

"Y'know," she lets out a tiny huff, "I feel like an idiot having a conversation through your bedroom door."

I assume Matteo is with her unless she got the jump on him and laid him out just for kicks. I chuckle at the mental image as I throw the sheet off and put my feet on the cool floor.

Out of respect, I push down my morning erection and even stooped to pick up boxers, putting them on as I head to the door. I finally open it and immediately lean on the frame with my eyes half open giving her the full-frontal view of my abs. Let's see how she likes this.

"The vision of you in shorts and a tank top is my sole motivation for getting out of bed. Period." As my sleepy gaze runs up and down her tight body. I enjoy the fact that it's extremely obvious that I'm ogling her to throw her off her game. She's mind fucking me as she's wearing next to nothing.

Her bright pink sports bra strains across perfectly natural C-cup breasts, and she even has the fucking matching running shorts and pink shoes. It's designer, but I've never seen it before, and I'm beginning to think she has stuff custom-made.

"Pink? Really? I wouldn't call that an indiscreet color to trot around in."

I prepare to warm up. Do we have all the information on her? Because coming from her family, she's too put together. It's like she's the block that doesn't belong with the rest of the group of rectangles.

"The sun isn't getting any cooler, so I suggest you get dressed and meet me downstairs ASAP." Her words hit me like a face full of ice water, and her green eyes cut through me, unfazed by my half-naked physique. Maybe I misjudged her.

I stand straighter and give her a half salute. "Well, aren't you the drill Sargent?"

"I didn't get this way by lying in bed all morning. You might look like you're in good shape, but can you run?" She spins on her neon sneakers before walking away, taking the steps downstairs two at a time like its part of an obstacle course.

"Oh, yeah, when are you having the barn converted to a gym?" she hollers over her shoulder.

"Soon," I respond, my answer ambiguous because I haven't ordered the equipment yet, but she doesn't need to know that. I'll have someone shop with the list.

"Good," I hear as the front door opens.

Christ, I better get down there.

With no time to spare, I throw on gym clothes and hop around the room on one leg at a time pulling on my sneakers before racing after her.

Shit, she's hard to keep up with.

I'm a numbers guy at work, so most of my work is done in my head. When I'm not working out in my head, I'm working out in my bed, but that's been a while, so I've resorted to servicing myself. I mean, that was sufficient until Francesca showed up.

I can't believe I think of her before I fall asleep. Her emerald eyes and perky smile make me want to be accommodating to her every whim. I even enjoy it when she gets a one-liner over on me. I like our wordplay.

When I make it out the front door, I catch Francesca doing stretches. I copy her moves and act like I'm a pro at this even though it's been years. I notice Matteo getting in his Range Rover, which he then pulls up and sits waiting on us. Not a bad idea to be vigilant on a normal day, but Francesca is, well . . . not normal. Besides, one can't be too careful.

Having Matteo close by and Francesca around all the time, it's beginning to feel like home week with my old soccer buddies from our recreation league days when we hung out all the time eating, playing, and exercising.

Matteo is watching us from a reasonable distance and that implies we're all getting less paranoid about each other. Francesca calls out to me bringing me back to reality and I'm chasing after her.

The morning mist rises off the road and the sun breaks through the cypress trees providing ample shade and then we run at a nice clip. A gentle intermittent breeze rustles the leaves and gives me goosebumps as it passes over my skin.

From the corner of my eye, I take in Francesca's full breasts, bouncing and straining to break free of her sports bra. They're beautiful, big enough to be more than a mouthful.

She catches me looking, so I fall behind and decide this is the better view, following her firm round bottom. As if she can feel my eyes on her ass, she picks up the pace. Fuck me, I have to run faster.

I can tell by the way she makes this look so effortless she's a natural runner. And I am not. The treadmill I use isn't the same as running in the elements.

"Glad to see you can keep up," she saucily teases me as I stare at her long legs and study her footwork.

"How many miles do you run?"

"Don't think about it," she replies without sounding out of breath. "We'll go as long as we can. A person can pump weights and get away with terrible breathing habits. We'll see how you do at the first hill. Then we can make adjustments."

"Great," I try to sound enthused. I admire her unwavering commitment to keeping her physique in top condition, but it's not like we're training for the Olympics.

I get it. She lives in a man's world and needs to hold her own. For the Contis and the Calabreses to overlook her probably hurt her mentally and emotionally.

Any hope she had of changing the chauvinistic mold

inside the mafia was probably a huge disappointment both personally and professionally.

By now, she must realize that men in this line of work are sexist, more so than in any other organization, and it's not just her, the guys have their pecking order as well.

After a half mile, the effect of the rising humidity takes a toll, and my breathing and getting enough air in becomes a struggle.

"Relax, slow your breathing," she instructs, slowing our pace. She taps her sports watch and seems satisfied.

I follow her instructions, and to my surprise, it helps.

"Let's stop for a water break," she suggests before leaning up against a tree and reaching around her back as I hold my breath, hoping Matteo frisked her.

I breathe easy when she pulls water out from the holder she has around her waist.

She takes a few swigs before putting it back and extending a leg up on the tree to stretch her thigh muscles, then stands on her toes and rolls forward to stretch her calves.

While she does the same to her other leg, she pulls another water from her waist belt and hands it to me. I thank her and open it, but wait until she drinks her water again before I do the same. Ladies first.

"The first mile is the hardest," she says between sips.

"Followed by the second?" I jest, bending over my knees to catch my breath.

"Let's just say, after you work your way up to two miles, you should be in your zone, and then you reach a point where you feel like you can run forever."

"Really? I never had the fortitude to do anything other than soccer, and that's more a game of sprints. I don't know what possessed me." I stand, running my muscular forearm over my brow to wipe away the sweat that's running down my face.

"We can turn back and do suicide drills in the yard, then cool down once we're home."

Home? I can't believe she's letting me off that easy. Who am I kidding? I'll be lucky to make it there without dropping.

AFTER WE FINISH our first workout, I approach the subject of the club. It's been gnawing at me for weeks. I didn't anticipate her ending up here in the midst of what might become bigger issues involving another mafia, one that's international and has ties in places I don't even know the names of. They are known to operate on three continents or more.

"Sure thing, we need to find out if the Albanians know anything. No sense in making an enemy when we might get the information in a more subtle way," Francesca suggests.

"They aren't pleasant people. You know all too well the types of people we deal with in our seedy underworld. I don't want you in harm's way or on their radar."

"Hmm, well I guess we'll just have to be careful. Matteo let me do some research the other day and I'm starting to plot what I know from the Conti and Calabrese camp and the players I can identify here."

"Great, but I want you at the club tonight. The sooner we deal with these Albanians and find Sofia, if that's even possible, the happier I'll be. Then we can go our separate ways," I reaffirm our deal.

I don't know why I'm being pissy. She's done nothing wrong. In fact, she seems pretty fucking normal, which confuses me even more than if she was a nasty, cold-hearted bitch like I expected.

But I'm not getting the reaction out of her that I desire, and I'm troubled by this. My cute one-liners and roguishly handsome morning charm usually work on the ladies, and yet she shows no signs of letting her frosty, professional exterior shed a layer.

I'd be happy to get just a peek under who the real Francesca is, but she reminds me more of Dante as the days pass.

Speaking of hot women, I decided that I need to be serviced in light of the frosty bombshell in front of me. I should return Carla's text and set up a date. I need to get laid. She deserves better than what I'm offering, but as long as we're both having a good time, what's wrong with that?

And I'll get the upper hand over Francesca by making her be my bodyguard for this date. I'll find out where her boiling point is because the sexual tension between us is making me crazy.

As for Francesca, she is turning out to be a tough nut to crack. She may be keeping it all business, but she's not succeeding in fooling me. Not totally.

Her heavy breathing when we're next to each other tells me everything I need to know. And to be nice, I send her to stores with Matteo to get what she wants while I shower, snack, and lie down to rest.

I have a long night ahead of me; however I can't stop thinking about Francesca's pert breasts and curvy butt. Her eyes flash from green to jeweled emeralds, depending on her mood. I'd like to think emerald is when she's hot and bothered as I notice it more when I'm closer to her and they are green when she's with others.

I lay staring at the ceiling and missing her which is crazy because we just met and she's down the hallway. How do you miss someone you don't even know? I mean, what do we have in common besides a shitload of money and a fondness for nice cars?

And we're both mafias. That's a huge plus. We understand our world and our places in it.

The only shared experience I can add to that list is her attempt on my life, followed by an interrogation in a damp wine cellar. Not exactly the stuff you hang your hopes on or tell your grandchildren.

What can I offer her? She doesn't need me. She's a self-sufficient package, and if it were not for her obvious contempt for men in general, she could have any man she wants.

I roll over and punch my pillow. I'm going to have to show her what I'm made of and quickly. Six months passes in no time, especially at her age, surrounded by horny Italian men.

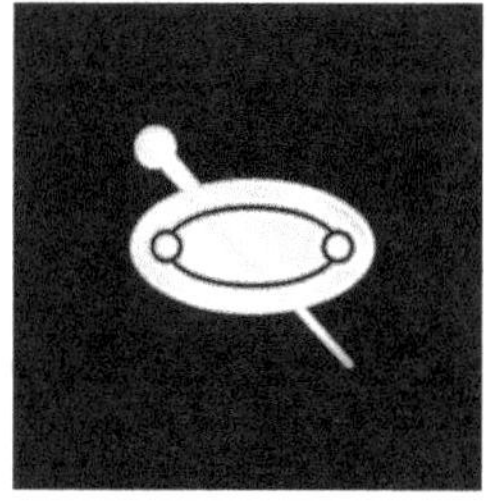

13

FRANCESCA

Damn if Sal's not hotter than that soccer player, Beckham. He casually stands there like the king in this castle knowing full well his naked chest is popping out. He makes himself look so innocent but he's trying to throw me off my game and I have a job to do.

Until Sofia is found, I can't let up. Each day lost means she's slipping away.

And fuck me. How can I live and work with him flashing those abs and pecs around? For sure, he can withstand quite a few of my punches from the eye candy shot I got this morning.

His face is as close to perfection as I can imagine, and I love the morning stubble on his face giving him that rough yet not-so-rough vision that turns me on.

I'd love to run my hand down the side of his face, feel the roughness under my manicured natural nails, and cup his chin, pulling him into me, but I'd never touch him like that.

His grey eyes remind me of his moods, and even if he wasn't the top echelon in the family, I'd never be so forward with a man I barely know and certainly not one that is connected.

I vowed to myself I'd never marry anyone in the family, which means no dating. If I don't date a bad guy, I won't be tempted to marry one.

It's not the life I want. I have this small window in which I might escape my past. I'll be fine if I can keep my mind on work and stop these rampant thoughts driven by lust and loneliness.

Besides, it's more important that we find Sofia. That's why I came here and why I'm staying. It's strange how fate changes our lives. I came to kill Sal, and now we are teamed up to find Sofi and get the low down on the Albanian mafia encroaching on his clubs. Sal has proved useful in many ways.

I think my bra top makes his dick pop, and now that I'm dressing for my first recon mission at the club, I have a cute smirk on my face as I know I have the power to make him regret making me stay and work with him.

He'll be so horny he'll be picking up a girl from the club and fucking her up against the back wall of his office before long.

This house is very nice, and I feel like I'm on vacation except for Matteo and his gun and my locked bedroom door at night.

But in all honesty, I can't complain about my treatment, and I don't have unknown men behind hidden cameras watching me like they used to do at the Conti compound. I'm not sure where all the cameras were but I never took any chances, one wrong word and you become one of those that just disappears.

I spent the afternoon shopping for clubbing clothes and found some cute designer items and a small handbag with matching shoes. It felt nice to be almost on my own and doing things that are normal for someone of my age and stature.

We have no proof that the Albanians are behind the deal with my family, and I don't need any new enemies. I have enough from my own tribe. Actually, my own tribe might be more of an issue as I don't have any eyes or ears in the place.

The wake of a don creates a void that becomes a free for all, like the dash to get the *Goblet of Fire* and I have no idea who has an alliance with whom, so I'm really screwed.

I'm pissed they sent me up here with vengeance on my mind to take out Sal, but Sal showed me their accounts, and there are no transactions with my family, and I believe him. Why would my family lie to me? The two families have hated each other forever so it's odd they would make a deal of any kind. That is a fact.

I have to protect myself, and working under the dim lighting at the bar helps but it's not enough. A blonde who looks ripped like me is going to get noticed and that's not conducive to obtaining information while remaining an enigma. However, I can play the part of a fixer.

I don't know who my family's enemies are and where I might stumble over them so an ounce of prevention will go a long way in keeping me and Sal safe. I've taught him some quick moves in a short amount of time.

His brain is unbelievable when I watch him go over the computer screens navigating programs for accounting and coding things that only he would know. He was impressive. There, I admit it.

Tonight, I dress more like a younger version of myself, with a skintight dress that is electric blue, my bag, and blue shoes. I look like a mafia princess, alright. More importantly,

I look like I wield more power —power that extends beyond my legs, tanned shoulders, and hidden knives.

I grab a small purse slipping the strap over my shoulder. I have Mace in it, my fake ID, and a few essentials, like lipstick. I take my time stepping down the staircase, and Sal is waiting for me at the bottom as if he perfectly timed it. It's as if we're on a first date.

"Wow, who are you, and where is Francesca?" Sal asks, holding his jacket in one hand while Matteo stands in a suit that must have a gun tucked in it somewhere.

True, I'm stripped of the ties I had on earlier this week, and the running and a few moves we've been learning have toned me up. I also do Pilates in my room at night to keep my mind off Sal. He's off-limits now and forever.

"Good, my real identity is a secret. I'm Francesca Savona. It's always best to stay the closest to the truth when doing this shit," I state as I wait for Sal to open the door.

"You've done that alright," Matteo says his first words to me.

"Matteo, you finally found your tongue?" I tease as I breeze by him, and he opens the car door as Sal and I get in. Matteo slides behind the wheel, and we're off to the club even though it's ten at night.

"Just a heads up, tomorrow is my family's Sunday luncheon. We mix up the times for safety and seeing as how you are new and it's a sensitive situation, instead of leaving you at home, I'll introduce you to my mother."

"Moving lunch to another location will have Mom asking questions, so Dante and I made a decision for you to be there under your fake name. Only Dante and Juliet and our other brother Marchello will know who you really are. Well, Riccardo too."

"Is that the man that looks like the Israeli elite force?"

"That's him, alright."

"Oh, wow, is that a good idea for us to meet? I mean, my half-sister will be there. Surely Dante told her about me."

"It's all I got to go with," he says as he turns his palms face up —he's out of ideas.

"Oh, alright. I guess we have to make it up as we go along." I lay my purse in my lap and fold my hands over it like I went to finishing school.

I'm not sure how I feel about this. I'm not much of a family person and feel more pressure to perform for his family than I do for my job tonight. It's easy to beat the shit out of a thug; it's difficult for me to sip tea with women and not show my angry side to men that can hit on me, physically or emotionally.

I sigh as I take in the city lights of Florence that are bright enough to illuminate the sky as we drive down mountainous roads. We arrive at the club by eleven p.m. It's important to know the time which is why I'm wearing an expensive exercise watch. My phone is turned off but it's my burner that Sal returned to me.

I must have been a very good girl as I'm getting privileges. That, and the fact that I need to make a buy from these Albanians. Sal gives me a few hundred euros to use at the club to buy coke off these pricks at the club if they're even there tonight. But it's Saturday night and we have every reason to believe it will be worth their while to move coke and possibly fentanyl pills laced with heroin or other substances.

"Pull over here, Matteo," I instruct with authority.

He looks in the review mirror at Sal, who nods his agreement.

"We're not there yet," Sal replies.

"Sal, we need to exchange numbers and if I get taken or

something stupid happens, I doubt that they would know what 'O' stands for in my phone and if you get a call on it, never give out your real name."

Sal takes the phone from my hand, and our fingers bump into each other as my heart races, and my pussy is instantly wet and warm as he makes sure we both have the number in our phones.

Flashbacks of seeing Sal naked this morning run through my mind and my palms turn sweaty. I rub them over the hem of my dress.

"You, okay?" Sal's deep voice has a ring of concern in it, and it's endearing.

But it's game time, so I have to let it go and get back to business.

"Sure, why?" I snap.

Then, I want to kick myself for being defensive with him when he's being sweet for the first time since he brought me that cold cappuccino in the cellar.

Well, there's the cute banter he makes with me occasionally, but I just blow that off as a man who wants to get laid.

We continue to the club and get out of the dark-tinted SUV like nothing screams drug pusher or mafia more than the vehicles we drive.

Memories of my first night here at the Red Grotto, where I checked Sal out for the first time. I eavesdrop on the conversations going on around me as I circulate.

It's a place for those in their twenties to forties and wealthy older men with young women, very young women and I hope the Albanians are not running prostitution rings out of here as well.

I can't tell if they are escorts, or not. Some look too perfect if you know what I mean.

Guys younger than me are checking me out. I order a

Cosmo from the bar and then turn my back to take in the club and the clientele keeping my eyes discreetly peeled for the Albanians.

I'm looking for known mafia pushers and enforcers, but I don't have a photographic memory, and men can change beards by adding goatees and gaining or losing weight to alter their appearances quicker than women, outside of a bottle of hair color that is.

Sal slides his arm around my trim waist as I sip my drink. He catches me by surprise as my focus isn't on him, and at the same time, my body wants to wilt into his like a thirsty rose on a bush that hasn't been watered in months. No pun intended, but yeah, my so-called 'bush' is very, very dry.

"What's that for?" I pry, fishing for something but not knowing what exactly I'm waiting for.

"I think making you look like you belong to me will help us, besides, I'm sure you don't want most of these men hitting on you all night long."

He has a point. "Hmm, you did, did you? Likewise for you," I tease as I cozy up to him, making it look legit.

It's the first time since my instructor that an arm around me gives me comfort and I like the fact that Sal is close to me.

"Look at the guys over there," Sal says. I follow where he suggests with my eyes. "That's Argon, he's one of the street bosses. He was picked up a few years ago, did some time, and he's back and in business."

"He looks vaguely familiar; maybe I saw him in the news."

"I think his street crew is working a few of our clubs."

"So, what's our play?" I ask.

"I'm going to tell him I have some men and want to know

if he has some girls he may have just received from my brothers."

"Go get 'em, tiger," he says and slaps my ass as I turn to leave. Normally, I'd lay a man flat for that, but with Sal and our mission, the fact he called me 'Tiger' brings a new kind of smile to my face. So, I puff my chest out confidently to make my girls show.

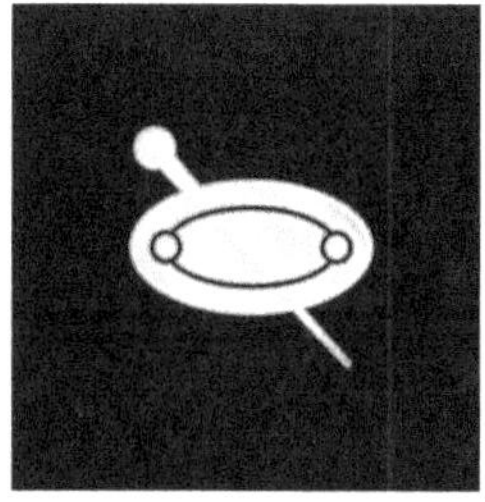

14

SAL

Francesca circles the dance floor and within minutes, she is buying coke from Argon's men, the same men who have been infiltrating my club for weeks. His men are trained to be fast and blend in very well, fooling an untrained eye.

They most likely grew up on streets in war-torn countries, and if you piss them off or look at them the wrong way they would just as soon slit your throat than look at you. Ruthless, even by Italian standards.

I'm nervous watching Francesca make a deal, and I'm relieved when she walks away in case Argon gets other ideas. They can sell in here until I put a stop to it because those in the mafia, don't ask for permission.

I haven't exercised my power yet because I want to learn more about them. Dante won't act until he has all the facts and can think about it, as a good don should.

Francesca meets me at my office, and we slip inside. She drops her purse and drugs on my desk. I open a packet of powder and put some on my fingertip.

"Blue is fentanyl, don't touch it," she warns me.

"Right, who knows what they put in it." I sample the white powder putting some on my tongue. "Seems decent enough."

"I asked if he had any girls for a private party. I told him I wanted pictures of the girls first. He'll text me a link." She offers me the details as if she's ordering pizza, her tone flat and unaffected.

Pulling out her phone, she presses on a live link that goes to the dark web, where we both look at her screen and search for Sofia.

"These girls all look Albanian, but that's not surprising. It's easy to pick up girls crossing the border looking for husbands. My brothers import girls from Nigeria and whomever they can capture at airports. The Nigerians smuggled here are looking for a better way of life based on the promises of jobs."

I agree, but this isn't adding up as I surf the pictures. "Where is Sophia? There must be more girls. I know the girls Fausto had, and none of them are here."

Francesca puts her phone away, clearly frustrated. "I agree, but where are they? Every day that goes by is another day that Sofia is gone and slipping through our fingers. I think Fausto sent me here as a decoy. Can you research ships in the port and have your men look around a bit?"

"What, me?" I ask innocently putting a hand to my chest, feigning innocence.

"Clearly, you have sources who know I'm on the outs with my family." She stares me in the eye. "Use them." Her tone gives me directions as if she's a boss.

"I'll look through ship manifests and see what I can find." I smile, liking her feisty like this and taking control.

"Great, and thanks, Sal. I'm afraid we might not find Sofia in time." Her voice fades in sadness, and I want to hold and comfort her, but I'm afraid it might put her on the defensive.

I'm not ready to make any move if it means I might drive her away. I'm looking to pull her closer. And if finding Sofia will make that happen, I'll do it.

Plus, we made a deal, and a Micheli always makes good on a deal.

"We should get back downstairs," I suggest, breaking the silence in the room and giving her a second to regain her composure before I gently place my hand on the small of her back.

"I'll talk to some girls at the bar who look like escorts, maybe I can get some new information out of them."

Francesca finds her optimism again and the brief flash I got that showed she still has feelings she's suppressing is quickly put behind her.

This is the first time I've seen her show any emotion other than anger. I admire her loyalty to her friend—her family doesn't deserve loyalty from her.

"Sounds good, let's go," I say as I lock the door behind us.

FOR LUNCH AT MAMA'S, we dress nicely but casually. This week, she put out a special spread of seafood and antipasti to impress Francesca. Mama is looking forward to meeting her, though I cannot say the same for the rest of the family.

Using a fake last name, Mama won't know she's really a Conti. The less she knows for now, the better. I can't have her thinking we brought the enemy to our door. When, in fact, we did.

"Dante," I shout out when I catch my brother leaning

against an umbrella tree in the backyard. He looks happy, and I'm happy for him. God knows he has the most stress out of all of us.

Everything fell on him when Dad died suddenly.

Francesca follows as I make my way toward him. Seeing Juliet leaning on her intended makes me happy, and it's a good time for introductions.

"*Ciao*." We hug and kiss. "Brother, I've missed you."

"Same here. This is Francesca. I'm sure Dante has told you we're not telling Mama who she really is." I turn to Juliet. "This is your half-sister, Francesca. Please don't be too hard on her. I know she tried to kill me, but trust me when I tell you, it would have happened if she wanted to off us. It appears that her brother, Fausto, set us up."

Dante stiffens. "What do you mean?"

"We've never dealt in human trafficking before. I'm sure they know that was all their dad. So why send Francesca up here?"

"That's a good question. I have a ship loaded with Calabrese drugs coming in very soon. Maybe they just want to take over our holdings at the port and screw us over again."

I can tell he's deep in thought as Marchello arrives and introduces himself to Francesca.

"Why the long faces? We're at Mama's for lunch."

"Marchello, how many men do you have and how quickly can they make it to the Conti compound?" Dante asks.

"I'd need a day to organize it and drive time. Why?" Marchello cocks his head.

"I think it's better if we strike first before this turns into a full-out war," Dante says, always the strategic thinker.

"Sal, see what you can find out about the Conti and Calabrese shipments. If I have guns on my ship, what do they have on theirs?"

"Good question. I think we need to find out."

"I know my way around and I can hack into the security cameras," Francesca offers, eager to contribute.

Mama calls us to the table and once we're around it I pour a limoncello martini for Francesca.

"Oh, no, Sal," she objects, but I know shit is about to get real and we all need to take the edge off.

Francesca sits across from her half-sister and the resemblance between the two is uncanny. I'm grateful they have different hair colors, or it might be more obvious that they are related.

"Congrats on your upcoming wedding," Francesca says as she sips the sweet lemony drink.

"Thank you." Juliet is polite, but she's reticent.

I would be, too if I found a long-lost half-sibling. They grew up much differently, but I hope that they can find common ground and get along once they know each other.

But who am I kidding? Francesca is on the run and not likely to be around after her six months, maybe not that long if we have a war brewing—one we didn't instigate and one we want to prevent.

Riccardo is quiet, but I can tell he's studying Francesca. He taught me always to know my enemy and never underestimate them. From our time spent with her in the cellar, he knows she's a spitfire and can kick ass as she's highly trained and proficient.

I realize she must have her mother's personality as she doesn't appear to be unbalanced, and she hates human trafficking as much as we do.

Besides, even Francesca let it slip her brothers are psychotic, and we know her father was too, so maybe that genetic marker passes only to the males in the family.

Dante is enjoying himself because Juliet is with him, but

behind his dark eyes, I can tell he's thinking of the Contis and the Calabreses and why they would want to start a war with us.

It's my day off, so we converse on light topics and catch up. After lunch, the women move to the kitchen to clean up while the men hang out under the shade trees to drink scotch and discuss business.

"I have a good haul this week, but a few gamblers are falling behind with the economic downturn," Marchello says, pulling out cigars.

"Don't let large tabs run-up. We'll never collect on them. You know how it goes. There are those who make their car payments every month and those who buy a car and never make one payment. It's the same with gambling and shipments."

"I know, but the shipments of drugs I move are all paid on delivery. No way am I on the hook for that." He smiles and lights a cigar.

It's hard to believe my little brother stepped up after Dad died. We all did. I'm glad we're all able to work together so well. Dad would be proud of us.

Besides, we need to take care of Mama and keep the family name alive. I'm sure Dante will have the first heir since he's getting married first. Ha. The most unlikely to wed brother is the first to walk down the aisle in the local Catholic Church where we were baptized. Who could have seen that coming?

My phone vibrates, and it's Carla. Eureka! The woman finally returned my call. I excuse myself from the table.

"Hi Carla, how are you?"

"I'm fine. I know it's Sunday, and you're with your family, but do you want to join me for a drink later?"

"That would be great. How about our favorite spot by the Arno? We'll watch the sunset if it's not overcast."

"Sure, sounds great. Seven, okay?"

"Perfect."

I hang up and notice Francesca does not look pleased. There's no way she heard me, so I suspect she reads lips. She needs to get over it. Tonight, she'll be part of my security detail, and she better not let her personal feelings compromise her job to protect me.

I would make a play for Francesca, but I don't believe she will ever get over her anger issues with men. As for letting any man past those concrete walls she built around herself? Doubtful at best. Her resolve borders on unnatural, and I don't have time to be her psychologist.

She's here to find her friend and sniff out the Albanians.

Dante puffs at his cigar and blows his smoke into a perfect ring that drifts away before finishing his scotch. He stands first, and we follow to say goodbye to Mama before we join our security details and clear out.

Marchello will be readying the troops in case we need them, a large and expensive operation involving many men, some whom might not come home.

But as Dante said, we can't sit by and let the little pieces of shit that have Conti DNA and Calabrese blood tarnish our name. I can tell Dante is already working on how the scenario might go down.

Meanwhile, we're on our way home for the afternoon siesta.

"Get your rest. I have a date tonight, and I want you on it," I inform Francesca.

"Righty-oh," she replies flippantly.

"Hmm, really?"

"Sorry, yes, sir." She sits up straighter, but her continued attitude tells me she doesn't appreciate me telling her what to do.

People like her are disciplined and respond best to their trainers who they respect above all others. Does this mean she respects me or not? I shrug it off as her anger issues and head upstairs. I may never figure her out and the sheer thought of that turns me on and my neck turns warm, and my chest is tight. I need air. And I need to get laid tonight otherwise, I'm going to go crazy if Francesca doesn't give me an in to get closer. The subtle smiles and the physical closeness while training together daily drive me insane.

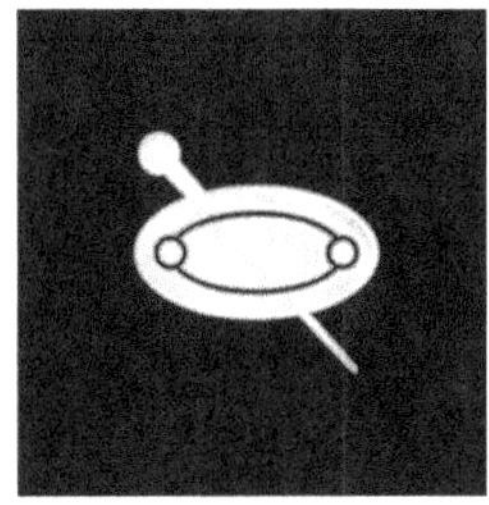

15

FRANCESCA

I lay in bed and stare out the window, watching the white clouds float by through the tree limbs of an old birch behind the house.

At night, it looks eerie as the light of the moon is broken up by the swaying branches, but I find it comforting. Is it the darkness in me or the fact that it's unique? I look for patterns in nature just like I look for patterns in people.

Who is this Carla and why is he meeting her? Is she the one who left stuff in the bathroom I'm using? Is she pretty? Wealthy? Of Florentine breeding? That seems to be a checkbox that has to be ticked here, and I have no idea why. I don't understand this thing about Florentines.

However, it's a big deal among Italians here who have money or prestigious backgrounds. All my questions will be answered in time I suppose. Maybe Sal has pressure on him to marry Carla. She could be one of the clans in their organization.

Just the same, I'd rather skip tonight's tête-à-tête. Witnessing the two of them is not my idea of fun. And yet at the same time, I can't stop thinking about what it would be like to be on a date with him.

A real date, one where I'd get to dress up and enjoy the scent of his cologne that mingles with mine. Maybe an incredible wine that compliments copious amounts of food and conversation that isn't about work.

But it's not me he's with and I only glance at the reacquainted lovers sharing an evening drink to make sure he's safe.

Sal mentioned that they are implementing a plan to check into my family and the Calabrese's involvement in human trafficking. They agree something is amiss, and the Micheli family doesn't take lightly to false accusations. I overheard something about my dad killing his men years ago when the families were at war to cover up a double cross.

The Michelis have plenty of reasons to hate us. I'm surprised they have taken me in, but I'm anxious to head south. We can pick up with the Albanians later.

Turf wars happen all the time. In all honesty, it's been a while since things sparked this far north, so I know we're all deluding ourselves if we expect this calm to last indefinitely. It's just not the nature of our 'business.'

I can't figure out what skin Fausto has in the game with Calabrese unless he's being paid well to deliver me to the enemy or he's got another trick up his sleeve. He counted on me coming here to avenge my father's death, and I fell into the trap.

I am tough, but my weakness is loyalty and empathy for the girls. My brothers knew this and exploited my weakness. And I fell for his lies. I know better, but I'm human after all.

His world is much larger with a wider swath of personalities. Personalities he's known for years through Dad, the same with Mario. I'm not savvy with all the games they play.

I bolt upright in my bed of crisp sheets that remind me of spring with the freshness of daisies when I realize they might be in this together. They both mastered manipulation a long time ago, I didn't expect either of them to use it on me. I should have known better.

I should have known that Dad's death changed everything for all of us as well and that they had their reasons for getting me out of town. I wish I knew what they were.

The only proof of human trafficking was paperwork showing money exchanged between bank accounts, and he could have easily forged it. Now that I can put the pieces together, I realize he hung me out to dry.

Whether he wanted me to die attacking Dante or not, the potential was very high I wouldn't return from that mission no matter how good I am. And he wanted me to go after Sal, not Dante.

I run my hand through my hair and lift it off my neck and shoulders as I'm hot. Damn. I have so many questions. With me out the way, meaning I wouldn't be making waves and making my brothers look bad, Mario would be the Don if Calabrese didn't take over. Or, if he takes out Calabrese, which might be easier after Calabrese thinks he's safely in as Don.

Maybe he went along with Calabrese because he wasn't set up to be successful in his bid to take over.

This makes more sense to me. I've been duped, as have the Michelis.

Fausto and Mario would need help solidifying their bid within the new regime and eliminating others without getting their hands any dirtier than they already are.

Plus, my brothers would inherit more of Dad's estate. Everyone I know is all about the money, and I had to fight for what I received.

Remorse takes over. Maybe I'm partly responsible for Sofia's disappearance. Maybe the family just wanted to erase Sofia to distract me in an elaborate plot. In the process, I became a loose end. And is Guido in on this as well? Could the three of them be this tight?

Financial gain is not the only factor that motivates my brothers. Their need for more power and more money is never satisfied. In the mafia world, one must be ambitious, ruthless, and devious . . . willing to go to extremes to obtain more spoils of war. There is no vacation from the pursuit of more, more, more.

I lay down once more, and I toss and turn. It's futile. I can't get my mind off Sal's hard as fuck body, and it's making me restless and agitated. Or is it the mere insinuation that he and Carla might get back together?

The moves we make on the mats practicing, and his deep voice is all I need to send my hormones crazy with lust.

Dammit, I don't have a vibrator either.

I need to get off, or I'll go insane, so I reach down between my legs and caress my nub with one hand and play with my nipples with the other. It's not hard to imagine Sal's strong hands cupping my breasts, tweaking my nipples just so before he leans over to kiss me, gentle at first. Then, he's claiming me as his woman for everyone to see.

Arching my back, I close my eyes and envision Sal's face as I come and softly whisper his name. It passes over my lips like dandelion fluff blowing away after a wish.

Relieved, I'm physically better but find I still can't rest so I throw on one of my brand's designer loungewear and head downstairs. I can't deny that I could feel safe in Sal's strong arms. I get a dose of it daily when we have the opportunity to practice basic maneuvers in the yard.

The barn isn't totally set up yet, nor is it weatherproofed, but it will suffice with some mats and a kickboxing bag until it's finished.

Sal's mellow attitude kept me calm when I found myself tied up in his cellar. We've moved past that and my hatred for him is slowly disappearing, or rather, shrinking like a violet from too much sunshine, namely his charismatic smile that makes me believe it's just for me.

But who am I kidding? He's friendly with everyone. He's the oil that makes their family machine work so well.

He smooths over arguments before they become arguments. He mends the fences between bosses, and I've only been his shadow for two weeks.

The sound of his voice before he enters a room cheers me up and his presence only makes me want him more. I find myself like all the other women he encounters, pathetically yearning for him to touch, kiss, or hold me in a situation that doesn't involve work or me passing out.

What will I do if I find out my family set me up and that the Michelis aren't as evil as I thought? What do I do with my life then?

I head to the kitchen and make a tomato and olive oil sandwich. Matteo joins me, and I ask how late we'll be.

He shrugs. "One never knows."

I can tell he's not particularly happy about the turn of events, either.

He suggests we suit up. I put on my new pantsuit and jacket I bought to hold my ID and weapons. When I check my reflection in the mirror, I barely recognize myself. I look like a CIA OP one sees in American TV shows.

It's dark when we roll out. I walk behind Sal and realize I just screwed myself as soon as I get a whiff of his earthy cologne. I'm relieved when Matteo opens the car door for

Sal. I hate to be more subservient than I already am. Matteo drives as we make our way down the hill and into town.

Along the way, the men talk. Me? I'd rather have a relaxing night at home reading a good suspense book. I try to control my thoughts but I'm a bit miffed that Sal is taking time out to get laid, while Sofia is still missing.

My issues aren't the Michelis' priorities, and I get that. They have a huge family to manage and I'm not one to them. If they don't start looking for Sofia soon, I'll have to escape, and risk being hunted by everyone.

We arrive at a quaint late-night wine bar and before I enter, I can tell Carla is already there. She a stunning blonde, pretty enough to model, waiting in a cozy booth in the back. She's speaking in Italian as Sal greets her with a kiss on both cheeks and sits. The waiter approaches. Sal orders a bottle of red wine.

I let out a heavy sigh as I cover the restaurant being left alone to witness the two while Matteo checks the perimeter. My legs need to move so I walk past them getting reacquainted, and check out the kitchen before returning to the dining room.

Matteo and I find a table across from Sal and sit facing opposite directions. We are not expecting trouble, but we need to be ready to fly into action.

Matteo asks the waiter to bring us some coffee and speaks to Carla across the way because they know each other from former liaisons she's had with Sal.

I use it to feed my anger and leverage it to keep the walls around my heart closed. They need to be refortified. And I need to get out of here like last week.

I turn away to dodge any introductions while Matteo glances at me before sipping his coffee. Talk about weird and awkward. Yesterday's lunch was enough family for me.

I've never had a normal family gathering that wasn't about work. The next score and outbursts from Dad and him fighting with Mom calling her a whore and a useless piece of shit are my memories.

Then, he'd take shit out on me, like if the sauce wasn't hot enough he would slap me in front of my brothers and dinner guests. Dad never cared how anything looked. The messier, the better.

I shouldn't be surprised my brothers treat me the same way, only it's not physical as I would kick their fat asses. Their need for money is a close race with a need for more pasta, in my opinion. They are playing to their strengths, the street smarts I wasn't privy to growing up.

Out of the corner of my eye, I take in the reunited couple, and I can't make out every word. However, it sounds as if Sal is trying to finesse his way back into Carla's life.

It doesn't sound sincere, so why is he even bothering to meet? It's possible Carla wants him, or they both want sex. I can't blame either of them as I turn my gaze back to the street and the establishment's front door.

It appears the two are progressing past their initial uneasiness when their lips meet over the table giving each other a severe lip lock as Sal pays the bill.

We stand to leave as we check out the street, with them taking their time in between me at the front and Matteo following in the rear until we reach a sports car on the street.

Sal puts Carla in her car after a not-so-passionate kiss and she drives off.

Matteo scratches his head and lets out a short, indiscrete sigh as we look at each other in bewilderment wanting to know what the fuck just happened.

Questions are inappropriate. I assume the woman either has some dignity or her feelings have changed. We make our way to our vehicle and head home, an uncomfortable silence hangs in the car.

"She'll call me, that's all," Sal volunteers as he fastens his seatbelt and ends the awkwardness. "Baby steps," he murmurs even though he doesn't have to say anything.

"That lip lock looked like more than baby steps. I'm surprised you didn't get more tonight," rolls off my tongue like I'm talking to my best friend.

"Remember who you are talking to. Trainer or not, you work for me." His harsh words cut through the air. He's angry with me, not Carla.

Shit. In all honesty, I forgot he's the brother to the don. In my clan, a throat could be slit for less.

During the ride home, I can't tell if Sal is hurt by Carla making it an early night or relieved. I, for one, am not happy he dragged me on this wild goose chase and would have made me wait while he got laid if they did hookup. Is he just flaunting her in my face to make me give in to him? It's too simple of a manipulation.

Besides, we're not in a relationship and I blow off his reprimands when he delivers them but underneath my tough exterior, his opinions of me matter.

It's a rare occurrence when I care how a man looks at me. With Sal, I even care what his opinion of me is and that's just me.

He could have gone on this date without me. All he needs is Matteo. I don't know why he insisted I go with him unless he's expecting my brothers to send someone after him. Which I seriously doubt because if that was the case, he'd remain at home, and safe.

I need to check in with my grandmother again. She has access to a wealth of information and keeps me in the loop. She's too smart to be outfoxed by the younger generation even though she's old school and well into her eighties. She hates technology and refuses to use a cell phone or replace her antiquated television. I mean what's wrong with a smart TV?

We pull up to the house and get out. After Matteo and I check to make sure all is clear, there's nothing left for me to do so I head to my room.

"What's the matter? You jealous?" Sal taunts, stepping in front of me.

Tonight, he has been insensitive and the display of affection with Carla hurt. The two of them make a good-looking couple. Carla is not short of cash judging from her fancy sports car and her Birkin handbag that has a three-year wait list. Did he plan the entire evening just to prove he can get his way with anyone?

"I don't give a damn what you do, I'm here for business, not pleasure and we have a deal," I remind him.

He grabs my arm as I turn to go.

"I can have Carla anytime I want. I just didn't care to bring her home tonight," he boasts puffing out his broad chest.

"Don't let me stop you." I yank my arm free and take the steps two at a time.

I slam the bedroom door closed, but I doubt he noticed. Reaching in my jacket, I pull out my knife and open my dresser drawers to find the rest of my knives. I throw them, one at a time, at the back of the door, picturing Sal's face.

There is a knock on my door.

"What?" I'm annoyed.

"Can I come in?"

"You own the house, and apparently, I'm still your prisoner."

The door slowly opens, and seeing the knife in my hand, he turns, looking at the door.

"You're going to fix that," he says, turning back, his stormy eyes turning to ice as he focuses on me.

He makes his way toward me, and my back is up against a wall. I have no room to retreat. I can't back down, so I stand my ground.

"What do you want?"

"Tell me, were you jealous tonight?" His body is inches from my own and his warm breath caresses my cheeks.

"Never," I scoff trying to turn my eyes away.

His large hand slides over to cup my chin and cheek making me look at him.

"I think you are lying. I hate it when people lie." The underlying threat lingers between us.

I can't start lying now, he will never believe me again. "Why are you here?" I change the subject, hoping to throw him off guard.

"I heard the noise and was worried that someone might be in your room."

"You don't think I can take care of myself?"

"I know you can."

"I'm fine. You can leave." My voice is stern but unconvincing.

"Why should I go?" he taunts me and for a moment I get a glimpse of him without his tough exterior, like when we're training, focused, relaxed, not all huffy and controlling like he is tonight.

"I don't need you. I don't need anyone. I just want to find Sofia, but you wanted to get your cock serviced earlier, and that's wasting time. Every day we are not looking for Sophia, we are wasting time." I'm consumed with worry for her, but it dissipates as my attraction to him gets hotter with each barb that passes between us.

"You need me. You just don't know it. Do you want to go up against your family alone? There are too many of them, and you know it."

"I…" His physical proximity scrambles my thoughts. I'm holding my breath for no reason.

He leans in and says, "Face it, *diletto*, you find yourself attracted to me."

"Never." But my words don't ring true, and we both know it.

We're at a stalemate until our worlds collide, and finally, he takes control, leaning in and his warm lips find mine. The knife is still in my hand, and I could stab him. Funny, I no longer want to kill him. I let my knife fall to the tiled floor, where it makes a clatter.

I'm naked, bathed in vulnerability, as he unbuttons my blouse and slips it off. His hands explore my body, caressing me with his long, strong fingers, running them down my arms and up my naked back, giving me goosebumps that run down my arms and legs. His hands slide to my neck, where he tightens his grip.

With his hands around my throat, he has total control, and I can't move my head. I have no choice but to look at him as he pulls me closer, and the pressure of his lips intensifies. Instead of being frightened, I'm turned on.

It's hot to have a man come on so strong, so confident, knowing he's dangerous enough not to take shit off anyone and that he could order my demise tomorrow.

Grabbing the back of his head, I angrily kiss him back. Our mouths nip and tease each other before his tongue goes down my throat. We can't get enough, and I'm sucked into a whirlwind of sensations.

His shirt comes undone, and we both shed them. He unclasps my bra with just a flick of two fingers. I don't care about anything now, and it's just the two of us, and our bodies glisten with sweat.

He unzips his pants, which fall silently to the floor. He's naked now, and his cock is hard and ready for me as he unceremoniously flips me on the bed in one move.

I'm impressed by his adaptation of the moves I taught him. He's on top of me, looking into my eyes, and in the soft lighting, I catch the heat in his breath, and the desire in his eyes sears into my soul. He's making his claim. I'm his.

I can't think. All I want is him. Our mouths fly over each other's bodies, driven by anger and lust, hungry as wolves on the hunt for food in winter. He sucks on my neck, no doubt leaving his mark for surely there will be a bruise tomorrow.

He slaps my ass, and I'm surprised to find that I like it. I use a move on him, flipping him on his back, where I pin his shoulders to the bed so he can't move.

He smiles at me. Beads of sweat cover his neck, and his chest hair is damp when I run my fingers through it. I pull on it hard, wanting to punish him for earlier. He chuckles before flipping me under him with one arm wrapped around my back, taking me by surprise.

"You are mine, Francesca. Don't you ever forget it." With that he enters me, hard, driving the fact home as a moan of pleasure and pain leaves my lips in the form of surprise that gives way to pleasure.

It's been so long, I'm tight and feel every inch of him in me. I tighten my muscles around his thick cock, making him gasp and moan.

I can't hold back a small smile and squeeze his cock again.

His breathing is coming faster and faster as he holds me

down and pounds into me. I like his roughness, and my release is building inside me, reaching higher and higher until we peak together, crying out in the dimly lit room.

Holding his body over mine, he catches his breath and pulls me to him briefly before he rolls over.

I have no idea where this leaves us. The situation just became more complicated.

We're not teenagers, and I don't expect a warm snuggle session afterward, so I'm surprised when he pulls me to his chest.

"Stay with me after this ordeal is over, Francesca."

I can't believe my ears. He's asking me to stay here with him. No matter how I might want to, I can't commit to a man in the mafia.

His question poses too many vulnerabilities for me. To live with his family is declaring war on my own. I swore never to fall for a man in organized crime as I'd hate to end up on the losing side of any relationship dispute.

"I can't," I whisper, so low my voice doesn't sound like it's mine.

He's quiet, and I turn on my side to get a good look at him and gently place my hand on his chest. His face is void of emotion.

"Look, I have some bad news," he states ominously.

"What?" My first thought is that they found Sofia.

"The word on the streets is that your brothers are looking for you and ordered a hit."

I bolt upright, my hands falling away from him and clutching the sheet around me.

"What?" My head is foggy. I let my guard down, and now my worst fears materialize.

"I'm told they tapped your grandmother's phone. She still uses a landline, and your burner phone is the only thing that prevented them from knowing exactly where you are, but they will figure it out soon enough."

"Right."

"We'll mobilize and head south tomorrow."

He gets up, and after a delicious kiss on my lips, he dresses and walks toward the door.

"You're leaving?"

"I can't lay next to you and not stay up all night doing what we just did. We both need sleep. Get your rest."

He closes the door behind him.

Rest? Is he for real?

Fuck that.

I'm heading out tonight, and I'll take his car because my Rolls will be recognized. I pack a small bag with my work tools and some clothes, all black of course.

While Matteo is out back smoking, I know the alarm is off, and I slip downstairs and out the front door. I push the car while it's in neutral and hop in before I get in, start the engine, and escape without a sound.

I left a note and hope he understands and won't be too pissed. I have to strike my family first while I still have the element of surprise.

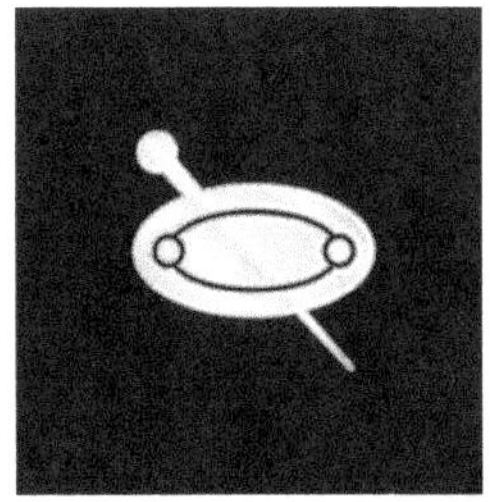

16

SAL

I wake up energized and slightly buzzed from last night with Francesca. Stretching in front of my window, I can't help but smile, remembering how her eyes turned dark with jealousy when I brought up Carla.

I tug on jeans and a polo and head downstairs. I'm the first one up but I sense something is wrong. The energy in the house is different. I call out to Matteo to check on Francesca as I head back upstairs.

Matteo opens her bedroom door, and we find ourselves staring at pillows arranged under the blanket to look like she is sleeping.

She's gone.

Shit!

I should have been more convincing when I asked her to stay, but I never dreamed she'd leave in the middle of the night.

Was it me that drove her away? Or the fact that her family has a hit on her, and she doesn't want to bring it to my door?

"Fuck, when did you see her last?" I yell at Matteo.

"She was with you. I assumed she stayed with you. I didn't check on her last night, boss. I'm sorry. I fucked up."

"It's not entirely your fault. We miscommunicated," I grumble.

It's my fault. I should have never toyed with her emotions. I couldn't stop being happy. No. I had to push her, and I pushed her hard, alright. I should have never dangled Carla in front of her. And I could have been more attentive to her after we had sex. I never make love—that's too personal —and I won't risk falling in love just to make a woman happy after sex.

"Well, tear her room apart, look for any clue that might lead us to her. I'm sure she went back to her family. And be on high alert in case her family sent a hitman." Leave it to the Contis to be despicable and ruthless. "Her brother set her up because she has compassion for those girls and her best friend," I add, growling. "She might know too much about them and they will assume she's sided with us if they know she's been living here."

I'm worried. I never worry about women. Her life is in danger—in fact, we need to mobilize now. No more training, no more emotions. It was fun while it lasted, but I have to get back to being 'Sal the fixer' or she'll never come out of this alive.

I wrestled with claiming her since I met her. I don't need more responsibility. But I made her my responsibility, and now, she's in a terrible situation because of me.

Granted, she came after me, but she doesn't have the heart of a killer unless it's necessary for her own survival. I knew that when she attacked me because she had me dead to rights.

The phone rings. It's Dante. He's concerned about the

Albanians who showed up in another club last night and wants to send a message. I let him know about Francesca and tell him we need to prepare to head south. I'm not about to sit on the sidelines.

"We can't fight on both fronts at the same time," I inform him, telling him what he already knows.

After a moment, he asks, "Are you sure Francesca went south?"

"As sure as I can be. I told her about the hit her brother ordered. Knowing her the way I do, I bet she wants to strike first when they least expecting it."

"Hm, you know her that well, little brother?" and the cockiness in his voice tells me he knows we're something more.

Am I that transparent?

"Okay, no jokes about it, you know me, always the player and don't worry, I never fall in love."

Or have I let my guard down?

"Sometimes I think your heart is darker than mine and what our life would be like if not for this darkness casting shadows over our once pure souls."

"True, but women have a way of getting to us nevertheless, eh?"

"Yes, so south it is. I'll call Marchello and let him know. I'm coming too."

"Brother, no, you need to stay and protect our territory," I plead, but he's already hung up.

Granted he has men of his own, but Dante, being the don, has to be protected above all others. God knows I don't want to be the head of the family. As it is, I have my hands full between Francesca and worrying about the Albanians.

Today the increasing pressure of being surrounded by my

enemies is real. From the Albanians in the north, who are muscling in on our territory, to the Conti/Calabreses in the south, who have always been a pain in our ass. The squeeze is coming whether we like it or not, it's inevitable.

And now, Francesca is caught in the middle of our feud with her family.

There are no good avenues to negotiate alliances in the mafia world because it's each family for themselves. Nowadays, we're into so many different money-making ventures that it's more and more likely to step on each other's toes.

It's not like we all use the same playbook, but we do primarily use the same methods to make our money. There are times we need each other to keep business moving and profitable, like the use of the same middlemen at times but we'll never know. A middleman who opens his mouth is a dead man.

There are levels to each of these money-making endeavors and Dante oversees the entire operation. Who do we get the drugs from? Are they reliable? In the end, the final sales have to be accounted for because the drugs and money go through a few hands, and any hand can take them.

I help launder the money; I'm good with the business side of illegal activities. Some may think I'm a geek, but I have my strong suits when called upon to do whatever must be done.

When things go sideways, the middleman might pay the ultimate price. And right now, Francesca is a woman on her own without a family. Without a doubt, her brother set her up to get into the Calabreses' good graces. With Francesca out of the picture, Mario and Fausto have everything to gain. I should have seen it coming and I'm beating myself up as if they've captured her already.

Matteo returns from Francesca's room with a board of pictures who are the players and note cards with information tacked to it.

"Here, she works on this at night." He hands me a cork-board with pictures and pins, and locations all labeled.

"She did this? She's left us the keys to the kingdom." I marvel as I study her layout. She has written 'Girls' next to a picture of shipping containers located at the port.

"So, the girls must come in on that dock." I point to the area designated on the map. "And if they come in that way, they can leave from there or be transported in vans to other locations. By the looks of this, they are moving them in both directions. But they can be anywhere by now." My voice falls off.

"That's a large percentage of their revenue stream, and if Francesca wanted to shut that down, it would have screwed up her brothers' chances to take over after Gio died," Matteo adds.

"This would explain why they want her dead. It's always about money or power. Francesca's share of Gio's estate would go to the brothers. It's clear from looking at this board, she has a lot of information on their business dealings. Amazing insight, considering she has no position inside their organization and only some security expertise."

"If she built their security, she would know how to break it," Matteo adds.

But his words bring no comfort to me. "It also means that they know the same and may have already made changes. This has been planned out for some time," I answer, rubbing my hand over my chin in thought. "I think they want us to look bad, and no doubt cut us out of the port altogether, but I don't know how."

I make an espresso and find a handwritten note next to the machine.

I needed your car. Hope you don't mind. Francesca

"We need to go," I yell to Matteo. It's not like he's that far from me. I'm just that keyed up.

No one is going to lay a hand on Francesca while I'm alive.

Matteo finds another car on the property, and we head south with the trunk packed with tons of firepower and bags of cash. One can never go wrong with untraceable Euros, greed is a powerful motivator, and most can't resist, especially in the mafia and the outer players who will never be part of the family and are used and discarded like the paper wrapper around meat from the deli.

I have guns and explosives, but I know Marchello's group will have more.

From the map Francesca left behind, it appears her family is heavily involved in supplying most of the syndicates with their drugs. Fausto could have shown her a bank account with money in it and our names on it. I would never know. Money buys access and documents can be forged.

As a result, our family has been pulled into a war we never wanted to fight. We were lulled into a false sense of security with the Calabrese's taking over instead of the eldest son of Gio Conti.

So maybe interrupting their supply of women and drugs will slow them down. Cutting off the influx of money is an effective way to fuck up any organization. When men don't get paid and deals fall through because of negative cash flow, they get pissed off. These men have connections and small armies because every syndicate has a need for them.

It's no secret the Contis have been our sworn enemies for three generations. Unfortunately, our feud didn't end with

Gio's death. Now, it appears it just made things worse. It seems he raised his sons to hate us until the end of our days.

Little do they know their days are numbered, and Francesca has sided with us. I can't imagine what Francesca has in store for them. I hope she's still alive. She's too beautiful to go through the type of torture they will use on her.

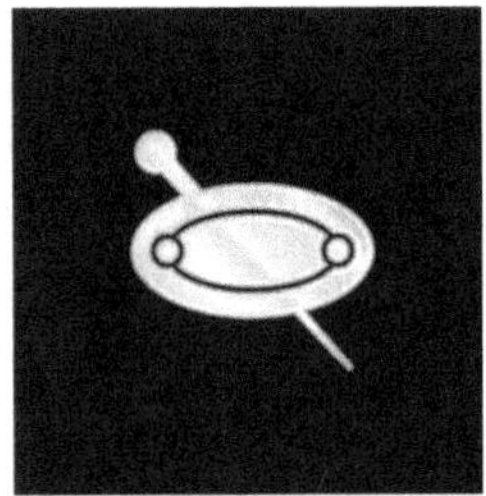

17

FRANCESCA

One thing I remember Dad saying is that cocaine's current and future market is in Europe, and he made a fortune by effectively smuggling tons of it from South America and Mexico through his port.

Some get cut when it gets here, the rest comes ready for the street. It's a cheap drug at its origin but when it's shipped overseas, it becomes very lucrative, and his foresight built our empire.

Europe is just now catching on to the drug trends that the Americans have more or less abandoned. The don has to know these things in advance to avoid showing up too late to a party that started without him, unable to move his product, and out millions in lost revenue.

I might be just one person, but I can fuck up their operation before they catch me. And hopefully, I can find the girls and set them free before they are moved further from the compound. Assuming they are still there. It's a great red herring to send me on a wild goose chase and then use that to put a hit on me.

It makes sense that if cocaine is worth more shipped to

another European port, the girls might be as well. I recounted details I heard here and there and decided there is no better place to hide them than under my nose. My bet is that they are still there.

Dad did business all over Europe, but Germany has the highest number of trafficked women, so I think that might be where they are going.

Dad was a true narcissist and psycho. He never thought much of anyone, and he hated all women. It's a no-brainer that Juliet chose Dante over him. I hear she was between a rock and a hard spot from tiny comments Matteo made when we occasionally talked.

As for my brothers, they must have falsified incriminating evidence to show the Calabrese in order to get a hit put on me. There really is no other reason for it. If they find me at the Micheli compound still alive, they will assume I spilled secrets to the Michelis . . . then I'm a dead woman, no matter what. There is no way I can talk my way out of that situation so it's imperative I don't get caught.

I pull into a five-star hotel not far from my family's compound. I picked this place because I'm driving Sal's Maserati, and I don't need it getting stolen.

My family will think I'm lying low and will be looking into dives and holes in the walls. They won't suspect I'm not the docile little mouse. If they thought beatings and degrading talk would destroy me, they thought wrong. I'm stronger than they will ever be.

I'm underdressed for La Dolce Vita Hotel, but the staff is used to it from the swarms of overweight and many unappreciative American tourists who dress more for comfort than style. Most don't care to learn about our culture and appreciate our love for the finer things in life. At least I'm not wearing sweatpants and sandals.

Pulling my hoodie over my hair, I check in using cash and a fake passport. I'm keenly aware that I'm close to the enemy's nest and try not to act too jumpy. It's serendipitous that my hair color is blonde and not dark, as they won't expect that, and I hope it will help me keep my identity in the shadows.

I wish Sal were here. Even though I'm not sure we can trust each other, he has a way of calming me with his laid-back energy.

We had sex, angry sex that melted my armor. Like a snail without a shell, the vulnerable feelings were overwhelming, and I couldn't stay. Flight or fight, they say, and I don't want to fight with him anymore.

The news of the bounty on my head pisses me off to no end, and my brothers will live to regret that. Except for Angelo Calabrese, I'll make them all pay. Who, if anyone, was in on my dad's death? It doesn't really matter, and history can't be rewritten. It's the past, and after our final confrontation, that's where it will stay.

I would hate it more if our own family killed Dad. My gut, along with the shreds of evidence point to the Michelis. Can I hate them when they took out such an evil person? Someone I despised myself?

I'm second-guessing my motives and find that not all mafia families have to be mean to their women. The Michelis are under my skin. I'm not numb, and the hatred I hold in fades to a lighter shade of grey when I'm with Sal.

Sal. Will I ever have a chance to tell him I wanted to say "I'll stay." Will he understand? I'm sure he knows more than I do about the families. He's been part of the inner circle for years, while I've always been on the outside looking in.

How can I make him any promises when I'm not in a

state of mind to make good decisions? If I come out of this alive, which is a long shot, I hope our paths cross again.

I have cameras in the car that I need to install in spots they don't know have great vantage points. When I did the security years ago, I looked for choice locations just in case I needed them in the future. The future is now.

It's odd that I hadn't seen much of Mario, my oldest brother, in the months following Dad's death. This concerns me because he's not one to lie low. Like our father, he enjoys showing off.

I need to get these cameras up before dawn. Security gets a bit lax around three a.m. when the guards go outside to play a game of dice or smoke cigarettes to keep themselves awake.

I hide the Maserati in the woods, gather a soft black bag from the trunk, and walk over a mile to reach my destination. Hiding behind a low perimeter wall, I look through binoculars to check out the compound that had been my home.

Normal night movement as far as I can tell. I hide cameras up in trees and other unseen places pointed at the compound. Sneaking around in the stillness of the night, I'm sweating and thinking of Sal. What is he doing? How is he? Will he forgive me for leaving?

I'll need to break in and use my infrared light to check the building. But first, I need to check the locations where they house the girls. I need to get into the port or crack their computer system and find the manifest they use on the paper, which is a pseudonym for humans. I have no idea what it might be.

Damn, Sal could easily get me into the port hidden in one of his men's vehicles. I want to call him, but I can't bring myself to ask for help. "A Conti needs no one," Dad would say.

But I'm feeling less like a Conti by the minute. I can fight and make strategies with the men Dad used. But I draw the line at using women for profit, which makes me an outcast and puts a target on my back.

Fuck.

Fuck, and fuck.

I should have known it was only a matter of time before my narcissistic brothers figured out how to get rid of me once and for all.

They must be planning to take over the Calabreses. When they kissed Angelo's ass so fast, I knew it was a ploy, had to be. My brothers will never bow to anyone, and their word is worthless. Angelo should have had them whacked if he wanted to be safe.

My word is good as I have a different circle of friends and contacts.

Dawn is coming so I return to the hotel to get rest. Tomorrow I'll scout all the locations and note their routines. All the key players need to be accounted for. Damn, I need my computer, the one that Sal took.

I fall into a deep sleep and wake up from a nightmare that I can barely remember. Someone is under our compound, and there are gated doors, there is yelling, someone is in pain and shouting.

I sit up in bed, my heart racing, and my tank top is soaked in sweat. It takes me a minute to remember where I am. The dream was so real, but I couldn't make heads or tails of it. Unable to fall asleep again, I get up and start coffee with fresh beans that grind and produce the perfect cup of espresso.

I down it in a gulp and step into the shower. As I close my eyes and let the hot water wash over me, I can't forget Sal's eyes as he looked into mine and asked me to stay. I'm not sure what to make of it, but I know what I wanted to say, I just don't know if I can do it.

I wash my long hair and blow dry it, not sure why I bother as it will only be under a hoodie or a ball cap later.

As soon as I turn the blow dryer off, there is a slight knock at the door—three quick taps like a code.

Wearing only a towel, I grab my .45 from the nightstand and move to the side of the door.

"Francesca, it's Sal, open up."

Shit!

I twist the deadbolt, and the door swings wide enough for him to enter. Sal's jaw drops when he sees my hair done and my body damp from the shower.

"What are you doing here? You scared the shit out of me!"

"How do you think I feel knowing you are out here all alone? Are you crazy?"

"Maybe," I snap back clutching the bath towel tighter, as if it will protect me from . . . what? My heart is beating out of my chest.

The fact that he pierced my armor, the armor that was never to be compromised. I'm ill-prepared for these feelings. I don't know how to surrender to anything. How can I give him what he's looking for?

"I'm worried about you." He pulls my laptop from under his arm and hands it to me. It's too hot for the jacket he's wearing, so naturally, I assume he's concealing a weapon.

"Thanks," I say, taking the laptop. Getting mad at each other isn't going to help anything. Part of it is pent-up sexual frustration, and I breathe deeply to inhale the scent of him and notice his slightly tired face. It makes me want to reach out and touch him, but that's not going to fix it.

"Where's Matteo?" I ask, placing the laptop and gun on a nearby desk.

"Gathering intel and supplies. He'll be gone for a few hours."

"Hmm."

"That's all? You run away—"

"How did you find me?" I ask, alarmed that he knew where I was. He knows my alias, but how did he know where I'd be?

"GPS in my car," he says with an emphasis on 'my'.

"Oh, right. Well, good thing you aren't still hunting me," and the retort is out of my mouth. It's a bad habit I use to defend the wall I built around myself years ago.

He lets out a tiny *huff* and ends with a soft chuckle.

"No, nothing like that. I'm here to help. We all are. We have tons of men on the way." And with that, he steps inside, takes me in his arms, kicks the door closed behind him, and locks it.

I don't know why he trusts me so much, except for our shared hatred of my brothers, but I'll take it. It's common ground and ground I'm familiar with so I release the tension in my body and let him hold me.

Holding my towel with one hand, I wrap one arm around him, pulling him to me.

"I'm glad you're here. I missed you."

"I missed you too. But mostly, I was going crazy without you at the house. Nothing is the same without you, Francesca." His lips gently descend upon mine as I surrender to them.

The warmth of his lips melts me like sugar in hot tea. When we take a break to breathe, his eyes are no longer cold and barren, but full of mirth and brightness. He uses a finger to trace the right side of my face down to the top of my towel that he dispenses with so quickly I don't notice because I'm craving him more than I've craved anything in my life.

These are new emotions, and the wave of anxiety propels me to run. I have an undeniable attraction to him I can't deny. I want him. I want all of him.

"I—" His lips are on mine, warm, inviting as we continue to kiss and this time, it's soft and gentle. We're not feeding off our anger. Soft gentle kisses that make my knees weak and my body tremble under his touch.

"Later," he replies as his hand moves down to cup my breast, making my nipple hard before he brushes his thumb over it.

My pussy is pulsating as I stand naked before him, wanting him more than anything in the world. I never knew what it would be like living without him, and I don't want to find out because I know that I would hate a life without him in it, he ruined the sanctity of my solitude.

His slender fingers roll my nipple between them with the expertise of a seasoned lover, and I don't know why I should be surprised. I'm sure he's had his share of women over the years.

"Mmm . . ." I let my head tilt back as his kisses move to my ear, his tongue licking the outside before circling inside, and chills run up my spine.

He continues down to meet the nipple, chilled from the cool air in the room, but the heat between us is short of nuclear fusion.

He teases my nipple with his tongue, circling it before taking it into his warm mouth. My back arches, his tenderness taking me by surprise as I run my fingers through his hair.

He picks me up, wrapping my legs around his waist, and walks me to the bed, where he lays me down gently. I touch myself and watch him undress, shucking his clothes in record time.

He joins me in bed and picks up where he left off, his kisses making my skin tingle as he works his way down to my clit. He massages it, causing me to raise my hips to meet him, to get more of him. His touch is gentle, circulating around my entrance, teasing me, exciting me with one hand while the other is still on my nipple, gently rubbing it and giving it a slight pinch.

I moan, it's been so long since I allowed myself to be vulnerable with a man, let alone a man I swore I'd never love —an enemy of my family, a man who works for a syndicated family.

I want to protect myself, but the fire of desire races through my veins. I'm addicted to him. I want more as the pressure of his tongue on my nub is building, I begin to sweat small beads of perspiration on my neck, and I'm close to coming, but I don't want to come this way.

I rake my nails across his taut shoulders and down his arms. With the slight amount of space between us, I start at the bottom of his abs and dig my nails into his skin as I rake my fingers up. A moan escapes from his throat before he raises himself over me.

Our eyes meet, and our lips devour each other with urgency as he grabs me around the waist and rolls onto his back with me on top. I grab his huge, hard cock with a slight curve between my hands and rub it around my opening, covering him with my juices as I do so.

I can't hold off any longer. I must have him. I slide his beautiful cock inside me, tightening my muscles around him, making his entrance into me a bit painful but giving us a taste of togetherness in only the way lovers can truly fulfill each other. Ecstasy overcomes us as I lean backward, dragging my fingers down his chest and slowly moving my hips, getting a feel for our rhythm. His eyes widen, and his breathing quickens as he watches me move.

Grinding my hips into his, the excitement builds as he plays with my nipples. Every time I move forward, his palms touch them softly, and when I move backward, they barely touch, creating a heightened level of anticipation. Between the fire ripping so deliciously through me and the thrill of an orgasm pulling at me, I'm suspended between two worlds, and I don't want this moment to ever end.

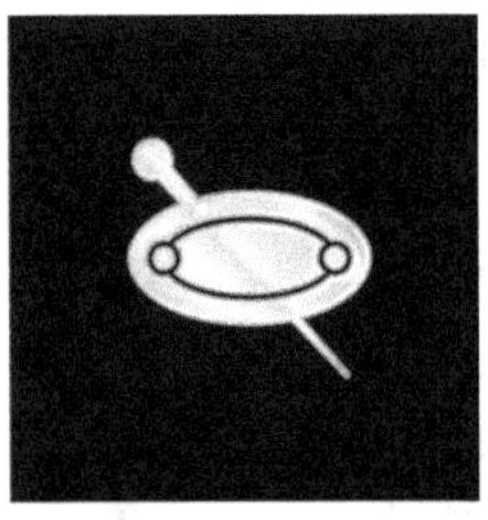

18

SAL

Giving up control in bed is the only time I give up control. But I have to hide it. I enjoy watching her face contort with ecstasy before her head falls back and a moan escapes her lips.

She's on the brink of her orgasm. I let her ride my hard cock for as long as she wants. She leans forward, her hungry eyes searching mine before she kisses me passionately.

The sex is different this time.

It's not angry sex. It's not revenge. We're meeting each other as equals, giving and taking of each other's bodies and hearts within the confines of an intimacy I've never experienced. I'm married to the *famiglia*, but it's the furthest thing from my mind.

I'll enjoy this and repent at leisure. It seems to be the way of our cursed life.

My cock pulsates inside her tight walls. When she moves, I feel her muscles squeezing my cock and watch her body shudder, knowing she's on the brink of one of her loud and multiple orgasms.

I run my fingers down her back, feeling beads of sweat

building up. Even though we've only been intimate twice, I know she's going to explode, so I squeeze her nipples the way she likes, adding extra pressure to stimulate them so she comes harder.

"OH," she exclaims, and I stop squeezing to grab both breasts so I can rub the tip of her pert, erect nipples with my thumbs. She explodes, coming loud as she yells, "Ahhhhh!" and "Ohhhhhh!" for what seems like minutes as she has one climax after another.

Her muscles constrict around me so tightly that she stifles my orgasm. I don't mind delaying my pleasure because the excitement will build again, and I will come even harder later.

My cock is drenched in her come, and it pleases me that she can feel that much passion. She told me she's never been with a made man before. If she's violating her steadfast rules to be with me, does this mean she's changed her mind on that?

She slumps onto my chest, her arms and body wrung out from the intensity of her orgasm. After two hours of physical love making, we're weak from the exertion. But it's not over.

In one swift move, I flip her under me, and she relaxes, relinquishing control, which surprises me. I glide in and out of her, slowly at first, milking the sensations.

Raising one of her legs over my shoulder, I can dive deeper into her. I wish it was her heart that I could dive into, but I don't know if she's ready for an emotional commitment. My huge cock fills her up and I have a feeling she's going to be sore tomorrow.

I hold her hair so she can't move and lean down, devouring her mouth with mine as I pound into her, taking long hard strokes. My desire builds to the breaking point, but I hold back. I enjoy the control I have over her and I'm not willing to give it up. Or am I lying to myself? Can I control her?

One thing is certain, I'm not cutting myself short when the pleasure leaves my lips in a soft moan I can't contain, nor the incredible feelings that are welling up in my chest. Feelings I never allowed myself to experience or take hold. Feelings for her I was able to ignore until she left. Then I realized my world isn't the same without her.

How can that be? She wanted to kill me. She's the daughter of my enemy. She could kill me just like I could kill her. I think they call that mutually assured destruction. What would happen if we came to blows over a difference of opinions? Have a war with knives?

I'm in love with Francesca. She's cracked my resolve to never fall in love and won my dark heart, making me feel things I've never felt before.

Succumbing to my innermost desire and physical pleasure, I explode with a loud groan. It's the most intense orgasm I've ever experienced. I brace myself on top of her, my dick pulsing and slowly softening, before rolling to her side and pulling her to me. I wrap my arms around her like I'm never going to let her go, and I have no intentions of letting her go. Ever.

Pushing strands of damp hair away from her face, I gently kiss her cheek. She's flushed with pleasure, and her face is glowing.

"Are you ready for this?" I ask as the morning light is turning into early afternoon. After hours of tossing each other around the bed, the bed sheets are nowhere to be seen. The cool air in the room is welcomed as we're both hot and sweaty.

"I've already started," she answers calmly, so calm it's scary.

I'm glad she's on our side, but even with all our men it's still going to get ugly, and there's no clear victory in any mafia war. There are so many intangibles. If we have a bit of luck, we might be able to pull this off.

If is a big word.

We're going to have to fight together if we are to have any future. My women were all high-end snobs, but Francesca gets her hands dirty and knows her stuff. This is not a typical security job. It's dangerous work. Her family is the most notoriously ruthless crime family in Italy, which scares me the most.

Clearly, she misinterpreted my question. When I asked if she was ready for this, I meant *us*, not the impending war. Maybe that's her way of deflecting. Maybe she's still not ready for a relationship and will disappear after this bloodbath is over.

But if she doesn't face her feelings now. When?

I guess it will have to wait. Timing is everything or so they say and right now we need to get ready for war.

As if she's reading my mind, she springs from the bed and walks to the dresser as if I'm not in the room. She's comfortable in her nakedness and I can't take my eyes off her body as she checks her guns and loads some clips.

Besides the guns and ammo, she has a bulletproof vest, knives, and weird-looking canisters. This woman is fucking awesome.

"I put up cameras outside the compound, and I have infrared handheld cameras to use when I get inside."

"What? Are you crazy?"

She turns to me, her body still glistening with the afterglow of our lovemaking. I'm horny again just looking at her.

"I have to be, a bit." She gives me an all-knowing wink.

"I can't find Angelo Calabrese anywhere on the compound, and that's not like him. He's vain and likes to be seen."

"That is odd. What could possibly be going on in there?"

"I'm going to find out."

I bolt out of bed. "Oh, no, not by yourself, you aren't. Besides, the boys are coming." I pull on my jeans. "You might want to get dressed. Matteo will be back at any minute."

"Damn, forgot about that." Her cheeks blush as she looks down at her naked body.

"This is my fight, Sal," she says, putting on a bra and panties. She's so stubborn sometimes I'd love to smack some sense into her.

"It's our fight. They are my enemy too. They would have double tapped you on my soil, in my house, if that's where they found you, so it leads to my door again." I clench my fist and teeth in anger while looking for my shirt.

"As if once wasn't enough." Her hollow tone conveys the emptiness she feels inside. The sudden death of her father changed her world overnight, and it's not over. The nightmare she's been living for years still plays on a continuous loop.

"Fine. We'll all go, I know a way in. I know their routine. We can do recon tonight," she acquiesces.

I sigh with relief that she'll let Matteo and me help.

"Matteo can be our lookout," I offer.

She nods in agreement and pulls on worn jeans with holes in the knees and a black shirt.

"Look, it's time for lunch. Let's grab something to eat; what do you say?" I ask, glancing at my watch as I button my shirt. It's one already.

"Fine, I am a bit hungry. But we need to stay off the grid. The area is crawling with the goons."

"No kidding."

She pulls her hair up, twists it, and puts a pin through it to hold it in place, the same pin she wore to the gala. But I notice this one is different from Juliet's. It looks like it's made from titanium, and the end isn't sealed like a knitting needle.

"Your hair pin . . ."

"Yeah, deadly poison on the end," she says like it's nothing, while pulling on a hoodie. It's hot out but it conceals her identity.

"What—" my jaw drops. I should be scared, but I find I'm intrigued. "What's in it? You had it the night of the gala."

"Yes, well, it's always better to come prepared. If I couldn't snap your neck or someone else came in, I could prick them with this. The poison, ricin, is encased in a substance that melts once it's injected," she turns to me with a stone-cold expression and continues, "the puncture is no bigger than the sting of a mosquito."

Fuck me she's gorgeous and brilliant. And deadly.

Just touching the wrong end of it could have killed anyone of us, at any time.

"Oh, and here." She tosses me a small vial with a tiny needle in it, the kind used as a butterfly needle to draw blood, but this one looks a little different. "That can cause anyone to have a heart attack, and it's untraceable," she informs me with a wry smile.

Here, I believed I had her disarmed by my mastery of banking and computer skills not to mention my prowess in the bedroom. But this is Francesca, taking everything she touches to a new level. She's more akin to a ticking time bomb. I believed I was safe with her in my house. Now, it's obvious she was letting us believe what we wanted. We were never safe. I feel deceived; duped, and I'm not liking it.

So why did she stay? Is she really working as a double

agent? It wouldn't be the first time. But I know the sparks between us are real. Now, I'm doubting if we'll ever be free from our families, our careers, and our pasts to build a future together.

She renders me speechless at times. Can I trust her? I'm trained to trust no one, and so is she. The situation's outcome can't be predicted and that makes me nervous. I need to shake all these doubts and focus on our mission.

"Does your family know about all of this?" I jump back into her state-of-the-art killing implements.

"Hell no, my greatest asset is that they underestimate what I'm fully capable of. It was no secret that Sofia was my friend, and you know what happened to her when her marriage deteriorated? Missing. That's how divorce is done here. That's why I'll never be with someone in the mafia."

Her words sting. No, it's more like shrapnel ripping through my heart. I have my answer when I least expect it. I'm a fool to think she'd change for anyone, but I know she felt the chemistry between us. One can't achieve the levels of intimacy we did without it.

For a moment, I feel like I've stepped out of a time machine and into a foreign country where women are sold as slaves and auctioned off for a herd of goats. Only this is my country and my time. I never knew men did this to their women, the mothers of their children.

It's inconceivable and reprehensible, and I want to make all of them pay just as much as she does. I'm all for doing what needs to be done but this goes against my fast, loose and dark morals.

"It's true," she says, throwing what looks like a tube of lipstick in her purse. She usually uses a pen to outline her luscious lips. Lips I'd kiss now if I weren't still annoyed at being played.

"Is that a new color?"

"No, it's a gun, one-shot deal." She saucily looks over her shoulder to check my reaction.

"What the hell are YOU?" I groan.

I feel like I'm seeing her for the first time, half disappointed that she's not separating me from the monsters she was raised with. The other half is from the fact that she constantly raises the bar on her spy and assassination craft, which is so over the top I can't help but be impressed with her no matter how much I might be pissed at her for her leaving me.

She gives a cute giggle that turns me inside out and walks to the door. Cracking it open, she checks the hallway, and motions for me to follow before swinging it open.

Outside the hotel, we run into Matteo and walk to an obscure restaurant away from the crowds to grab a panini.

Sitting with her back against the wall, she asks the waiter to bring her another sparkling water as she nibbles at her sandwich, savoring every bite. She never takes her eye off the door, always looking for anything suspicious. Our new guys have gained so much knowledge and experience from watching her.

She also trained me well in the few days we had at the house. I can hold my own better in a surprise attack and I can now break a leg without a baseball bat.

I owe her freedom, but who am I kidding? With her skills, she could have left at any given time. So why didn't she is still the nagging question running through my mind when in the past it's always been focused on my op.

And where did all these gadgets come from? Did she have them on her, or in her, when she was in the cellar? Her bedroom? Or did she have them stashed in a storage locker?

Or a bug-out bag that most criminals keep for that what-the-fuck moment when they realize they need to run.

The only direction I want her to run is to me, not from me. But that conversation will have to happen on a different day, and I can't let my disappointment that she doesn't appear to have the same feelings for me interfere with our attack. This mission is too important for both of us.

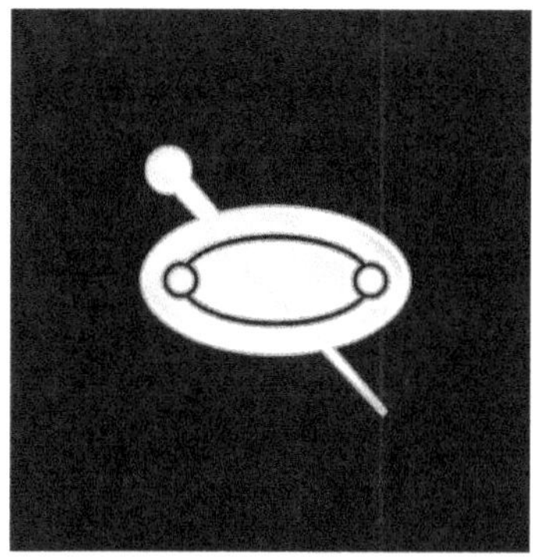

19

FRANCESCA

Night has fallen, and I don't know if it's my imagination or the unaddressed tension between Sal and me after hooking up at the hotel earlier. But the unnatural stillness filling in the air is suffocating me.

It's hot as fucking hell even though fall has started. My black pants aren't helping my mood. The sweat is sticking to my legs. My pussy is still wet from Sal.

It seems things changed after I showed him more of my dark side, but I developed it out of necessity, and I'm not sure he understands that. We both have to protect ourselves and our families, only now, my hand has been forced, and my brothers need to pay.

The humidity clings to me like a tree fog to a windowpane. I'm sweating profusely. My long hair and the hoodie produce more sweat to run down my neck and face. It's not the look I want Sal to see. Especially when compared to Carla. I'm sure I look more like a homeless person tonight and an unsavory one at that.

I'm not used to caring what men think of me. I've met

them all with indifference, with the exception of Sal; he's different. A killer when he needs to be, but the changes he's made in the bedroom can't be ignored.

I can't resist his touches and soft caresses, though none of this fits with his usual demeanor of all business and strategic planning for the family's best interest.

Night has fallen, and I don't know if it's my imagination or if there is an unnatural stillness to the air that clings to me in the form of humidity that has me sweating profusely. Of all the nights, tonight has to be the one when the clouds hang low in our valley, pregnant with rain.

A storm is imminent, and so is our attack.

We stalk around with shadows inside the compound. These walls were made over five hundred years ago. Rocks from the coastline have served their purpose and kept us safe.

But not today.

My *famiglia* cuts deep, and while it's not easy to escape the clutches of one's clan, ours is made up of many. Most are due to the lower birth rates, as we're all Italians by birthright. The fact that each family under our umbrella of protection is another loyal servant who helps to feed the entire infrastructure.

Sal keeps his eyes peeled and at times walks with his back turned to mine to make sure the coast is clear. I scan the lay of the land in front of us as we dip into the shadows dodging guards who are getting a smoke or are ready to bolt for shelter as lightning drops around us.

Ahead, guards having a cigarette are visualized and we find a different route to the building where I expect to find Angelo. Only it's empty when I peer through the dirty window.

We duck behind a commercial trash bin, and I pull my

laptop out of my backpack, immediately connecting to the Wi-Fi. It would be easy to turn off their security but that would tip our hand too early.

"Dumbasses didn't change the log-in," I mutter.

Once I'm in Mario's files, I hand my computer to Sal. "Here you are the number guru. What can you make of this? Maybe we can find out what he's up to."

With Sal pulling up numerous documents, I pull out my binoculars and ask, "When is Marchello arriving?"

"Any time. Not sure exactly. The phone is on vibrate, and I'm waiting on an update."

"Hmm, well, Matteo can notify him if we don't make it back. I need to be within twenty-five feet of the building to find out how many men are up there with my thermal camera. I still haven't seen Angelo, which makes me think foul play might be afoot."

"Where should he be?" Sal asks, taking the infrared binoculars from my hand, and I can't deny I like the closeness of us working together.

He takes in the people in the building, then hands me the binoculars before turning back to the computer screen as we crouch on the old pavement under our feet and knees underneath the overhang of the house to keep the computer from getting saturated.

"His office is on the top floor. But those men in the window look like my brothers, given their height and weight," I surmise, looking through the binoculars.

I lift my camera, and no one else is in the building. "My brother is in Angelo's office." That's surprising.

"Isn't that unusual?" I ask, knowing I answered my own question.

"Extremely," he replies, tapping like an evil genius on my gaming laptop.

Sal looks at me, and it's not like I'm a killer or his captive. I feel the warmth in his eyes for me. I'm something more to him, and we both connect intimately without touch. It's as if we've both broken our own barriers, and we've let intimacy enter. It takes my breath away, but I cover it up with a sigh.

"Looks like your brothers have numerous shell companies and a shipment coming in tonight of canned bananas. No doubt they have cocaine packed in that." He's talking out loud as I scan more buildings around us.

"I should get a closer look."

"I'll go. You can't be caught," Sal offers.

"I know the compound," I argue while putting away the binoculars.

"I memorized your map," he quips, flashes me his sexy, and gives me a quick grin.

"Right." I roll my eyes and continue, saying, "When we come back, I can hide some explosives in the room where they torture people and some spaced out around the compound, so we can blow this place up anytime we want."

His look is priceless even in the shadows.

"Well, if we need to," I add, softening the delivery of this other side of me.

"Gotcha. We've seen enough here." He folds the laptop and shoves it into my backpack.

"But—"

Sal touches my arm, stopping me. "Let's head over to the port and identify where the bosses are. I can get you in there on one of our trucks. They would never think we are working together in a million years."

"Good point." I whirl around and make my way down the hill, walking close to the expensive cars that belong to the high-ranking bosses.

"Maybe the girls or Angelo are held there." Sal's looking around like an eagle, leaving no corner overlooked, and Matteo has our back with an AK-47 at the ready.

I'm beginning to think Sal is an excellent addition to my team. We played hide and seek with the guards back to the forest, where we stashed the black SUV with plates registered to one of Sal's shell companies.

"Maybe your crew knows something," I add, and I must admit the danger is turning me on, and so is Sal. We're a good team, and he's not a stranger to this world we share. I never realized I knew so much, but it's coming to me like a natural gift, memories treading together like a computer network. It's making sense now, and all those little tidbits over the years create a complete picture of the empire.

The three of us make it out of the compound hike back to the black vehicle where we cover it with brush lying on the ground.

Sal calls one of his foremen on the phone to come out and meets us. Matteo sits in the front, next to the driver, as Sal and I stand in the back of the box truck in the dark as we make the twenty-mile drive journey to the port being jostled around.

I'm trying not to bump into Sal, but it's impossible, and finally, I grab onto him as he holds onto a strap that dangles from the top of it, a strap I can't reach.

I grab him with both arms as the backpack is on my back, and he has one on his as well. We're so close, I can hardly bear to be near him like this and not kiss him or touch him intimately.

But this is work. I hope we'll have time for pleasure later. There is a possibility that neither of us will make it out alive.

I hear the brakes squeak and we roll to a stop at the guard-house; the soldier buys his excuse to come back so quickly, saying he had to pick up a worker.

We start to move, and we're past the checkpoint.

"Dante is on his way too," Sal informs me.

I take in a sharp breath, surprised.

"No, he doesn't need to be here. I don't want him to risk it. Please tell me you can change his mind," I plead with him.

"You know how the Micheli men are—once we set our mind to something, it's hard to change it. Besides, he's the don, so I can't question or press him too hard. It would make him look bad in front of others."

I lean my head on his chest as darkness is now our friend. Matteo opens the tiny window to our area from the cab part of the truck.

"Where to, boss?"

"Park at dock number nine. It's ours, and I'll look for Pietro. He used to work at my club, so he'll know me."

The door closes and we're in the darkness once again. We come to a not-so-smooth stop and bang into the side of our box. Then the back door swings open, and Matteo offers me his hand to help me down.

My hood is over my head as there are cameras everywhere.

"I'd turn the cameras off. I don't want to tip our hand," I offer as we walk casually into a warehouse that has a small office inside it.

"*Ciao*," Sal introduces himself to the manager of the docks who is in his late forties by the looks of his expanding waistline and willingness to help he doesn't have much skin in the game.

"So, what can I do for you?"

"We're wondering if you've seen Angelo Calabrese lately."

"Come to think of it, things have been weird around here lately."

"How so?"

I let Sal do all the talking. The less they know of me, the better.

"He usually is out and about, but even the threat of rain won't keep him inside for days."

"Days? That's odd. Where are his men?"

"Some are at dock five; that's all I know, it's very hush-hush. That's the only rumor I've heard all week. It's been slow."

"Great. Well, let me know if you see Calabrese." Sal scribbles his cell number on the blotter on the man's desk, littered with soda bottles and wrappers from microwaveable food.

"Mind if we walk around a bit?"

"It's your dock," he explains. "We've pretty much left it alone since Calabrese came in. Conti was an ass. Made our lives hell hoping we'd pull up and leave."

Sal nods. It looks like he knows this, and I don't doubt it.

"Thanks." Sal shakes his hand.

I stifle my gag knowing how sticky his hand is going to be after that exchange judging from the porn on the small computer sitting on the corner of his desk. This would be missed by most visitors as there is no sound coming from it to give away the dirty secret.

We walk away as if nothing out of the ordinary is going on.

"We need to check out the warehouse near number five, we should find something there. The entire place can't be empty. It's busy twenty-four-seven every day but the holidays, and even then, there's still work that has to be done," I inform Sal.

"Okay. But stay behind me."

We play cloak and dagger using the moonless night as our blanket to cover us for safety, and when we get to the warehouse, we open it, and the stench can't be denied that there has been human cargo here.

"It's got to be hostages," I whisper.

It's a smaller warehouse, and I can tell the stench is from body fluids, and the floors are filthy. There are shackles and some beds. We walk around and duck when a flashlight shines through one of the few windows and then moves on.

As I turn, my foot hits something on the floor, and I trip. My hand hits a latch, and I find it to be in an odd place. I nudge Sal, and we put our ears to it. We can't hear more than a clatter here and there.

I pull out my infrared gun and give it a go. People are moving below us. So, this is how they did it. Hiding the girls underground makes sense. No one would ever think he'd spend the money to build a cell under this building.

"The girls," Sal says to me with a questionable lilt to his deep voice that is louder than a whisper.

"Must be." I'm afraid to give in to the excitement that it will this easy to find them. "I think there are about twenty-five. There might be guards there, and they must be moving them somewhere soon. They can't stay down there for long periods of time, too much work to feed and take care of them, it will draw attention with that many men coming and going for no reason, the building is empty."

"True. But if we barge in now, we jeopardize our surprise attack and we don't have enough men until Marchello gets here."

"Right." I look to him for a suggestion as soft light bathes us from a streetlight outside the doors.

"We'll assume it's them. We still haven't found Angelo."

"That's what's so weird, he loves for everyone to kiss his ass. He'll walk around just for people to suck up to him and make him feel important. Or inflict some pain for a perceived wrong," I add.

"There are ships coming in tonight. One is from Colombia, but it's from a company I couldn't find anywhere. Then, there's our ship. But Dante said he's slowing it down as he didn't want it in port until afterward."

"Good. What was the name on the manifest?"

"Luigi Oil Imports and Exports. It sounds so odd," he comments.

"Fuck."

"What?"

"Fausto always made fun of Mario ever since that video game came out in the nineties, I think it was. The name . . . Mario truck, no Mario Cart, the other brother in it was Luigi."

"You think it's Mario's company and shipment?"

"Must be. They move the coke around in the bottom of the vats of oil. They keep moving it around from port to port making drop-offs and the girls could be on it and shipped around as well for that matter."

"We have a window of what? How much time do we have?"

I pull out my laptop.

"Not that long. Someone is bound to come by soon if the girls are down there."

"Right." Sal looks at me and asks, "How fast can you get into the system?"

"Ha, they never took me off, I'm in. Let me see." My fingers fly over a keyboard that's so worn it's glossy. "There is a ship due to arrive in four hours."

"Four hours? It makes sense, it will still be dark out when

they load the girls and unload the coke. I'll text Marchello so we'll be ready for them when they arrive."

Sal texts on his burner phone, then puts it away when he's done.

"We need to find your brothers." He looks at me.

"I know. And the only other puzzle piece is, where is Angelo?" I ask with trepidation. "Let's go looking around. There is a torture room under the old wing of the house."

"Not another old wine cellar?" Sal mocks me as I pack my bag and immediately jump as a lightning bolt hits the ground outside the window.

I hand him the infrared camera.

"Very funny, but yes, more of an olive oil and wine cellar. We added to the house when we remodeled so Dad made a state-of-the-art one. He figured no one would ask about the old one, and no one did. It's a short flight down under the back of the house."

"I'll follow you," I say as he leads the way. All the while, Matteo has his weapon at his side to remain inconspicuous yet prepared. We all have our eyes peeled and exit the port in the box truck, uncover our vehicle, and make our way back to the compound.

Guards are in positions around the house. We wait in the shadows as the sky opens and a heavy rain soaks us. The men go inside to stay dry, so we take our opportunity to get closer to the cellar and Sal uses the camera that shows three people.

Sal motions that he's going first and waits for lightning to make a noise before opening the exterior door. He heads down first with his gun drawn and I pull mine.

A heavy, shallow breathing voice is heard. "Yeah, well, soon it will be over."

"Ha, you thought you had it all. You were so full of your glory that you never looked around you to notice that you were just a stooge for the Contis." The other one lets out a light cough as cigarette smoke fills the air.

They must have been down here for hours, if not days, judging by the air that reeks of smoke and stale bourbon.

The step under me gives way, causing a grating, not loud but enough for them to hear. Or did they?

Oh, where is the thunder when I need it? I pray to myself.

We hear footsteps, and I don't want to use my gun, but in the end, our lives all come down to the inevitable—it's them or us.

Sal raises his left hand and puts up three fingers, motioning them forward.

He's going in, and the wooden steps let out a tiny creak.

Sal steps into the room with lightning-quick speed and kicks the heavy-set man in the groin, bringing him down with one large thud.

I go into action with the man behind him, who doesn't have a chance to grab the gun around his waist.

Matteo has his AK-47 poised if I need it at the door, but I have my man wrestled to the ground with his arm twisted behind his back as he kneels at my feet.

"I'm going to—" he yells, but I cold cock him between the eyes, and it's lights out for him.

Sal has a rag shoved in the other man's mouth as he's now face down on the cement floor.

I feel the dampness in the air, and my hand hurts from breaking the guy's face, but it feels good at the same time.

I toss Sal some zip ties, and we finally have a second to look at the prisoner.

"Angelo." I'm in shock as I take the gag from his mouth and cut his zip ties. He owes me for this. "What the fuck?"

"Your fucking brothers are going to die like the rats they are!" I can tell he's been roughed up as one side of his face is messed up with bruises and dried blood from his broken nose.

I cut the ties that keep his ankles to the chair.

"Angelo Calabrese?" Sal asks.

"Who are you? Oh, wait, you are part of that fucking family from Tuscany. Forgive me. I'm a bit foggy."

I offered him some water from the table nearby.

"What are you doing here?"

"Not my first choice of places to be. Untie my hands," he demands.

"First things first, how did you wind up here?" I ask.

"Your brothers had their own agenda. They ran a side deal with the Colombians for coke when I had a supplier from Mexico. They undercut me, stealing my drugs and sealing my date with death. They hung me out to dry. Everyone will be looking for me."

"I find that hard to believe. You've been in charge of many of Contis' businesses, so surely, you know the business inside and out as the underboss." I put my hand on my hip, debating whether he's that stupid or been duped.

"Before they overpowered my men at the old warehouse by the port, they made me call a big meeting and locked everyone in. They took me prisoner and brought me here. I've been here for two days waiting for his fucking ship to come in. They're going to kill me." He gasps and turns to me. "They're going to kill me as soon as the ship arrives."

But his story is plausible.

"You don't see my men anywhere, do you? We can't stay here. Someone comes every two hours to relieve these baboons," he says, looking around in a panic.

"Are the girls kept underground at dock five?" I ask.

"Yeah, and no one is guarding them. They will unload the coke, put them on the ship with barrels of olive oil, and send them up the coast. When the ship gets to Trieste, they'll be handed over to a middleman who will take them the rest of the way to Germany."

"And what about the coke coming in?" Sal asks.

"The Albanians are waiting for it. We're just the middlemen on that. I didn't want to get in bed with them, but Mario insisted it was a good move."

"Albanians, you say?" Sal pipes up as he puts his gun back in its holster, suddenly very interested.

"Yes, Albanians. Francesca, your brothers are into a lot of shit, and they want me to be the fall guy if anything goes awry." I can tell by his rapid breathing that he's anxious to get out of here, and when he tries to stand up, he all but falls on Sal before we catch him.

"Looks like it already has," Sal's chuckle slips out.

"We need to move." Matteo runs down the steps. "Compare notes later. Let's haul ass," he orders, leading the way up the stairs just as two goons are coming down. As if on cue, it thunders, and Sal shoots them both with his .45 because it has a silencer on it.

Besides, the AK-47 would be overkill on just two people.

The men Sal shot fall backward as blood stains the rock walls, and he double taps them in the head as we move by, just to be sure we won't see them again.

He puts another magazine in his gun as Matteo leads, and I help Angelo walk down the road. He's weak from being beaten, and his body is stiff.

"I'll help you, but you've got to help us," I tell him.

"I'm with you. Your brothers can't do this to me and my men. We're trying to be better than Gio because the men don't want more of the same." The way his bloodshot eyes look into mine, I believe him.

"It appears my brothers have been double-dealing for

some time. I'm sure Dad taught them all the tricks of the trade." I look up to Sal, who agrees and throws his head to one side.

"Angelo," I whisper, "is Sofia with the girls?"

"I think so," he mumbles as he struggles to stay conscious.

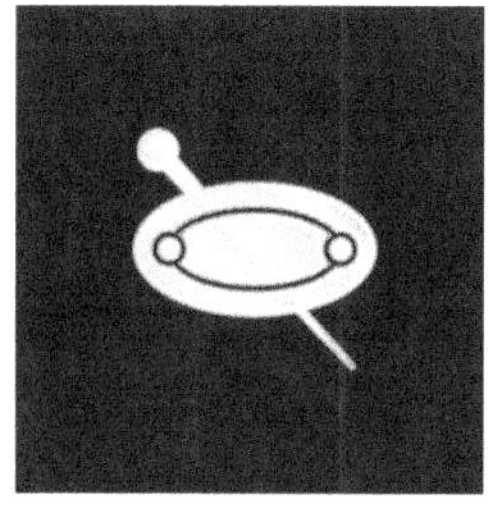

20

SAL

We wait in the shadows of the trees, and due to the cloud covering, the humidity is building up. I'm keenly aware of Francesca crouching next to me as we are peering through the trees outside the wine cellar, but It's the quiet before the storm that will rage inside those walls tonight if everything goes according to plan.

Lady luck is on our side tonight when the sky opens, a light rain at first, then, a downpour. The men on guard go inside to dry off and grab warm coffee on the top floor of the house and in the yard.

It's approaching midnight and we use this as our opportunity to sneak out of the wine cellar, weaving in and out of cars.

"Is this a convention?" Francesca asks with sarcasm in her voice.

"Appears to be a coup if you ask me," I reply, drawing my weapon.

Francesca's is out as we move along the tree line behind a long driveway, and hope no one notices us as we approach the pool area.

The rain in my face is running into my eyes and it clouds my vision momentarily.

"Are you okay?" I ask Francesca, but knowing better—she's such a phenom.

"Yeah, fine." She slides her knife back into the holder on her belt to hold Angelo with both hands.

My cell phone vibrates as we reach the pool area.

We park Angelo on a lounger, where he passes out.

"Pronto." I listen, then hang up. "Everyone is in place to hijack and torch the trucks with Angelo's stolen coke. That will effectively fuck over Mario and Fausto." I look up to Francesca. "Do you have a problem with that?"

"It's never easy with family, but we have to do what we must to survive tonight. They forced our hand, and I can't walk away." Her voice conveys the sadness of a woman who is loyal but knows she has to do what must be done to stop them to save her friend and the girls.

"My brothers will create a diversion, and that way, we'll be able to get out of here," I say.

She nods with a sigh of relief.

"We definitely need them. We only have so many bullets," I mutter.

"It's a brilliant plan, Sal." She leans her head into my face in relief, and we share a tender kiss before she moves away, whipping out her laptop.

I love how her mind works. It's chilling she's so well-versed in this life, but it's the biggest fucking turn-on I've ever encountered.

I text Dante, giving him the game plan. We'll free Angelo's men when we're sure they're on our side, or when we need more firepower. Until then, they can wait.

"Once my brothers send everyone out to the truck fires, he'll be left with a skeleton crew. Dante and Marchello can breach this place," Francesca says as she crouches with her techie software behind a lounge chair. "I'll be taking their security system and communications off-line now." She taps the computer key extra hard.

"You're so fucking brilliant." My devilish grin might not be seen in the darkness that surrounds the glow of the pool light. But things are going to get hotter around here, and for once, it's not because Francesca and I are in close proximity to each other.

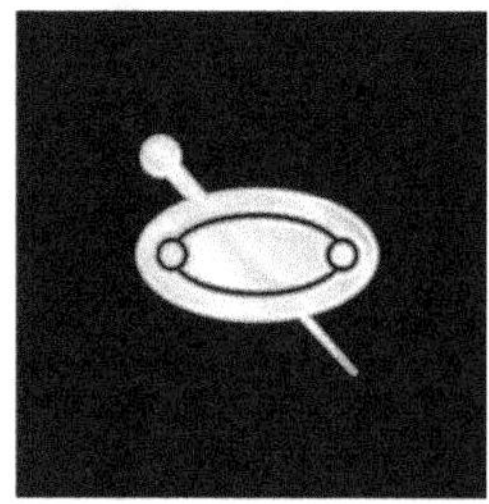

21

FRANCESCA

"As soon as the men leave, we can get out of here," I take a seat momentarily, slide the hood off my head, and it falls heavily on my back as we wait.

I wring my hair out before putting it up again. My wet hoodie is sticking to my back like a spitball. I gulp water from the stash in my backpack and hand it to Sal.

He chugs water. "It's not safe."

"You have a better idea?" I stand and remind Sal who he's talking to with my posture. Technically, after tonight, the family belongs to me.

Fuck.

"You stay with Angelo. I'll go when my brothers arrive to create a diversion."

"Hell, no, I'm going too." Besides, I outrank Sal.

I don't see this ending well because this position will make it impossible for me ever to have a man who truly loves me. I'll always have to question their motives and loyalty.

And to marry any man outside of the family or another mafia family for alliances is not going to look good to my men when they've been trained to hate Sal's family. But stranger things have been known to happen.

As don of the family, I'll have no life, I'll never be safe, and I'll never be able to have a family. Men won't say it, but there is a higher rate of mortality for those at the top of the mafia hierarchy, and the number of men that could be my suiters has just been reduced to zero.

"Fine." He gives in and checks his gear before swiping a sleeved arm across his eyes to clear the water from the rain.

The target on my back is nothing compared to the target there will be on it once I have the seat. I'll always have the threat of assassins just like Dante, and they will be people I don't know or wouldn't suspect.

There will not be any downtime for me now. Not until I have total control and respect for my family. A family of many families and off-shoots that make the entire machine work.

Peace is always sought over war, but it's only a matter of time before someone gets greedy or skims money, and they have to be dealt with. I will have to give those orders. And then there is the bigger picture—the turf wars, new upstarts, and moles within our organization.

I'm no fool as to how Calabrese ended up where he did. It took more than my brothers' cunningness. He didn't need much help, but some of Angelo's men had to be involved in their scheme.

But I don't have time to dwell on this; it's just a conspiracy theory that plays in my mind. I need to focus on storming the compound, making my brothers pay, and finding Sofia. Thankfully, she's still alive from what Angelo told us, and I pray to God it's true.

"Alright, I guess we'll be able to get out despite the

chaos. But what of Angelo? He's pretty weak." Sal reads my mood and knows I'm not sitting this out.

"He'll be safe here. The compound will be empty, and once we free his men, they can get him." I shrug. I have no loyalty to Angelo other than my promise to free his men. I owe him nothing. But they will only be freed if they are on my side and help our cause. I'm confident they will. Being locked up for a day gives a person lots of time to think and get pissed off.

I pull Sal aside. "Besides, if he doesn't last until morning, he's lived longer than he would have if we didn't rescue him. I'm fine with that."

"Me too," he concedes as he dries off his weapon and pulls a new clip out of his vest, loading his gun again.

We hear a loud explosion, and we look toward the road. I see smoke and fire billowing in the rain which has dissipated.

"That's our cue," Sal gives me a tentative look, and we both turn to Matteo puts two fingers up, using them as directional cues for us to move forward.

"Let's move," Sal reiterates standing directly behind Matteo. "Mow down anyone walking. Protect Francesca first and foremost," he tells his number one man.

We break into a run for the front gates, and I chuck an empty water bottle over my shoulder.

Vehicles leave the compound like ants to a picnic, and no one thinks twice about us as we arrive safely at the road. The low-lying clouds and mist blur our vision, but we are still able to make out numerous fires, and more explosions flare up over the hillside.

A huge vehicle comes toward us, and I prepare to pull back, but Sal recognizes someone in it as a friend and not a foe as. Matteo comes to a halt and starts rattling off in Italian.

I can't suppress a smirk when I realize it's Dante and

Marchello in the front with men hanging out the windows waving at us like they're a boy band. Well, they are a band of sorts I guess, and I take a second to enjoy the familiar sight of friends and . . .family. Yes, we're a brotherhood, but family.

They stop. "Brother," Dante smiles, "it was splendid. Get in, get in."

No sooner are we in, with our feet barely on the floorboards, the door isn't even closed, and Marchello taps the side of the vehicle, saying, "*Andiamo. Andiamo.*"

"Where to now?" Marchello asks calmly as we drive.

"The port, we need to free the girls and intercept the ship coming in from Colombia that has Mario's coke on it, and we're giving it to the customers Angelo promised it to, not the people the Conti brothers screwed over," Sal replies with a grin to convey his excitement.

"A reverse sting," I mumble. Great brain on this man. I love it.

"So, we're setting Mario up? Love it, little brother." The glee Dante has with the plan isn't lost on me.

I smile in the darkness amid the stench of sweaty men who are as wet as us.

"I'll let you guys handle that. You'll need most of the men. Drop me off at dock five for the girls; I only need a few men," I say as the vehicle creeps down the road to the port.

"Like hell," Sal objects.

"I can handle it," I insist.

"Mario still has men out there looking for you, it's not safe."

"It will never be safe. I have to find out if Sofia is there."

"I'll do it with Marchello and a few men," he offers.

"I have to see with my own eyes." He knows he's not going to win this.

"Is this a lover's quarrel?" Dante's voice is one of curiosity and experience.

His keen sense of human interaction throws me off as he's actually talking to me like I'm in the family. His family.

"It's settled. Marchello, let's bring a few men as they'll need to drive the girls out of here, so save your best soldiers for the compound and wait for us."

"I'm on it." He talks into his mouthpiece, giving directions as we arrive at the port, his men shoot up the guard house, and we arrive at the dock.

We roll out of the vehicle as Dante runs to Mario's port master so he can secure the ship coming in. Out of the corner of my eye, I can tell he argued as his blood is splashed all over the booth's glass.

Sal, Matteo, and a few of their men follow us to the girls. Sal opens the lid that leads down, extending a ladder from the warehouse used to get the girls out.

I attempt to walk down first, and Sal shoots his arm out to stop me.

"There might be armed men in there."

I pull out my gun. "I got this."

Sal follows me and we find the girls huddled against a wall, living in squalor. They are scared and thin, looking more and more like they were primed for a Hannibal Lecter movie, as creepy as that sounds.

My eyes are searching the faces for Sofia.

"We're here to free you," I say in Italian and English, as I have no clue if they speak either language, while Sal and some of the men help them up the ladder.

They are weak and can't move fast.

"Sal, we need to get them medical attention."

"We will, let's just finish up what we need to do first, huh?"

I scan all the girls, "Sal," panic sets in, "Sofia isn't here."

"Fuck." He clinches his fist as he's put his weapon away to not frighten the girls.

"Where can she be? Did Angelo lie?"

"Doubtful, but we'll find her before the night is out."

I have a feeling he knows something I don't but I there's no time to grill him. We only have two hours left to get the girls safe and the coke going in the right direction on Dante's trucks because we blew up most of Mario's.

We are the last to leave the dungeon and we take a minute to make sure the van is ready to take the girls for medical care and those crimes go against my brothers. There are too many of them for him to prevent them to be material witnesses no matter who my brothers paid off in law enforcement and witness protection programs.

But the reality is that they are the first girls to ever escape, and most will just want to go home, and not risk their life with a trial if my brothers survive tonight.

"Have someone call the media for the hospital, Sal, please," I plead with him. "You know the girls won't be safe, it's the only way I can think that will subvert an all-out attack on them at the hospital. Mario has other hands in this trade, we don't know if who is gunning for them is out there for them or us, for that matter."

"You don't need my permission, it's a great idea. Use your burner phone."

"Right." I whip it out and dial quickly, speaking so fast, I have to repeat myself as I give the biggest tip of the century to the media.

I hang up the phone and look at Sal as I re-do my hair. I'm a hot mess. Jittery with excitement, the mix of real combat, being so close to Sal, and the final confrontation being upon us is a drug in itself. I'm buzzing.

"We'll find her, she has to be here somewhere. There are lots of places left. Angelo didn't know where she was but said she was alive. She could be anywhere, even at the compound," Sal offers hope in my despair.

I appreciate his attempt at hope, and I realize I can't give up now. I've come so far.

Sal checks in with Dante. The ship has been secured, and now, we need Angelo's men to load trucks and get them out of here before the *polizia* arrive.

"Let's go to the dock where Angelo's men are," Sal suggests. "You know what this means, right?"

"That I'm the new don."

"Yes." I know he's proud of me, but the sadness in his voice can't be camouflaged.

"It's all so fast, I don't know what I want, Sal. I ran away from all this, now it's in my lap."

"Think fast." He coolly walks toward the Jeeps Matteo is driving slowly, giving us a chance to hop on the running boards to the other dock with the storage unit, just as Angelo had instructed, there is a storage unit, and inside it is approximately fifty men.

Their faces are filled with confusion as they don't know if they will be mowed down with our guns or saved.

"Look, I know I'm a Conti," I shout so they can hear in the back. "I'm not like the rest of my family. However tonight, we liberated Angelo Calabrese and we're here to set you free. If you want to remain part of the new family going forward, stay and help us take the compound, if not, you can leave no questions asked."

The men are all talking amongst themselves.

"We have to move! Now," I yell taking control of the lull in action. I'm pumped up, I'm out for a whole new level of vengeance.

The men are well trained as they all follow my orders and Matteo tosses them their guns that were collected and leaning up against a wall. I'm sure they were made to leave them here before they entered.

They load up and our men are with them because we can't totally trust them, but we have more firepower with them, so we tipped the outcome of this war in our favor as we head back to the compound for the final showdown.

22

SAL

The rain is soft, and it reminds me of lying in bed with Francesca at the hotel. Alone. Serene. Giving into the emotions and passion that I've denied myself for so long. Just the two of us, loving each other. No family business, no distractions.

I'm brought back to the present by the sound of the large tires humming on the ride as eight of us are in the SUV heading to the family compound.

"Your brother will be prepared, so don't take any chances," I warn her.

"That's why I have this." She tugs on her lightweight bulletproof vest.

I made sure Marchello and Matteo wore them as well. Most men don't, but I knew tonight would be akin to guerrilla warfare, and I was correct in my assumptions. Never underestimate the enemy.

One thing about fighting with family is it's easier to anticipate their moves as people rarely change their routines or habits. And Francesca knows this family inside and out, so

I'm relying on her to not give in to her familial emotions when we need her to show no mercy.

"Dante has the men we left and he's loading up the trucks to move the product as we speak," I say, leaning close to Francesca's ear so she can hear me. And even though we're sweaty, wet, and nasty by all admissions, I still want her. She always turns me on.

Whenever she walks into a room, I want to grab her and hold her to me, protect her, and make love to her. I'd love to tell her that I love her, but I don't know if that will drive her away again.

The chemistry between us warms the air, and I'll settle for that . . . for now.

"Great." She gives me a weak smile of gratitude.

I nod, acknowledging her acceptance of help, as no other words are needed.

Thankfully, the trucks that were blown up are miles away and will keep law enforcement away for some time. The compound is isolated, and, logically, we'll have the ground swarming with detectives and backup before long.

"I hope we have enough time to get there before they bug out." Francesca's voice quivers, partly because she's been in wet clothes for over two hours.

I fish around in the vehicle and find an old airline blanket, put it around her, drape my arm over her tired shoulders, and pull her into me.

She leans her head on my shoulder and seems to find a moment of solitude as I feel her body relax against mine, which warms my cold heart.

The gates to the compound are closed, and what is left of Mario's men have refortified the compound. This was to be expected.

I give directions to the soldiers in our vehicle, but it's

through our earpieces, so I know Francesca can't hear what's going on. It's logistics. We've practiced tactical formations and wall breaching before we came. I left her out of it as it's dangerous, and I want to keep her safe.

The guys in the back bring ropes with grappling hooks on them and we park a half mile away before we make a run for it.

We have to break in, and men will be lost. Francesca might be hit or fatally wounded.

"You sit here, let us get in, and I'll come and get you," I order Francesca as I sit here on our side of the wall.

I can tell she'd like to make an intelligent comment about how she's going in with us, but instead, she remains silent. This alone tells me that she's exhausted, and we still have the final confrontation ahead of us.

I wish I could spare her, but I can't. She must face her demons.

I give the command, fifty of us breach the wall, and the gates open. I send Matteo to retrieve Francesca, and he brings her to me. She's regained her composure and again holds her weapon with steady hands.

The rain stops just as we breach the house with Matteo and Enzo shooting and bodies dropping. We enter the upstairs office not knowing what we'd find.

One of Dante's guards, Enzo, is wounded on the way in. I'm not sure if he's alive or dead, but I pull him out of harm's way as we make our assent up the stairs, bullets raining on us as we take out one man after another and I shield Francesca.

But it turns out Mario and Fausto's greed made them misjudge how fast we'd get here. We've had the place surrounded for the past half hour. Surely he knows an attempt to get away is slim at best.

Matteo and I head to the office upstairs. The office was

once held by Gio Conti himself. Even though it was a place I had heard about for years and it's one place I wanted to see—but not as a prisoner. There is no way I ever would have imagined that I'd be standing inside these four walls.

Walls that made deals for years, but I wish the walls could talk since I'm here. The cunning man had his ways about him that threatened every connected family and extended well beyond the borders of Italy.

Rumors precede my vision; however, I find they are accurate. The office is filled with antique furniture, heavy satin curtains that are holding years of cigar smoke, and a huge liquor cabinet filled with the most expensive collection a man can buy.

There is also a large gun safe for every weapon imaginable and wines. He loved the best whiskey and the best wines, including boutique wines that are rumored to be rare and exquisite with unique flavors.

And in the middle of the room, behind that large imposing desk are her brothers, with bags of cash holding Sofia.

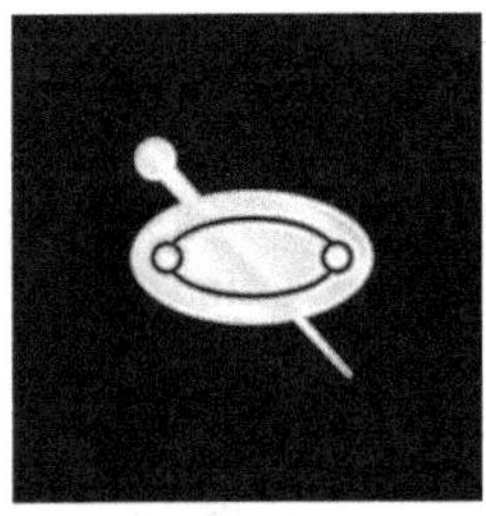

23

FRANCESCA

I'm cold, but it's more than being wet. Looking at my brother's makes my bones chill. Part of the freezing cold in my body is because my brothers are bastards, but they are still my brothers. The same brothers I ate gelato with on family vacations at the beach.

Before our Dad turned them into monsters. Clones of himself. Maybe I was the lucky one after all. Maybe they spared me being the same as them.

I'm grasping at my mixed emotions. It's one thing to suspect them of being capable of these things. It's another to witness the devastation and the trail of treachery we uncovered tonight.

The chills aren't just limited to my bones. My teeth start to chatter and my hands remain steadfast on my gun.

I don't have the strength to go on, but I have to pull my strength from Sal for now as I can't be weak in front of my men or his.

My men. The gravity of the situation will have to wait for another day. We sped through the mountains to track down my brothers and rescue Sofia before it was too late.

I'm thinking I'm so glad I didn't go this alone and that my brother probably has some nasty surprises in store for me but Sal has my back. I'm about to be overcome with emotion knowing his family is helping me fight my battle but I stifle it.

No tear will escape my eyes today. I can't remember the last time I allowed myself to cry, but Sal moves me with his loyalty when he owes me nothing.

"It disgusts me to call you brothers," I announce taking my stand to shoot, we're all ready to pop anyone that gets out of line or trigger-happy.

"Sister, you are just in time," his raspy voice is not unlike my Dad's. "You want a cut of the profits before we leave town?" Mario has gained weight and I doubt he can run far. His eyes are bulging from too much liquor so his reflexes will be slower than ours. Still, he's no less of a monster.

"Put that down and walk away," I hold my gun on him, but he doesn't care.

"Like you can shoot me," he chuckles.

"Face it. You're ruined. We intercepted your trucks; we've stolen your shipment and we rescued Angelo."

"Bravo, little sister," Fausto laughs as he drains the cognac from the tulip glass that slams hard into the table, causing it to shatter in his drunken state.

My nerves are jittery and Sal senses this and moves in close behind me, his body touching mine. I need this man who has my back, he's done nothing to cause me to not trust him and everything to prove to me that he loves me.

We've been together night and day for over two weeks, and we are in synch so much it scares me and I'm always sexually excited around him.

"Relax little sister, I have what you want right here," and

as he bends behind the desk Sofia materializes in front of our eyes.

Sal and I prepare to shoot but the sight of Sofia disarms me momentarily. She is bound and gagged.

Her dark hair is dirty and stringy. The dark bags under her eyes extend into her once beautiful cheekbones. She's lost weight. I hope she was only a hostage and not made to work in the brothels. Or worse.

"I think we can let bygones be bygones. No?" He holds his gun on Sofia and Fausto stuffs the rest of the cash in a second leather duffle bag.

Fuck.

Fuck this. I think I can take Mario, double tap to the head but I still have Fausto next to him that would hit me unless Sal and I take them bought out at the same time.

"Just let her go, we'll let you leave peacefully." I stand at the ready.

"That would be too easy little sister. No doubt there are men crawling all over, I need a guarantee to escape safely."

"You're using a human shield. You are such a coward!" I shout.

"Well, maybe, but we're getting out alive, back away from the door."

"No," I stand my ground.

I hear a bang and piercing pain in my left shoulder as the impact of a bullet sends me staggering backward into Sal who catches me.

Matteo is our last line of defense.

"Let them leave," Sal says as he lowers me to the floor. Matteo holds his gun on my brothers as they disappear into the night with Sofia.

"Sofi . . we should have shot them first," I gasp as Sal takes off his vest, then his shirt, ripping it into pieces and balling it up to plug my shoulder. I've been hit as the bullet narrowly missed my vest.

"Thankfully, he shot you high, and not near your heart."

"Oh, so you know this?" I joke.

"We need to be sure; I'll call a doctor we know down here. You need to go now." I somewhat pass out as Matteo is talking into his earpiece.

I'm carried to a van and rushed through the mountains to a place with lots of animal noises. And dogs barking

I chuckle at the irony of it, but it hurts.

I see faces I don't know but Sal is with me so I'm not worried.

I receive an IV and drift off to sleep.

UNBEKNOWNST TO ME, Dante had men in the van that was their getaway vehicle and as soon as they got in, they were disarmed and tied up. Sofia was rescued.

They escaped before the polizia arrive at the house as the fires of the trucks covered up the noise at the compound.

Dante and Marchello had the great pleasure of taking Mario and Fausto to meet their drug connections without the drugs. They were turned over to the Albanians in exchange for a future favor.

As Sal told me, they figured they would be able to make their deaths interesting. Even in my haziness, I know Dante and Sal didn't want to be the ones to kill them. Neither wanted it to be an issue that would become us or our families. Sometimes there is honor among 'thieves."

Or, as it turns out, our families.

"Sofia?"

"She's safe, we took her to a hospital where she was treated." Sal gently lifts a cup of water to my dry lips and it brings back memories of our first coffee in the wine cellar.

"We've put Riccardo on her for now. I know you won't be happy unless she's with you when you're on her feet again. She was put in with the girls but never made to do what they did."

"Thank God."

"She's very fortunate, and very lucky to have you as a friend."

I grimace.

"Something I said?" Sal asks.

"This is painful. Damn," I clutch my gut with one hand and use the other to feel my wounded shoulder and push the button on the pain drip.

"Yeah, but you'll do much better in a few days. The good thing is that you'll regain full use of your shoulder."

"That's a relief."

Sal takes my hand as I lay on a narrow bed with clean linens and an old quilt.

"I want to take you back home to recuperate. We've been doing this dance," he wrings his hands in his lap, but I can tell he's showered, shaved and his yummy cologne drifts over me.

I don't know if the painkiller or his cologne is making me float.

"If anything happened to you back there…"

"I know," I whisper.

"No, I don't think you do. I love you, Francesca. I never thought I'd love anyone, but you're everything to me."

"And you are everything to me, Sal," and I reach my hand out laying it over his.

"But you're a don now, I'm just in the family, the opposing family."

"Hm. Complicated. Still clinging on to that damn bachelorhood title like it's an Italian girl's virginity."

He gives a hearty laugh but wraps his hands around mine.

"I've had more time to think about it."

"You have, but if we can beat the Conti brothers and foil their big play, there's no telling what we can accomplish together," I grin. "Now, kiss me."

I longed for his lips. It doesn't matter where I am, I want him with me. He's the first man I can trust to have my back, and he's had the trial by fire. I feel confident that there isn't anything we can't overcome together, and it feels nice.

It's a feeling I have to get used to. Love. How complicated we make it and how simple it can be.

But I know we won't have an easy go of it. There is so much to be sorted out but for now, I return his kiss as it deepens and his hand slides under the sheet.

I'm naked and his hands find their way between my legs and my pussy is wet with anticipation.

"Who's here?" I mumble.

"No one close enough to hear you screaming with pleasure, but the place is guarded. Heavily."

He slips out of his pants and shirt, sharing the single bed with me which makes it hotter and more challenging due to his size, and my inability to move.

He slides over me, kissing down my body as he flings the sheet to the floor.

I grab his hard cock with my one good hand for the moment and guide him into me. I want to possess me.

"You are mine, Francesca, never forget that."

"You are mine."

"I am," and he enters me making me gasp at how he fills me completely and we find a rhythm that doesn't jar my shoulder as we climax together.

DAWN COMES in through the tiny window, and I hear dogs barking. The door opens, and breakfast is on a tray, left by a woman in a maid's uniform who leaves as quietly as she came.

Sal stirs. I'm laying on his shoulder and arm that, by the groans he's making, have fallen asleep under my weight of the night.

I have no idea how long I've been here, but I do know it's daytime, and I have to get to the compound and figure out what's up with the situation.

"Who is at the compound?"

"We left Angelo there with an ironclad provision signed that he's temporarily acting on your behalf to keep the family together. We figured you needed a few days and he's the best man for the job. We couldn't be caught there."

"No, of course not."

"And Sofia?"

"She's with my family, I'm sure Juliet is taking good care of her. She can't be around to be questioned, and we don't know if Guido is one of the dead or injured."

"Good call."

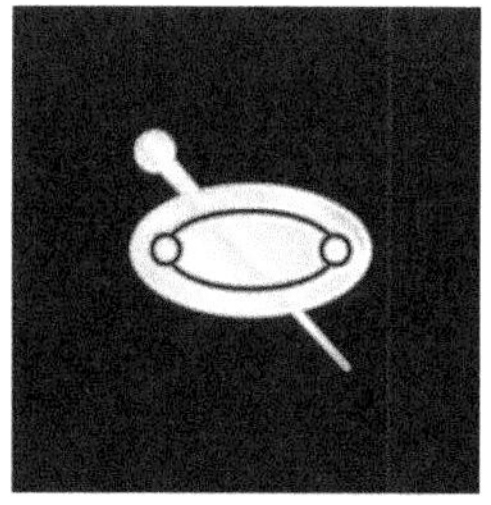

24

SAL

I drive Francesca back to her compound and turn on the TV in her old room, which we've been sharing. A news flash comes on, and it's an update on the missing Conti brothers.

"Breaking news. The Conti brothers, Mario and Fausto, known racketeers of the mafia, have been found dead after what appears to be a local war. This is just coming in, but Mario was found shot execution-style in the river near the compound. Fausto was found strangled in his sports car. There are no witnesses at this time."

"Wow." I expect Francesca to be shocked and am surprised she's taking it so well.

I turn to her as she stands to dress herself. She's so stubborn, insisting on doing more than what the doctor recommended.

I help her put a blouse on her stiff shoulder that needs immobile and take the opportunity to kiss her lips.

"No trace of us at the compound?" she asks.

"Bodies we might not have been able to recover but that's normal. There may be questions. All of Italy knows Gio has many enemies. As long as it's not one of our main guys there, it'll be hard to trace them to us. Still, we don't like to leave our men behind. We're different than most."

She nods and bends to pull on her jeans, and I can't deny that I enjoy watching.

"Stop." She catches me.

"What, I can't admire the woman I love?" I pull her back into me, so my hips are aligned with her butt in front of my hard-on.

She turns and lets out a grimace as it jarred her shoulder. "What are we going to do?"

"Well, we can make love right here, that's my vote." My mischievous grin makes her laugh.

"Or we can go to our business meeting with Angelo. I know the bosses will be there after that," she replies.

"You're not fun," I say and slap her ass. "Right. Okay then, I can't be there with you. It will make it look like we're taking over your organization."

"I know." She pats my crisp designer shirt before rolling forward on her toes to kiss my lips.

"Please get word to Sofia that I'll find out about Guido. I know it's not safe to contact her right now."

"I'll be sure to. I'm going home for a few days. Give you some time to adjust and get things squared away here."

"You have a few men with you. Do you mind leaving Matteo with me for now?"

She looks at me with those gorgeous green eyes, eyes that belong to the woman who is in love with me, and I can't refuse her much, least of all a man to keep her safe when I'm not around. I understand her completely. If anything, our raid of the compound answered all my questions, and I understand her better than before.

"Sure, *il mio amore*."

"I love how you say that." She smiles before slipping into high heels and putting on a suit jacket.

"I'll be here when you get out of the meeting."

"Thank you." She walks toward me with all the confidence in the world, but I don't know how I would handle being in her position.

"No need to thank me for anything."

"Without you and your family, this wouldn't be possible. Not that I wanted this position. I just wanted Sofia and the girls freed."

"I know."

But inside, I'm dying to know if she will choose her family business over me. We both can't own her heart. I won't share her, but I might have to because I believe she is the new don. And I don't want to live without her.

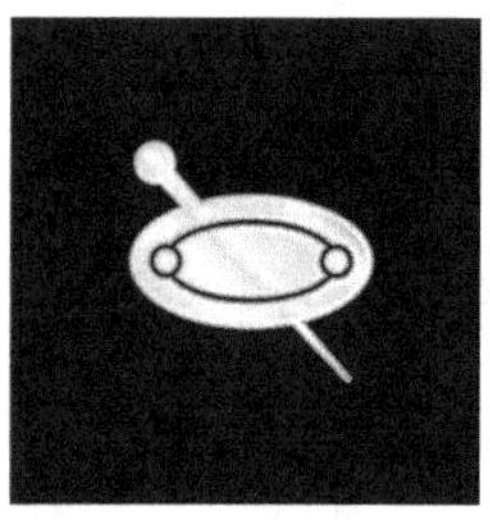

25

FRANCESCA

The meeting with Angelo went easier than I anticipated. It didn't hurt that I saved his life and freed his men. In the middle of the meeting, I hear the church bells ring from the monastery up the hillside, and I take it as a good omen that this union will be blessed.

"Angelo." I shake his hand and sit at my father's desk as he and his *consigliere* take their places.

"Francesca, so happy to see you doing so well."

"Thanks." I need some whiskey to take the edge off. Luc, Angelo's right-hand man, pours for us.

"All of us," I offer when it's customary for just the don and top members to drink unless invited.

I raise the glass to my lips. "To a prosperous relationship."

"*Saluti*." We chime in unison like the bells.

"Look, I know there is resistance that I'm a woman in a man's position…"

"You are Don, make no mistake about it, Francesca," Angelo says as he scoots to the front of his chair, looking none the worse for wear. His stitches are healing nicely, and his cane is only temporary.

"Thank you, Angelo." I tilt my glass to him as I let the warm whiskey do its job of taking the edge off the pain in my shoulder. The bandage is changed daily, and the scar will be minimal.

"I'm bound by my duty to take over the family seat, but I'm more modern. I don't want to be tied down. I want to be able to travel, and I need trusted men in positions to do the daily work."

The men nod in agreement.

"What do you propose?" Angelo asks.

I glance at Matteo at the door. He's a welcomed sight in a room of men that I'm not sure I can trust.

Never trust . . . never trust.

And yet I trust Sal and broke my own rule.

"I want to run operations from here. I'll be appointing an independent accountant to oversee the books and he has a forensic accounting background. And, Angelo, I think that since you are indebted to me, you would be the most loyal. For now, you are to run the business. Your men speak well of you. But make no mistake that I will not tolerate human trafficking of women or men or children."

"Agreed."

"Good. We'll work out the pay for everyone based on what we have found and what you all have said. I'm sure we can arrive at an equitable situation."

"For sure, *Signorina*."

"I also want Guido, Sofia's husband, found dead or alive." I set my empty glass on the thick wooden desk. "That's all for now." I take a deep breath before standing.

Everyone stands. We shake hands and kiss both cheeks before the visitors make their leave. Matteo is armed and I take comfort in his shadow as we head to the living room downstairs where Sal has had the maid prepare an afternoon lunch for us.

"I hope you are hungry." Sal pulls the large chair on the terrace out for me.

It's afternoon but the weather has changed, and winter is coming as the leaves rustle in the cooler wind, and the sun is obscured occasionally by clouds.

"My appetite is coming back," I answer as I sit.

"Great, our favorite panini and fresh fruit."

"I don't want you to go," I admit.

"I understand that. In fact," he sits opposite me, "I'm flattered. There was a time you didn't want to be in the same room with me and you certainly wouldn't have accepted help from anyone."

I chuckle as I drink my fizzy water. "I know. However, I have a temporary command staff in order here and they are to find Guido. I can't rest until he's found."

Sal nods. A few strands of his dark hair fall over his forehead making him look rugged when combined with the day's growth of hair on his chin. "What?" he asks as my sly smile appears.

"You're just so doable. I like the rugged look."

"Well," he puts his napkin in his lap, "I might have to keep it then if it will keep you around."

"I can't wait until we don't have to spend a night apart. But order has to be restored first."

He, of all people, understands the position I'm in.

"When you are ready, come to Florence."

"I will."

We take a long siesta to make love. His new guard has driven his car down. He has little with him to pack as we've been on the go the entire time.

"I do long to see you and your family again." I hold his face between the palms of my hands as I kiss his thin lips before he gets in his car with Maurizio.

"I know. I wish it was over."

I fear he might doubt my commitment, but I can't become weak for love. I can love, as much as the timing sucks, and I can't give him up.

Visions of Carla entered my dreams last night when I thought he was proposing to her. I'm sure that relationship is over, but at the same time, trust is new to me. Trust is good until it's not and even when I speak the words, I'm hoping I'll stick to them.

I know I'm damaged. I never wanted my brothers' lives to come to this end. I hoped they would change, or that it wasn't so bad. That they weren't truly bad people, but they were, and they got the only ending that was fitting for their crimes.

Not to say I'm an angel for taking over the family business. I'm not one to take vengeance unless it's earned a response from me. And I realize that my vendetta against the Michelis was really to blame them for what my dad did and the man he had become during the years of feuds and wars.

It doesn't excuse my dad's actions, but I'm not sure I want the title I've inherited either.

I'm the last of the Contis, and it makes me sad. Sure, I have a half-sister, but she'll never be accepted at the table. Besides, she didn't grow up in the life we've become used to.

I take my clothes off, crawl into bed, and the tears come. I give way to years of pent-up anger and sadness. I cry for the family I wanted, the family I had, and the family that was taken away from me by this life.

I miss Sal. I can't wait to meet up with him and, Sofia and the rest of his family. I mourn what I wanted from my dad—the love I never got, and I hope that in time I will find peace.

We are all responsible for our lives and the decisions we make are our own.

And now, I have to make mine. Will I become the don and pick up where Dad left off? Or is there another path for me?

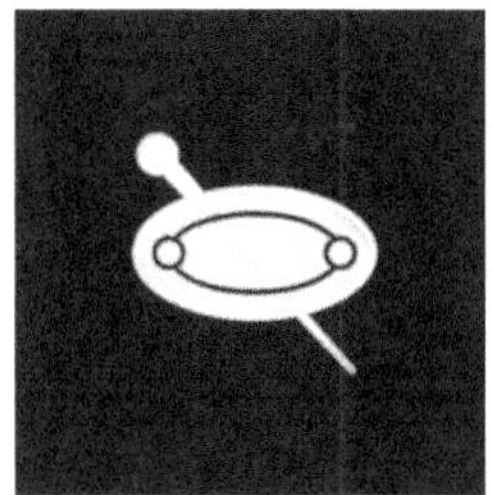

26

SAL

The days feel like years since Francesca last walked these hallways. The house is empty without her, and on top of it, she has the comfort of Matteo, and I'm with my next in line, Maurizio.

Sofia is at the house with Mom, and both are under lock and key. Until we have located Guido, Sofia may not be safe. But Mom is guarded inside, and out, just like the rest of us.

Francesca and I talk daily, but mostly it turns more to business and how she can wash more money than it is phone sex. I'm worried that she is becoming the true leader of her family and that her love for it might replace her love for me.

Carla welcomed me to town with a text. We're just friends now. I was wrong to lead her on just to make Francesca jealous.

On the other hand, it forced Francesca to take me out of the friend zone of patriots who worked together and kept strict rules of engagement. She viewed me differently after that date. She saw me as a man who has game and isn't just a thinker, or bar owner. I'm also a man who won't bend to her will. But I'll be by her side.

I have a will of my own, and I usually find a way to deal with people effectively with the least amount of force used if possible so they can become a potential ally in the future if need be. Making friends along the way can pay off.

Meanwhile, I'm back into my routine going to bed with an un-serviced boner every night as I listen to Francesca's sweet voice.

I don't want to hound her on when she's coming up. Even if it's just a visit, the ball is in her court. I've gone to the ends of the earth for her, so now, it's time for her to decide.

A month is enough time to get her affairs in order. Will she come to me, or will she send for Sofia when it's safe for her to return home?

I head to work, and damn if Argon isn't in my club. He's the boss of the local Albanians in my territory and now I know he was getting his coke from the Contis. I'm pretty sure they recruit girls from their country as they have rough lives and people are desperate to leave it.

I don't want to make waves as we're lying low after Francesca's family feud. But boy, do I want to send a message to his pompous ass. Parading around in my club like it's his.

How long do we have to hold off before we send a message? I hate Argon and it's irritating the hell out of me every night I see his pompous ass in here. I'd love to meet him in a dark alley, but I can't go against my brother.

I'm sure Dante is cooking up a strategic plan. We like to set things up so that these things are taken care of without us being in the picture. No need to implicate ourselves when we don't have to. Which is a brilliant plan.

On a positive note, Enzo got shot in the leg, but he is on the mend and expected back to work any day now. We lost a few men and we made restitution to their families for their service.

Tomorrow is Sunday dinner at Mama's house, and as much as I love to see my brothers, I feel the sadness that Francesca isn't here . . . again. Are we just slipping away or are we going to move forward?

I make it through the night, spending most of it in my office doing books but not really concentrating. I go downstairs and have a bourbon neat. I hate to think I'm sick over a girl, so I brush it off to co-workers as if it's just stress or exhaustion.

I head home, and when I get there, I find a sports car parked in my driveway, only it's not mine. I look at my guard. "She's here," he whispers.

My heart beats faster and my feet move without thinking. I enter with no idea of what to expect.

"Sal!" Francesca jumps into my arms and hugs me as soon as I'm through the door.

"My love, how are you?"

"Fine, fine." She kisses me, and this is so much better than the daydreams I've had of us seeing each other again.

My lips claim hers, and I twirl her around just because I can. She's dressed in skinny jeans and an off-the-shoulder top that shows me she's had time to get a tan and looks sexier than hell.

Her hair is softer as I run my fingers through it, feeling the silky stands I've grown to love. I think she left it blonde to go with her new life.

Her fingers grab my hair before she rubs her chin against mine as our eyes lock. Our lips meet, and it's going to be fast and rough make-up sex because I can't wait to claim her taut body.

Her full lips and round ass—that I love to pound and

make bounce against my balls when I'm overly excited—is minutes away.

She rips off my shirt. Four hundred euros spent, no biggie. I pull her shirt off over her head and let her down long enough for her to wiggle out of her jeans on the living room floor.

As soon as she's done, I move her to the area rug under the glass coffee table and nearly break it into a million pieces just to get it out of the way.

I'm a crazed man. I can't get enough of her as I take a deep breath of her and the light airy feeling of being at the ocean with a hint of jasmine mixed in warms me. She seems better, softer.

Changed.

She returns caress for caress and nip for nip as we play and giggle before I kneel before her, on my knees, my hard cock in front of me, and she says those words that drive me crazy.

"Make me yours."

I don't hold back as I plunge into her, and she lets out a gasp, taking me in fully before I glide in and out of her, and her walls tighten around me.

I'm rough from years of the streets, but I've found love because of her, so I slow my pace, turning my hard and fast fucking into making love as if a light was lit. I tenderly touch her breasts, taking one into my mouth as I massage the other with my large hand.

It's been a month, but it feels like an eternity, like I'm exploring her body for the first time.

She moves her hips against me and slows my rhythm and her hands roam over my body and she digs her nails into my rounded butt cheeks until I gasp.

"I missed you," I whisper as I bend over to suck on her neck.

"I missed you, too." She smiles and tugs at my chest hair, and we move in sync as we come together.

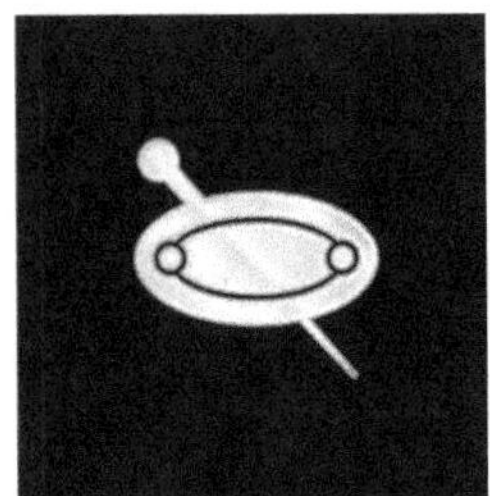

27

FRANCESCA

I can't believe Sal is even sexier than I remember. Funny how a month can make me forget little details, the smoothness of his skin, the hair on his chest, the cologne I love on him. . . the little things that add so much to one's memory, that build up over a lifetime.

And I should know given how many lives I had to take to find Sofia and as it turns out, liberate Angelo. Angelo better make good on all his promises, because if he doesn't, I have a few cement blocks for his feet.

And I'm not kidding.

We risked our lives for him and his men, but in all fairness, many of those men were loyal to my father. I'm just saying that as the new don, I have to keep track of favors given and favors asked, as there is no other way to keep it fair.

But so far, I have more people who owe me so I'm feeling more confident day by day.

On the flip side, I have to make sure bosses aren't too indebted to me as they will look weak. It's more complicated and cutthroat than politics in the weird American reality shows make it seem.

I found Guido, he had been murdered and now Sofia is safe. I told her family I'd have her get in touch with them as soon as possible so they can hear from her themselves and that her enemies are gone.

For now.

I'm not a little girl who needs to have basic things explained to her. I know that peace and prosperity will last so long and then a boss or another family in our clan will want change with something and the political drama will start up again.

Being a don means putting one fire out after another, and dealing with many different personalities all the time is wearing thin.

I can understand why Dons want to whack half their crews sometimes.

Is it just my patience or the fact that I miss Sal terribly, and my pussy is itching for a road trip . . . or a quick ride in Dad's jet! I forgot that I have more toys at my disposal now.

Ha, I have all the perks of Dante! Imagine that.

And imagine that I hated him and his family so much that my attempt on Sal could have taken me out and with just cause.

But I hope to be a long way from here soon. The world is open to me, money is flowing in, and I think I need a vacation.

Sal surely deserves one. I need to do some research and plan it. I'll surprise him with a trip as soon as it's convenient.

Making love with Sal is like a dream and I can't believe I'm here.

I had time to adjust my mind from work and living in the

compound and meetings as I needed to set up new businesses to clean money.

Turns out cocaine is a huge money maker and the further I can ship it and truck it, the more I get for it.

I bought myself a few things, no longer reliant on my dad or brothers for my monthly allowance, and it feels good. Of course, I do have my own brand of workout wear and loungewear from my time as a fighter and trainer.

Endorsement money is great, there's no way I'm working that hard and not making a living off my mad skills. One way or another . . .

We moved to the bedroom before evening, and before I know it, Sal is stirring beside me and birds are chirping.

I can finally hug Sofia today.

Sal grumbles, "Where do you think you're going?" as he pulls me back into bed and whispers sweet things into my ear in Italian.

It's early afternoon and we meet Sofia at an outdoor piazza with beautiful fountains that have been restored in Florence, just under the huge statue of Michelangelo where everyone drives by in their limos on Saturdays to pose for traditional wedding pictures.

Sofia is standing near Enzo getting a gelato. Enzo looks like he's recovered, and I give him a hug and thank him for his help.

He's shy and gruff as he mumbles, "Don't mention it," but I've never had so many loyal friends and employees help me before, and to think that he came to fight on Dante's behalf touches me.

Sofia is taking in the fountain eating her favorite lemon-flavored gelato in a yellow sundress with white spots on it. It's so retro fifties and looks adorable on her.

"Sofia!" I shout because I'm so excited I run to her and engulf her with my arms as she turns around.

Luckily for me, she's fast on her feet and we keep from falling into the water as we are laughing like teenagers and off balance as we hug and struggle to remain upright.

Sal is laughing behind me.

Part of it is the two of us reunited but the other part is that he's just plain ecstatic that I'm here in Florence, and with him.

I can't blame him.

For a while, it was easier for me to just stay at the Conti compound and work around the clock, but I don't want it to consume my life like it did Dad's.

And I don't want to turn into my brothers and live a lonely existence.

"Is it you?" Sofia teases and she's all smiles but I can still see the fear in her eyes, even with me.

"Of course, who else do you think would see you today?" I joke. "Relax, he's gone. You're free. Just promise me I get to approve of your next husband," I joke, treating her like normal and hoping it will force her back into society.

"I don't know if I can ever go back to *Casale de Sole*, even though it's where we both grew up and the compound is nearby."

I understand her sentiment.

"I know, and you don't have to." I hug her again and take a bite of her gelato to tease her. She always makes me feel light-hearted.

"Hey, that's mine." She turns away, pretending to protect her dessert.

"Come." I grab her hand and walk briskly toward Sal.

"So nice to see you looking so happy," Sofia explains. "But thanks to you and your family I'm here. I tell your mother every day that I am so happy she has such brave and honorable sons." She gives him a hug and hands me the gelato.

"I'm so sorry for all your suffering. Francesca has nothing but the best compliments to say about you. It was clear to us she wasn't going to let you go missing any longer than need be, you've needed this time to recover so we've not talked much at Mama's dinners," Sal explains.

"I love your mother; she's made it an easy transition for me and she's easy to be around." Sofia pulls her hair back and puts it in a ponytail as we speak as it's getting very hot.

"Let's have a glass of wine at the café." I point toward the square.

"Sure," Sal agrees as he slips his hand in mine and Sofia puts an arm through mine like old times.

I'm not sure if she's scared she'll be snatched again or if it's like our school days when we went to private school together. I don't care for now. Because I've been reunited with my best friend and she's safe and maybe she'll settle close by.

"Oh, don't forget to call your parents. They know you are okay and it's safe now."

"I will."

She's quiet a minute, so I change the topic to tomorrow's Sunday dinner for surely it will be a great family reunion.

SUNDAY AFTERNOON DINNER is outside under the trees at Mrs. Micheli's house.

A breeze blows up from the valley beneath us, and it's

welcomed – just as much as a small rain shower would help to cool things off.

"Sofia!" We hug and kiss at the door. She's making an attempt to blend in with the family and pretends she's fine when Sal gives her a light kiss on each cheek in greeting.

The trees give shade, but it's all we need without the sun. We congregate around the small garden fountain until the sun sets, giving us a break from the heat as the cold breeze of the night unfolds and moonlight emerges.

"Francesca, I'm so glad you are okay." Juliet gives me an unexpected hug and a kiss on both cheeks.

"Thank you. I confess I noticed that you have the save-the-date announcements on the desk." It's my lame attempt to make polite conversation as I take in her petite figure and gorgeous, but casual dress.

"Oh, yes, so many people to invite. I wanted a small event in Greve, where I'm from, but Dante wanted to invite friends and contacts," she says, rolling her eyes. "You know how that goes."

"Oh, yes." I let out the tiniest of giggles because I interrupted their 'business' at the gala this summer.

No doubt her wedding will be populated with other unsavory characters like myself and the hot men standing near us, all waiting to kiss the ring of the don and give their blessing on his wedding day.

"I'll help you with your wedding if you like," I offer, "I wasn't in a good place the first time around."

"But you are now!" Juliet cheerfully exclaims.

"Yes, very much so." I smile, "I wish you both the best of luck. I think you make a great couple."

"Thanks, my family still doesn't know the truth, that's rough. But they love Dante."

"That's good. I mean, is there any way to really announce

that you are part of a mafia family? They'd be too afraid to come to visit you. Better they don't know, then they have nothing to hide," I advise her.

"You're right. I never looked at it like that." She smiles a genuine smile that makes me feel welcome. "Come, let's go get the antipasti and bottles of water." She invites me to go into the kitchen with her like we've been friends for years.

"We should get together to shop for your honeymoon," I reply on her heels.

"Oh, that would be fun, it's so nice to have you here, I only have one friend from college that I can trust. You'll meet Ava soon—she's my maid of honor."

"Fantastic," I reply, picking up two green bottles. One holds a liter of fizzy and the other the natural.

Juliet picks up the antipasti and we make our way to join the men as they talk sports and no doubt, business under the umbrella trees.

"Francesca, how are you, dear?" Mrs. Micheli asks me as I head out. We met briefly at the door, but it seems I've piqued her interest.

"Mrs. Micheli. I'm fine, thank you. And you? Thank you for having me."

"Oh, no problem, there is always plenty of food. Any woman Sal brings around is always welcomed." She gives me a wink.

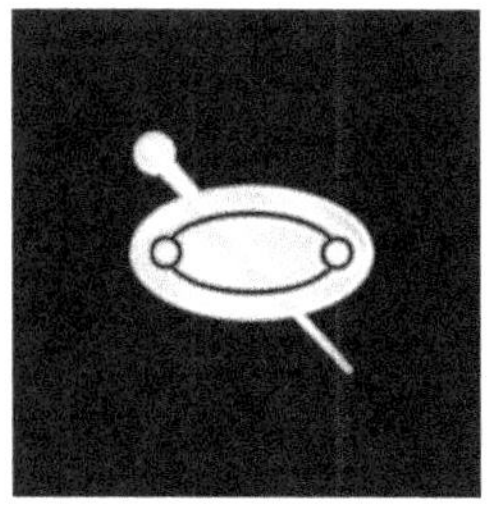

28

SAL

I wouldn't admit it to anyone, but my heart flutters when Francesca walks out with the water bottles. Mama brings the bread with a plate of olive oil.

Mama and Isabella are both dressed in flowing dresses, and I swear they are more like sisters than the maid and an employer.

Isabella smiles as she carries two bottles of Chianti, handing one to Dante to open.

He makes his way around the table, pouring wine into all the glasses looking so debonaire.

Juliet would be a fool not to snag him. They do hit it off. Their affection is genuine and evident by the fact that they can't keep their eyes or hands off each other.

I hope I can be so happy with Francesca.

Dante's older,more mature, and Juliet— she's smart and more stunning than she gives herself credit for. She's adjusted to her new way of life rather well for a small-town country girl.

She likes her work doing the company's public relations,

having finished her internship with the largest company in Florence.

Francesca sets the plate of food on the table, leaning over it carefully. She looks up after her hand leaves the plate and winks at me as her eyes light up when they meet mine over the antipasti.

That ill-fated gala where she tried to kill me is only a few months behind us, and yet, it's a mere memory. It's a funny story to tell our grandchildren eventually.

I'm in love with her, but I'm not rushing into marriage. She has traumas to work through, and I want the timing to be right.

We gather around the table and say a blessing as we hold hands, and silently, I pray for peace. I squeeze her hand before I let it go to sample the meat, olives, and slices of parmesan.

Mama made her famous meatball and spaghetti dinner. She's an excellent cook, and it dawns on me that I don't even know if Francesca can cook.

Riccardo is looking more polished than normal. I notice his goatee is freshly trimmed, and he's wearing new dress shoes.

That's odd, but then again, the man is a fashionista. Between his days as Mossad and now Mafia, I wouldn't want to be on his wrong side—ever.

Sofia hands him a bowl of fresh grated parmesan, and I notice that she blushes. It's so innocuous. I never would have caught it if I hadn't been watching with my own two eyes.

"This is the best sauce and meatballs, Mrs. Micheli. Will you share your recipe?" Francesca humbles herself to ask.

That's a first, and I sit back in my chair and take her in, making sure she's not touched in the head by the heat.

She feels my eyes on her. "What? I can't ask for a recipe?"

My eyebrows furrow over my nose. "I had no idea you knew what a pot was for unless you've weaponized it."

Dante and Marchello all but spit out the wine in their mouths before they have a gut-breaking laugh at everyone else's expense.

"What is that all about?" Mama asks.

"Nothing, Mama." Dante smiles and gives me an all-knowing glance.

Marchello takes a quick interest in the napkin he places in his lap and cuts up the giant meatball on his plate to escape Mama's prying eyes.

"You boys, I swear," she scoffs, but we all just smile knowing we're the only ones here who will ever know the story behind the looks.

The conversation returns to our week and what we've been up to, implying the normal things in life, like the spoon stuck in the new disposal I installed at my house.

Modern appliances aren't always what they're cracked up to be.

Francesca and I want to plant a garden, and when we have time, we still work in our makeshift gym in the old barn.

The guards even use it in between their shifts, and at times, we hear music blaring as we're out walking in the vineyards and vacant field that is filled with sunflowers.

I never knew this amount of normal was possible in my life.

But like those of us at the table who know the real world we live in most of the time, it's just a matter of time before our lives become chaotic.

The women clear the table and make conversation in the

kitchen, the windows and door open, so we get bits and pieces of their conversations as the wind blows.

We're sitting in our 'male only' section under the tree as Dante lights up a cigar and pours us each a Puni Vina Italian Malt Whisky.

We sit in the rusted and uncomfortable chairs, but it's tradition. Some of our favorite memories are watching Dad do this same thing with his bosses. And none of us can part with the chairs.

"That was funny at dinner. If Mama only knew a trained killer was sitting at her dinner table," I grin.

"Oh, my," Marchello adds, "you'd be so dead right now."

"Yes, but by whom? Mama or Francesca?"

"I think they both love you too much to hurt a hair on your tiny head," Dante teases.

"You might be right. I don't know. Both Sofia and Francesca had a rough go of it down there.

"I'm not sure she can open up, and I'm not sure she'll want to stay where she is forever. She was going to assume another identity and hightail it out of here when we met."

"Hmm." Dante takes a puff and lets the smoke float off into the night. I can't tell if he's deep in thought or just relaxing as he leans back in these terrible chairs and stretches his long legs out before him.

I look toward the house as I hear the coffee cups and saucers clatter and know the women will be having coffee talk next.

"So, now we've escaped the battle in the south with our lives," I make the sign of the cross on my chest and head, and tap both shoulders for good luck. "What's next?"

"The Albanians are going to try to muscle in on our turf. You know they were in another one of our clubs before the gala incident. I spoke to our friend from Florida at the gala after I went back to conclude business for us. The Albanians are aligned with the Sicilian Mafia, they're all over Europe and our friends in New York are very worried as they're so powerful."

"Their allies run deep," Marchello confirms.

"Yes, we don't want the wrath of other families on us, but a message has to be sent as we have to protect what's ours. The incident with the Contis' and Calabreses' was well-timed." Dante takes another sip of whisky, letting it coat his tongue, briefly cooling it before swallowing.

"The enemy of my enemy," I start.

"Is my friend," Dante finishes, and the three of us look at each other, smile, and nod.

We have an ally now, one that is even bigger than just what Gio Conti had built, as his organization now includes the Calabreses and their affiliates, the original family, the Rosellis . . . and we have a direct in through Francesca.

"I didn't do too bad with this girlfriend, it appears," I joke.

"Oh, girlfriend now, is it?" Dante slaps his hand against his leg as if it's a trick. "Seriously, she's chosen you, brother?"

"I think so, judging by how much we fuck each other's brains out and that she came back."

"True." He's resolved to the fact that Francesca is family.

She would have been accepted into our family if I married her, as it's not uncustomary for mafias to marry off their daughters to a rival in order to keep the peace.

However, the irony isn't lost on us that she's a skilled assassin and technology whiz who has successfully corralled our enemy.

She exceeded our expectations.

Who knew all it took was potentially getting murdered

with my zipper down and my dick out . . . and it wasn't even in a woman's mouth when she found me in the bathroom.

"So, when is the wedding?" Marchello asks me.

"What? What wedding? Dante is getting married in January. That's enough excitement for Mama for now."

Riccardo comes over and asks, "Everyone doing alright?"

"Yes, thanks for giving us a few minutes," Dante concludes. "Please ask Francesca to join me for a moment. I want to welcome her to the family." He dismisses us with his hand, and we carry our refilled glasses with us to join the women.

Francesca passes me on her way to Dante. "Did I do something wrong?" she whispers.

"No. If I know Dante, and I do, he's working."

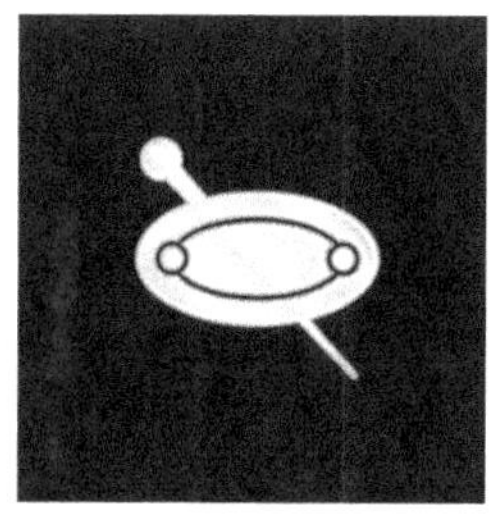

29

FRANCESCA

"Hi, Francesca, nice seeing you again."

I make my amends for not being free to visit with him before dinner.

"Thank you, Dante," I respond, unsure what to call him.

"I overheard you and Sal discussing a vacation you'd like to take. I have one in mind for the two of you, and you'll love it."

"And why would that be?" I'm being coy because he's up to something.

"I think you might be able to mix some business with pleasure." He rubs his right hand over his square chin before stubbing out his cigar.

"Maybe."

"Have a seat," he offers and waves his hand to the old, metal patio chairs. Sal told me they hate but hate the thought of getting rid of them more.

I gingerly lower myself into the chair.

"What do you have in mind?" I cross one leg over the other and lean forward with an elbow over my knee as if we're going to share a secret.

"Congratulations on becoming Don. It's about time a woman in Italy achieves such greatness." He motions to the alcohol in front of him with questioning eyes.

I nod. I can't turn down a drink with him—besides, I hear it's good stuff. He doesn't impress me as a man who goes cheap on anything, judging from the casual wear, Juliet's ring, and the lavish wedding I'm hearing about.

He looks good in a light-knit shirt that pushes the material far enough to show off his sculpted muscles. For a man in his thirties, I can tell he will age well.

"Thank you," I say, and we clink glasses with a "*Saluti*." He tells me about the drugs in the club and that it's time we make a subtle move but one that will be felt. It requires total anonymity, as the Albanians are strong, outnumbering us due to their connections around the world. He lifts his glass to punctuate his point. "But you know this."

"Yes," I agree, sipping the whisky. It warms my throat quickly, but I can suppress the slight cough my lungs want to make. "I have my issues with them, personal ones." I look into his eyes; we know we've reached common ground, and a contract has been made.

We're both stronger together, and a new family has been born. Now I have to take Sal on a trip to a ski lodge. Retribution is going to be served. It has to be ruled a normal cause of death to prevent an escalation. We don't want the Albanians coming after us, but a message has to be sent.

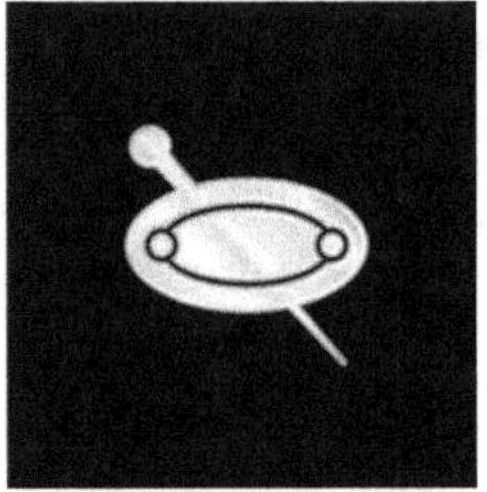

EPILOGUE

Sal

It's nice having family dinners on Sundays. Francesca and I have found a way to combine work and pleasure . . . and there is lots of pleasure. She even hangs out with me at the club.

A lesser man might be intimidated by a powerful woman, but to me, I'm just lucky she chose me.

"The wedding is coming up quickly," she says as she stalks up behind me at work, overlooking the quiet club below as we're ready to leave.

"It is."

"But you're nervous."

"Yes," I sigh heavily.

"Me too. You'd think those fucking Albanians would be grateful to us for handing Mario and Fausto to them, but it's not been acknowledged."

"I know. It's Italy, Europe, the entire world has gone crazy."

"Yes, it's all changed. So much has changed."

"But we have a happy occasion, and we'll be safe, then we have a vacation to look forward to." I change to a lighter topic before she becomes depressed over the loss of her brothers.

"Yes, we do, and it's a surprise."

"I don't like surprises. There are too many already," I complain.

"I know, but it can't be helped. I want to treat you for a change."

We turn and walk down the steps to our car, followed by our guards. I thought one or two was enough and annoying, but now it's more like four.

We make our drive home, and we both know this is the calm before the storm. The only difference is that we have a good idea of where the next battleground will be. It's closer to home, and I suspect Francesca will be in the middle of that too. We're going to the mountains to ski. Funny, I never pictured her on a ski slope.

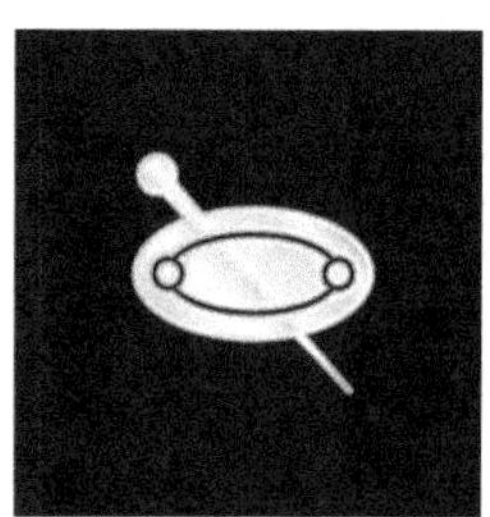

Continue with the Micheli family by reading Book 3 Dirty Bargain

Meet Marchello, the third brother and Argon's daughter, Prende. Both find themselves looking for who murdered Argon and what foul play may be afoot. The entire Micheli family is involved, as the killer's motives might not be as transparent as you think.

Exclusive for you is the special bonus scene for fans, and you can get yours here. This scene will give you a taste of what will kick off the events in Dirty Bargain. Dirty Vengeance Bonus Scene or https://dl.bookfunnel.com/f41ldmn2bt

FREE BOOK!

Bratva's Bride

https://dl.bookfunnel.com/px5mvpb293

ALSO BY ZOE BETH GELLER

Visit shopzoebethgeller.com

Dirty: A Dark Mafia Romance Series

Micheli Mafia

Dirty: A Dark Mafia Romance Series (Micheli Mafia)

Italian King: A Dark Mafia Romance (Micheli Mafia)Book 1

Dirty Vengeance: A Dark Mafia Romance (Micheli Mafia) Book 2

Dirty Bargain: A Dark Mafia Romance (Micheli Mafia) Book 3

Dirty Born: A Dark Mafia Romance (Micheli Mafia) Book 4

Dirty Deals: A Dark Mafia Romance (Micheli Mafia) Book 5

The Volkov Bratva Series

Volkov Bratva

King's Promise

Brutal Promise

Sinful Promise

Maine Megaladons (Football Series)

Faking it with the Football Star

The Player's Obsession

Maine Maulers Series

Maine Maulers Hockey Series

Rookie in Love

Jagged Ice

Hotter than Puck

Benched by the Nanny

Puck in the Oven

Pucking the Team Captain

Pucking with the Goalie

Sin Bin Hockey Series

Tyler: Hooked (Free prequel to the series)

The Sin Bin Hockey Series

Jackson: Against the Boards

Alan: Between the Pipes

Erik: Fire and Ice

Blayze: Slap Shot

Paavo: The Defender

Spencer: Penalty Box

Isak: Coach

Kaden: Game Time

Liam: The Enforcer

Jake: Roughing

The Sin Bin Hockey Series Box Sets

The Sin Bin Hockey Series Box Set Books 1-4

The Sin Bin Hockey Series Box Set Books 5-7

The Sin Bin Hockey Series Box Set Books 8-10

Facebook Fan Groups

Zoe Beth Geller's Hockey Pond Fan Group

Dirty Series Dark Mafia Fan Group

ACKNOWLEDGMENTS

Thank you to everyone who is following me on this journey. I hope you are enjoying this series. Special thanks to my hubby for his support. And as always my besties Mo, Aidy and Aarti.

ABOUT THE AUTHOR

Zoe Beth Geller lives in Florida with her grown kids and grandkids. When not writing she enjoys swimming, cooking and family nights.

She is the author The Sin Bin Hockey Series which is a collection of 10 standalone novels. There is a bit of continuity across books and do not need to be read in order.

Her spin-off series, Maine Mauler Hockey Series is a pro team series based, obviously, in Maine! These are interconnecting romances that can be read as a standalone, but this series has more team interaction between players and a series arc as well. It is best read in order.

Other works by Zoe include her dark mafia -The Dirty Series: A Dark Mafia Romance (Micheli Mafia). Starting off with Italian King, These books should be read in order as the plots and romances are involved and carry through the series. The series is expected to be 5 books when completed.

Stay connected with Zoe through her fan groups and her newsletter with updates on evolving news and releases at Newsletter sign-up

For your free book to the Sin Bin Series download Tyler: Hooked

Fan Groups

Zoe Beth Geller's Hockey Pond

The Dirty Series: Dark Mafia Romances

If you would like to review books before they are released please sign up to be an ARC
ARC sign-up!

ZBG Website

facebook.com/zoebeth.geller.96
instagram.com/zoegellerauthor
bookbub.com/authors/zoe-beth-geller

www.ingramcontent.com/pod-product-compliance
Lightning Source LLC
Chambersburg PA
CBHW071432200726
48294CB00002B/609